ESSENCE

ESSENCE

HAYLEY GABRIELLE

THE FATE OF HUMANITY RESTS WITH HER

ESSENCE
©2019 Hayley Gabrielle

Expanded Edition

Visit the author's website at www.hayleygabrielle.com

ISBN: 978-0-646-98709-5

CONTENTS

MY BODY SHUDDERS AGAINST A COLD SURFACE. An unceasing hum reverberates loudly in my ears and my throat aches—the sort of ache that comes from repressed tears, or holding back a scream for too long.

I try to force my eyes open, but each lid is sore and heavy like the rest of me.

Movement comes into my fingers first and I graze them across a smooth, hard surface. I must have sleepwalked and landed on the kitchen floorboards. I remember going there for a glass of water.

So then why can't I get up? Did I fall and hit my head? Have I had a seizure or something?

With all my strength, I open my eyes a crack. Blurred outlines swim in my narrowed vision, foreign shapes I don't immediately recognise.

I've been holding my breath, I realise then. As I let the air in, the incessant hum in my head eases up and the haze of the room shrinks into clarity. But it's a room I still don't recognise.

The floor underneath me is flagstone—not the wooden boards of our kitchen. There's a table beside me too. Its legs twist with intricate, carved vines and leaves rise in exquisite detail to a wide tabletop above. Not our kitchen table.

Panic rushes through me and with trembling hands, I manage to push myself up onto my knees. Everything spins. I squeeze my eyes shut and grab my head as if that might steady the sensation.

When I look again, the room holds. High above is a pitched ceiling with exposed, wooden trusses.

I'm dreaming. I must be. Or I really did hit my head. Hard. The only other possibility is that I've been kidnapped in my sleep, which seems unlikely.

I stagger toward the central table and see a rusted lamp there—the only light source in the room. The flame inside casts a gentle, wavering glow.

I back up a few steps and twist around to check behind me. My heel nicks something solid. Still battling dizziness, I stumble and find myself colliding with the flagstone again. My wrists take the brunt of the fall.

I release an exasperated, drawn-out groan. And my fingers ... they curl into something soft. Silky smooth. I lift my head off the floor and my stomach flips.

A sweep of ash-grey hair draws up into a widow's peak, framing a face mapped in fine wrinkles. Her nose curves gently to the ceiling, eyes closed and pale lips parted. She's wearing a gown that flows all the way down to her ankles, and her hands are flat over her chest.

The woman looks ...

I scramble to standing, breathing hard as acid rises in my throat. I cover my mouth and swallow it down.

Dead. She looks dead.

There's a ghostly pallor about her skin, and no rise or fall of breath. My heart thumps as I bend again to examine the body more closely.

The vacant, serene look on her face is evidence enough. Some vital cord of life is missing.

I've never seen a dead body before. There was an open casket at Tyler's granddad's funeral last year, but I steered clear. It felt intrusive to look. I remember watching people pass his coffin though, some crying, others drained of colour, praying, bowing, reaching in to touch him one last time.

I begin to feel the same as I did then—as though I should get as far away from this body as I can, because I haven't earned the right for the intrusion.

As I step back, I catch a glint of silver under one of the woman's hands. I angle my head, and so abruptly it almost knocks me back, a memory rushes at me. That thing on my desk—that marquise outline shrouded in shadow. When I came back to my room, I had seen it there. And when I touched it, I was drawn away. Sucked down into blackness.

Under the woman's long, narrow fingers, I can see it. The very same object.

A prickling energy starts to shift under my skin. For quite some time I simply stare down at the body—frozen.

"Hello."

The voice sends me whirling around. Flickers of light from the lamp draw a tall figure into focus against a wall thick with shadow. I didn't see it before. The flash of teeth, the broad brow and sharp nose. The gleam reflected in two dark eyes fixed on me.

She slowly emerges into the light—a young woman draped in a cloak, jet-black hair falling in glossy sheets to her waist. Her skin is pale around eyes so dark the pupils are lost.

I'm dreaming. I've got to be dreaming. I never woke up to get water from the kitchen. I've just fallen more deeply into sleep.

It all feels so real, even the stench of mustiness and wet stone. But I've experienced dreams before that have felt real while I was in them. This particular one, with the dead body and creepy lady lurking in the shadows, seems like a dream I should escape while I can—and soon, before it turns into something sinister my brain is too capable of conjuring up from all the horror films I've watched with Mum and Tyler.

I press myself against the wall and do a rapid scan of the room. A few feet to my right there's a door. An escape route, I hope.

My searching gaze cuts back to the pale woman, who is watching me carefully. There's a slick coldness about her that arrests my attention, and I momentarily forget about the door and any desire to flee whatever dark sanctum of my mind this dream might open up.

"Hello," the girl says again.

I open my mouth to answer, but no words come.

Her black eyes drop to the woman lying motionless between us. "The time before passes into the now, and the after. Human life is so trivial. So tragically fleeting."

I clear my throat and force myself to speak. "What's happening here? Who are you?" The sound of my own voice shocks me, as though I didn't expect to hear it back without the muted ambiguity that usually clouds a dream. Every word is clean and hewn into an illusion too close to reality.

The woman's full lips curl delicately at each corner. "Two rather vital questions," she trails into a soft hiss. "Neither will be answered in full. Not here. Not in the words you know. The truest answers can only be found when the veil is lifted and you see them for yourself."

I blink at her, deciding how much to indulge this elaborate storyline. "See what? What veil?"

The woman smiles. "Kayna." She glides around the table, her cloak whispering as it drags behind her. "That is my name, amongst others. Might I learn yours?"

"Uh, Abbey. Abbey Shader."

"Abbey Shader," she repeats. Her tongue slashes across her teeth, as though wiping them clean.

Another flash of reality sends shivers through my fingers, to my toes. Her voice—so real and close and foreign. It's beginning to crystallize. Stamp itself into a space of me that's becoming less and less familiar. Less and less *me*.

Kayna sinks to the body on the floor and reaches out a hand. Her wrist, exposed as her cloak shifts back, is pale and bony. She plucks the metal object from the dead woman's grip. "It isn't often that I have the honour of meeting with the Melder before the others," Kayna says, inspecting the marquise piece. There's a mottled, grey stone at its centre now, in place of the spiralling shadow that rose from it in my room. I also see a pin across its back. A brooch. "They tend to swoop in first," Kayna adds, with an impish smile. "Where is this one from?"

She's still looking at the brooch, and so I don't answer—until her dark gaze cuts to me again, rolling over my *Winnie-the-Poo* pyjama pants and white singlet top as she stands. "Well? Where are you from?"

"Oh." She was referring to me? "I'm not sure—"

"You are not sure?"

"Well, I was in my room ..."

Kayna's lips curl down on one side, as if her patience is dwindling already.

A dream. That's all this is. It *has* to be. Otherwise, I've gone freaking insane. Or ... what if I died in my sleep? And this is an 'after'? The thought propels my pulse into a panic.

Suddenly Kayna laughs. The sound is like cold water running through me, as tangible as the pain throbbing in my head. Her teeth are huge and grey, the canines sharp. I eye the door again.

"You can leave, if you wish," she says, suddenly serious. "But where would you go?"

I hesitate, gnawing on my lip in the hope that the pain might wake me up. I taste blood, but nothing changes. And so I pose, "Home?" as if speaking the word might beckon it closer.

Kayna grins. "Oh, Abbey Shader. You are a long way from there."

THREE

KAYNA HAS DRAWN TWO SEATS TO THE TABLE and claimed one for herself. She gestures for me to sit but I stay where I am, buzzing all over.

"Have it your way," she mutters. "You will grow accustomed to that." When I say nothing, she sighs and goes on. "You are the Melder, Abbey Shader. The Melder of all living things from Earth to Ethra. Try not to look so baffled—most receive it as an honour."

I shake my head with enough vigour to jolt myself into waking. But again, it doesn't work. So I grab the skin of my forearm and pinch. Hard.

"What are you doing?" Kayna inquires from the table.

"Waking up," I tell her. When the pinch fails, I take a deep breath and at the risk of looking like a total idiot, start to tap my heels together. "There's no place like home," I mutter. Maybe a pop-culture reference can bring me out of this, back to the realm I know it from. "No place like home. No place like home."

Silence fills me, and I expel a breath. When I open my eyes into a squint, the room remains, and Kayna is staring at me like I'm the Wicked Witch of the West.

"Okay." My voice is hoarse and even I can hear the terror trapped in it. "Okay, okay, okay." I start to pace, moving around the perimeter of the room. "This feels real," I whisper, mostly to myself.

But Kayna answers, "Quite real, I assure you."

I keep walking, tossing my head left and right.

"How can I put this ..." I hear Kayna mutter. "You are here because she is not," she says, more tersely.

I stop and look over at the line of her finger, arching toward that body on the floor.

"Where is *here?* Have I been kidnapped? Is this some sort of hostage situation? Am I a hostage?" Kayna only presses her lips into a tight line. "We don't have much," I add. "Money, I mean. Trust me. Mum earns enough for us to get by, but my Dad only gives us ..." I trail off as an awful thought springs to mind. From what I've heard—which is mostly snide comments from Mum—Dad is freaking rich.

What if someone is after his money?

"Honestly, he won't care," I say, driving venom into my voice. "I hardly see him as it is. He'll probably pay you to keep me."

Kayna's eyes harden. "You are not a hostage," she says. "You are the Melder. She was the Melder past, and now you are the Melder future."

I glance at the dead body. There is a high chance my kidnapper isn't entirely sane herself. "What's the Melder?"

Kayna extends her hand with the brooch resting in her palm, dark against her skin. "Take it. Wear it. It is yours."

I stay where I am. My mind trails back to where I left my phone—on my bedside table. If I *have* been taken, I'm out of reach. Off the map. Maybe a cavalier approach will get me out of here. "Well, I'm going to head off now," I say, walking backwards in the direction of the door. "I—thanks for the—bye."

I whirl and grab at the handle. A hand clamps down around my arm. I shriek and lurch away. But Kayna is strong, her grip like a vice and her face so close I can feel the chill of her breath, somehow ice-cold. How did she reach me so quickly?

"You can go," she says. "But if you do wish to return home now, you will require my assistance to reach the great tree."

The great tree? Freaking hell. Okay. She's a nutter. I'm officially locked in some dungeon with a nutter. But then if she had brought me here herself, why would she offer to get me out?

Unless she's trapped too …

Various scenarios whirl around my head, most of them totally ridiculous, but given the circumstances—I can't write them off. I incline an eyebrow, feigning calm. "Why help me?"

Kayna's gaze, darker than coal, locks with mine. "You will see." In one swift motion, she yanks at my singlet and fixes the brooch into place. "Leave this room and meet me outside the house. There is an important matter I must first attend to."

"Okay?" I frown and tentatively tap the brooch. Just an ordinary piece of jewellery.

Kayna hesitates, flicking her tongue against her teeth in a disturbingly serpentine manner. "Leave through the front door—and open no others on your way," she says. "You will find nothing good behind them."

I dispel any flicker of desperation from my expression. I'm almost out. Almost free. If I can play into this lady's weird game maybe she really will lead me home. "Front door," I repeat. "Got it."

Kayna leans in close to take the handle behind me, pushing the door open for me. I glance back at the body of the old woman, her ashen face almost blending with the stone like she's becoming a static piece of it herself.

Then I turn through the doorway. Down a few steps, a corridor stretches ahead. Light pours across the walls on either side, dipping into darkness where the day doesn't reach. Numerous doors are set into both walls, but my attention is drawn to the set at the corridor's end.

I step down onto a tattered, wool rug that leads all the way to my escape. Then I turn, just once more, to get another look at the striking, pale woman I'm leaving behind. I see only a flash of dark hair before the door clatters shut.

✻

Dusty cobwebs droop from shadowed corners and the air is musty and dry. I'm halfway along the dim hall—when a strange gurgle stops me short.

I spin on my heel. The corridor is empty.

Listening carefully, I retreat a few steps. Again, I hear the same sound, this time louder. I'm fairly certain it's coming from the door to my right.

I glance at the end door, chewing on my lip. But the gurgling noise transforms into a sharp cry, and I can't help but press my ear to the source.

The oak door is dusty against my cheek but I keep on listening. My heart pounds as the cry comes again. And again. Someone in pain.

Maybe I'm not the only one who was taken. How can I leave without knowing? Can I really trot along without finding out for sure?

Kayna told me not to open the doors. But whatever's in there, it doesn't sound like it will pose any great threat—more like it needs my help.

My compulsion to go in grows so strong I find my hand clutching the cold, brass handle. Then, brushing aside what could be very rational fears, before I can convince myself to walk away, I pull on the handle and shoulder the door open.

The room is full of swirling dust. I splutter through it as a writhing shape against the back wall draws my eye. Batting the blooms of dust away, I edge closer.

A head of silver hair breaks into view, followed by the body of a man. He's kneeling with his back to me, his hands bound by rope and striking the wall so hard I can feel the impact under my feet. I see that his feet are bound too.

The muscles in his back shudder as though spasms are running through them, over and over. His shirt is grey with dirt and torn under his shoulder blade, leaving a streak of pale skin exposed.

I'm not sure whether to run forward or backward. Indecision roots my feet to the floor.

But then the man twists himself around. Pain contorts his face, squeezing his eyes shut and his upper lip into a grimace. The expression looks like an intrusive entity, because I can see the degree of his beauty through it. Pristine. Unmarred.

A renewed rush of bravery propels me to his side. "Hello? Are you okay?"

The man's spasms cease for a moment and he hangs his head. I bend into a squat and reach out with three fingers to touch his brow—before jerking back. His skin is icy cold.

But now he isn't shaking. He's completely still. A sculpture of white marble, fine features and lean muscles. He's younger than I expected, with hair that falls to his shoulders like fine strands of ethereal silk. Up close he looks only a few years older than me, if I had to guess.

The man's eyes spring open.

I leap back, startled by the colour—an electric blue. A shade I've never seen on anyone before.

The man sits up straighter, his alien gaze shifting to the rope restraining him. Then again to me. I set my jaw and command myself to return the look.

"Hi," I say. A voice inside me questions the casual remark, whispers that I should feel more afraid. More cautious.

We've never met before, obviously. But for whatever reason, this man doesn't feel like a total stranger.

His gaze shifts to the brooch pinned to my singlet. And then, the flicker of a smile touches his mouth. "You came," he says softly.

FOUR

THE STONE ROOM, NARROW AS IT IS, SEEMS to shrink smaller still. "What?" I frown at the man kneeling in front of me. "Do I know you?"

He inclines his head, those strange eyes tracing my features. "In a sense."

"Who are you?" I ask, too baffled to channel any social pleasantry into the question.

"My name is Balvinder." He presses his fists to the stone and pushes himself to his feet. I'm startled by his height—a head or two taller than me. But I mask my surprise by folding my arms and pursing my lips.

"I'm Abbey," I tell him. "Abbey Shader. I found myself in this room—" I gesture behind me, "somewhere back there. I was leaving when I heard ... you."

Balvinder blinks at me, breaking the brilliant blue of his eyes only momentarily before re-focusing his gaze over me. My pulse quickens.

"You said you were leaving," he says. "Where did you mean to go?"

It seems an odd question to ask, and surely not the most pressing, given his obvious predicament.

"Uh ... home," I answer, glancing at the rope around his wrists. "There was a woman, back there, she told me she could help me find my way. But ..." I pause a moment, wondering how much to tell him.

His hands and feet are bound—possibly a reason not to trust the guy. I mean, what if he did something terrible?

But then if he were a serious criminal, would he really be kept in some dodgy stone house tied up with a piece of rope? And why do I feel like we've met before, even though I can't recognise his face?

"Look, I don't know what the hell happened, but I was asleep in my bed and then I dreamt that I touched this brooch." I tap at it for emphasis. "And now, somehow it's here and I'm here, but I don't know where *here* is. I think I—I might have been taken."

Balvinder regards me, unflinching through a lengthy silence. "Yes," he finally says. "You have been taken. But not in the way you think." He lifts his bound hands. "I can lead you home too, if you untie me."

"You don't know where I live," I say, suddenly wary.

For a second, it looks as though Balvinder is fighting a smile. "Abbey," he says. There's a resonance to his voice that warms me through. "I have answers to your questions, but first we must leave this place, and only you can untie me."

"Why me?"

Balvinder hesitates a moment, and then says, "Because you are here."

"Right." I squeeze my fingers into fists. "Do you promise not to kill me?"

A look of shock graces Balvinder's features, like the pain, wavering at his surface as though it isn't permitted any further. "Why would I kill you?"

"I just mean—don't make me regret this, okay?" I reach out to the rope and start wrestling with the knots. Cutting a quick glance up at him, I notice the gauntness of his cheeks.

"Why are you in here?" I ask. Balvinder averts his eyes and I hesitate over the rope. "It's a fair question, if I'm about to release you. Don't you think?"

"It is," he agrees. "I was brought here by ..." He flinches. Inhales deeply. "I can't say. But I did no wrong. Believe me."

"I don't know you," I say. But why don't I sound convincing? Why does it feel like a lie? And why am I still untying the rope?

Finally, it falls away. Balvinder wrings his hands out, and then beams at me. Any concern I might've had about his being free eases with that smile, and for some reason I'm smiling too—even as I bend to untie his feet.

His shadow doesn't scare me. For some inexplicable reason, I feel like I don't want to leave it. Even once the rope around his feet has fallen loose.

*

I'm not sure what I expected, coming out of the house. But what we walk into wasn't it. Two huge, stone columns flank the portico, and beyond I can see a river babbling before a cluster of houses that runs as far as I can see. In the far distance there are smooth hills and fields of yellow and green.

I'm in the middle of nowhere. Kayna was right—home must be a long way away. So how the hell did I get here?

I follow Balvinder across a lush stretch of grass outside the house. It was cold inside. But now the air fills my lungs, prickling and heating me instantly. I blink up into the sky and water fills my eyes. The sun is huge, beating down against my skin so intensely I can feel myself burning already. It's *hot*. Even for Melbourne, this kind of heat is unusual.

We head toward a narrow, wooden bridge arching across the river.

"It's so freaking hot," I mutter, tying my hair up with the elastic around my wrist.

"This is nothing," Balvinder says. "The sun isn't ordinarily this kind in Emba. The villagers will be in a frenzy in the fields, no doubt, taking advantage of it."

The villagers? Emba?

I spin back to the house we came from, inspecting again the mottled pillars at its entrance. They stand tall and polished, like the trunks of trees uprooted and lodged there. The entire structure is made of stone.

Balvinder has stopped beside me. He's looking back at the house too. "Centuries old," he says. "The villagers ensure they never get too close. Many who have ventured into the Petrified Forest have never returned, and so they believe the house is cursed simply because it was built from the stone of the trees. Most prefer to source their stone from the mountain quarries."

I swallow, feeling my eyes grow wider. Who exactly did I just rescue? King Henry reincarnated?

Sensing Balvinder's gaze on me, I do a quick side-glance and see his near-white brows inclining curiously. He points to the brooch on my singlet.

"Petrified wood," he says. "Cut from the trees. The curse is not really a curse, you see. It is all a matter of perspective, as most things are."

And then he starts walking again, leaving me staring after him.

"Are you coming?" he calls without turning.

I hesitate, glancing around once more before following on. "Do you know why I'm here? Who took me, I mean?"

"Yes," Balvinder says simply. He strides across the bridge without further explanation. More perplexed than ever, I follow. Rippling water flashes through the spaces between the timber panels under my feet.

We reach the opposite side and continue on toward the row of houses ahead. Balvinder stumbles a little and I reach out as if to steady him. He regains balance on his own though, and casts me a wary smile. "I'm all right."

I feel suddenly stunned by my willingness to lay helping hands on a perfect stranger. Mum emphasized stranger danger to me from the time I could walk, to the point where I was apparently super-suspicious of every nanny who came to the house. I'd cry and hide behind doors and under beds and we went through numerous women before I settled on one I was comfortable with—who had dark hair and blue eyes like Mum. Now, I tend to look at anyone and everyone with a skeptical eye.

But then Balvinder has that indescribable familiarity about him. I want to be cautious, but when I meet his eyes it's as though the film of my general distrust evaporates.

The houses appear to be connected—wood shingle roofs rising and dipping like waves above rounded windows. Small gaps are left at intervals between the structures and Balvinder leads me to the closest one, turning his broad shoulders to sidle through. I turn too, suddenly aware that I'm in my pyjamas.

Although, I doubt I'll be seeing anyone I know in this place. I'll need to find a phone to call Mum. She might know what happened.

Judging by the position of the sun, it's probably late afternoon, which means I've been gone all night and morning. Unless I've been here for days, unconscious. Unless I was drugged.

I shudder and push the thought away. Thinking clearly will be impossible if I let the worst possibilities in now.

We pass by a window in the avenue between the houses, and I jump as a curious face appears through it—a kid with reddish hair and a freckled nose. He watches me, his jaw slack, like he's just as confused by my presence as I am.

Balvinder and I step out into a large square. A tree occupies its centre, its roots twisted and drawing in and out of the dirt like snakes frozen in motion. The tree's bulging limbs shade nearly the entire space, and a gleaming plaque is set up beneath its trunk. I'm squinting in an attempt to decipher the words when I feel a touch on my arm.

"This way," says Balvinder, angling his head toward the opposite side of the square.

We pass a cluster of kids in loose, earthy dresses and shirts drawn together with strings. They're bustling around a structure built from sticks, stones and leaves, one in particular yelling orders at the others. Their giggles fill the square, but as we pass by, they all stop and stare at us.

"Act as you normally would," Balvinder whispers in my ear—the man with silver hair covered in dirt and torn clothes. He looks like an escaped convict and I'm in pyjamas and bare feet. No wonder we have the full attention of the square.

A few other people pass us, casting curious glances our way. Unlike Kayna and Balvinder, they all have skin tinted bronzy-brown, and strange clothes too. It's like I've stepped right into another country. Or another century.

"Where the hell are we?" I quietly ask Balvinder.

"Emba," he answers, like it's supposed to ring a bell with me.

The square, broken by dirt tracks veering off at every corner, seems mostly comprised of shops and places to eat. I don't see a payphone. Or a bus stop. No signs or sounds of cars either.

We reach a place with a low-hanging sign displaying some mythical, winged creature I don't recognise above the door. Balvinder gestures for me to enter first.

Inside, booths run the length of the left wall and a bar is set up along the right. Bottles of all shapes, colours and sizes hang from the ceiling above it, tied and left hanging by thin pieces of rope. They glint in the light from the front window, casting pools of colour across the room.

There are only a few other people here—a group of men covered in sweat and dirt at the bar, and two women speaking together in the nearest booth, one with a toddler in a flat sort of hat set on her lap.

Balvinder beckons for me to follow him to the booth in the farthest corner. The woman with the kid performs a brief but not-so-subtle scan of my pj's as I walk past. *Sorry lady*, I imagine myself saying, *but when you're abducted right out of your bed, wearing Winnie-the-Pooh isn't your biggest problem.*

My nerves are strung tight and my heart pounds, reminding me that this is serious. I don't know where I am, or what happened to me. Abduction isn't out of the question.

We've barely sat down before I burst out, "Tell me," studying the fine, angular shapes of Balvinder's face for any sort of answer. "Tell me everything you know."

"I will tell you what I can."

I clasp my hands over the table, partially in an effort to keep myself together. "Okay then."

"What can I get you?" I jump at the sound of a new voice. The woman stands beside us in a leather apron. She lays a single stem of wheat in front of me and waits.

I stare at it a moment before looking back to her. "Uh, I'm okay at the moment, thanks."

She walks away, frowning, without so much as a glance at Balvinder.

I pick up the wheat and roll it between my fingers. "What's this for? Entrée?"

Balvinder smiles a little. "It is a custom here. A declaration of welcome and a promise to provide."

"Huh." I drop the wheat. "So, you were saying ..."

"I was saying that I can tell you what is possible to tell you." He pauses for a beat, and a shade of yellow light cuts across his jaw from one of the hanging bottles. "I can explain why you are here, but I can't explain the condition in which you found me."

I swallow hard, holding his gaze and waiting for more.

Balvinder inclines his head at me, a wave of silver hair falling across one eye. He brushes it behind his ear. "We are in Emba—a village on the western continent of Ethra. You are here because you have been summoned from Earth to become the Melder between our two worlds. The Melder of the Essences."

I stare at him. "Sorry?"

"The Melder of the Essences," he says again.

"I heard you." I lean back, pressing my palms against the table's edge. "Is this some sort of joke? Am I being punked right now?" I do a rapid scan of the room, searching for cameras. Maybe Tyler set this up. It would be a fairly extravagant gag, but he's a fairly extravagant guy.

Finding no trace of recording devices, I turn back to Balvinder. "You can't be serious." He just looks at me, cerulean blue swirls forming in each iris like the colour itself is alive and roiling. I gesture to them. "You're even wearing contacts."

"Pardon?"

"Your eyes," I say. "They're not ... normal."

"Neither am I."

"Okay, what's going on?" I tap the table impatiently. "Tell me, or I'll leave."

A smooth calm evens out Balvinder's expression, seeming to reach out to me too and ease a fraction of my tension. "I ask that you listen," he says. "Once I am finished, you can decide what you wish to do."

I grit my teeth together, but force a nod.

"Our two worlds exist in parallel," he starts, "Earth—your homeland, and Ethra—where you now find yourself." I clench my hands together again and bite down on my tongue as he goes on. "Long ago, the Overseer fashioned spirits, and at the same time brought the Essences to life. The Essences were powerfully distinct. They provided choice for the spirits, and still, they exist in the air you breathe. Unseen. But they require balancing. And as the Melder, you have been called to balance them."

I feel my heart racing. The words rattling. I run them through logical trains of thought, but every one of them skitters into oblivion along with any semblance of sense.

Two worlds.

Overseer.

Essences.

Melder.

"I don't know who you think I am," I begin slowly, cursing myself for letting my voice wobble, "or what you think I have, but I have no idea what you're talking about. I need to get to Lane Street. Do you know where that is? Lane Street?"

Balvinder sighs, a gentle sound that eases out through his narrow, parted lips. "Abbey," he says, delicately. "I can get you home, but you must be open to what I am telling you."

"You're telling me that I've been transported to some parallel universe or something, right?" I snort and shake my head. "You really think I'm going to buy that?"

Balvinder's brow contracts ever so slightly, the blue of his eyes flickering in an unnatural way I've never seen. A chill spirals through me. "The brooch," he says. "It brought you here.

A piece of Ethra on Earth will draw a bridge from one to the other. You crossed that bridge when you touched the brooch."

"I—" I stop abruptly. Last night—in my room. I *did* see the brooch. The very same one. I saw it and I touched it, and that's when my memory blanks out.

Next thing I know I'm waking up in another room beside a dead woman and that lady with black eyes.

Everything feels surreal, until I really think on it, and then it doesn't. I do remember the brooch, there on my desk. I couldn't have been dreaming. I'd just woken *up* from a dream. I remember creeping down the hall to my bedroom after spotting a shadow in the doorway. I remember following it inside. Finding the brooch. The cloud of black spinning above it.

The memories are as close and clear as watching Tyler recline in my beanbag, or filling that glass of water in the kitchen, or sitting here now opposite this man with gleaming blue eyes that haven't left my face.

I turn to the bar, observing it carefully. The stools. The men gathering there and the sweat gleaming on their necks. My eyes catch on a tall boy behind the counter, towelling dry a long-stemmed glass.

He's wearing a brown, leather apron, and his hair—dark and tinged with the blue and pink light shining through the bottles suspended above him—is tousled around his temples. His skin is a lovely warm, copper-bronze colour, like I've seen on most people around here. But it's his smile that holds my attention. A half-hidden smile creases his cheek, coming to rest at a dimple as he listens to the conversation between the group of men opposite him.

His gaze abruptly flashes across the room—to me. He lays down the glass he was drying and tosses the towel over his shoulder, but his attention holds. Even from here I can see that his eyes are green, and gorgeous, and I should definitely look away now.

Something in my chest lurches and I cut my gaze back to Balvinder, finding him still watching me. I'm not sure what I want to say, but, "I really don't understand," is all that comes out.

"The Overseer," he says. "The one who summoned you—you need to meet him before you leave."

"When you say Overseer, you don't mean, like ... some type of god?"

The corner of Balvinder's mouth wavers. "A single word will never do him justice," he says. "Though, I suppose that works as good as any."

"And you're saying I've got to meet this—this Overseer? And then I can go home?" Balvinder gives a short nod in answer.

I shake my head, clenching and unclenching my fists under the table. "Maybe I'm the one going insane." Or maybe this is some sort of existential crisis triggered by that bald career counsellor, and I'm here to figure out whether I have a purpose and what I'm supposed to achieve in life.

Could my brain possibly have conjured up a scenario in which I'm vital to the universe in order to ease the pain of being just the opposite?

Balvinder straightens, shifting his gaze to the bar. "Would you be so kind as to order me a bolikon pie?"

I frown at him, unsure whether to question the command or the *bolikon*, whatever the hell that is. But it doesn't seem like the most urgent question, so instead I wave down the woman in the apron and repeat it back to her as best I can.

"He'll have the bolikon pie."

She blinks at me. "He?"

I return her inquiry with a shrug. "Yeah?"

The waitress nods, but walks away slowly, with that same frown she wore before—like she's confused over the *bolikon* too.

"What's a bolikon?" I hiss at Balvinder. "I've never heard of it."

"You will see."

"Ah, yes." I nod seriously. "Just like I'll *see* the Over*seer*, right? A god who created '*Essences*' and '*spirits*'." I wrap quotation marks around the words with my fingers. "This is crazy. I have to get back. Can you just point me in the direction of a bus stop?" Unless I'm stuck in some country town. "Or a train station, even."

When he makes no move to answer me, I shake my head and rise—just about bowling over the waitress, who's holding out a flat plate with a steaming pie.

"Sorry," I mutter, as she stares at me with a look caught between confusion and offence.

"You're leaving?" she asks.

"I'm leaving." I nod at Balvinder. "He's staying."

The waitress cautiously lowers the pie to the table and retreats.

"You're welcome, by the way," I say to him, gesturing to my wrists to indicate our unconventional meeting. "I hope getting you out of there wasn't a huge mistake." And with that I turn to the door and move fast.

With one last glance behind me, I see the waitress leaning in to whisper something to the green-eyed bartender. He looks right at me again, and this time I bolt.

I'm back in the square. The kids from before are gone and the castle they were building is now a pile of sticks in the dirt. I make for one of the dirt tracks to my left. Surely it will lead me to a road, at least, so I can get a sense of where I might be.

Scorching sunlight pulses against my skin as I march down a dusty path between two rows of those shingle-roofed houses. A man and woman carrying large baskets pass me by. Both glance down at my pyjamas.

The street ends abruptly and I start to shake my head at the fields of wheat extending before me for what looks like miles. A series of stables line the right-hand side. People bustle around them, bundling wheat and hauling baskets.

I turn and move slowly along the border of the nearest field. On my other side, vibrant vegetable patches are growing in rows of garden beds continuing on as far as I can see. There's a flurry of movement between the plants—farmers watering the soil with buckets. Their skin is deeply tanned and speckled with thick beads of sweat that roll down their faces in the heat of that sweltering sun.

My heart beats like a drum in my ears. Kayna said it, and Balvinder did too—I'm far from home. Now I'm starting to believe it.

FIVE

I'VE BEEN STARING AT THE FARMERS FOR A few minutes, mulling over my options, when I spot a woman with long, grey hair in the distance, watching me. She starts to stride my way, running her hand across the heads of wheat as she goes.

Men and women in the midst of tying sheaves drop them to acknowledge her, and even those cutting the wheat stop to nod. She must be a manager of sorts. Maybe she'll be able to help me.

A flicker of hope springs to life and I cross the distance between us. "Hi there," I say. "I'm just looking for the nearest train station. Can you point me in the right direction?"

The woman, whose hair drops to her waist in soft curls, regards me with stern interest from a pair of hard, grey-brown eyes. Wrinkles web their way around her eyes, mouth and nose, and deep grooves are set between her brows. "Our training stations are west of the square. Are you new to Emba?"

I blink at her. "Uh, yeah. I'm not sure—"

"There you are," says a voice behind me. I turn to see the green-eyed bartender stopping a few feet away. He's looking at me like he knows me. "Pacer Aubrin—hello. Abbey is a trader from Preo selling vessels for the tavern. Though I'm afraid she's a little lost."

Abbey. He said Abbey. He knows my name. How?

The woman straightens her narrow frame. "I see," she says, and then extends a hand. "It is a pleasure." I hesitate a second before returning the gesture. Her slender fingers clasp mine more firmly than I anticipated. "If you should need anything, I will gladly assist. We are always looking to broaden our items of trade with Preo. Please send Pacer Toryn my regards. I hear he has been unwell."

"I don't know—"

"Thank you Pacer Aubrin," interrupts the boy behind me. "Come on, Abbey, let me show you the tavern."

"I was just—"

"Follow me," he says.

The woman, *Pacer Aubrin*, apparently, offers a small smile and waves a dismissive hand. And so I go after the boy, who has already started off without me. I have to jog to catch up.

"She knows more than most," the boy says without looking at me. "But not everything."

"Knows what?" I ask, already panting from the heat. "How do you know my name?"

He casts me a bemused look, the sun showing flecks of gold in his eyes, but says nothing. Instead he angles his head to indicate a nearby, shaded wall. I follow him there, the heat creeping away from my skin as we escape the sun.

"Balvinder told me who you are," he says, turning to me. Great. Two madmen. It's a shame this one is so cute. "He also told me you didn't believe it. That you were trying to find a way home."

"Yeah, I am."

"What he says is true." The boy gives a quick sigh. "I can vouch for it."

A trail of sweat slips down my back and I shiver. "Who are you?"

"Zacharias Nellerwood." The corner of his mouth lifts in an almost-smile. "I prefer Zac, though."

Despite the absurdity of all this, blood rushes into my cheeks at the lingering attention of his dazzling, green gaze. "I'm Abbey," I say, looking back at the fields. "Although, you already knew that, didn't you. Balvinder told you my name?"

Zac nods once.

"Did he tell you that he thinks this is a parallel universe? That I've been taken from Earth to someplace called Ethra? That I've been brought here to balance spirits or something?"

Zac is silent, but a crease starts to form between his dark brows.

"I found the guy in a house over there, tied up," I tell him. "So, now I'm starting to think he might be deranged."

"He isn't deranged," Zac replies, the words clipped. "He told you the truth."

I press my lips into a tight line, and then let them go with a huff. "You can't seriously believe him?"

"Of course I do." Zac leans back against the wall. "This parallel universe—as you call it—is my home."

My brain starts to whir, piecing together everything I've learnt so far. Man tied up. Man tells me some freaky story about an Overseer and spirits and the rest. Wheat fields and farmers. That woman ... Pacer Aubrin. Pacer Aubrin? What kind of title is that? "Have I been brought to a commune?" I think aloud. "Is that what this is?"

Zac's frown deepens. "Commune? What do you mean?"

"Oh shit." I swallow. "I'm in a commune."

At that moment, a tall, pale figure comes into view from the street. "Oh good ..." I murmur. Balvinder slows as he approaches, his tattered shirt wavering in a warm, passing breeze.

"You found her," he says.

Zac whirls around suddenly. "Balvinder." He sounds a little surprised, or uncertain. I can't tell which. "I'm not sure I have helped."

Balvinder sighs. "We will return to the house and decide from there what to do next."

"I'm not going back to that house," I say, looking from one face to the other as flashes of stone and cobwebs and that dead body jolt through me.

"No," Balvinder says. "I meant Zacharias's house."

SIX

I FEEL NUMB AS WE MOVE THROUGH THE winding streets of the town. With every step I fall more deeply into considering the impossible, because this place—I can see it and I can breathe it. And now I have two people telling me the same story. It doesn't help that both have exceptionally pretty faces that seem to elicit some unfounded sense of trust from me.

They're strangers, I tell myself, as we walk through a narrow path between houses. We just met. Why should I believe anything they say?

At the next street we pass a cart piled high with bulging sacks of odd-shaped produce. Not only does the cart spark my curiosity—since we're not living in the fifteenth century, people—but I don't recognise the animal pulling it. Hairless, with a long nose like a horse's but ears flat and wide like a dog's, and paws instead of hooves.

I stare after it until Balvinder touches my arm to beckon me onward.

We come to an avenue of trees—pale leaves fluttering a little in the thick breeze—and I fall behind, just in case I'm being led to my death and need to bolt in the opposite direction.

Zac bumps into Balvinder and mutters an apology. Then he starts whispering, and I strain to hear it. "Where have you been?" he says. "She told me you were tied up. What happened?"

Balvinder glances at him but keeps quiet.

"Are you there?" Zac inquires. He glances behind his shoulder, eyes flashing briefly my way.

"I am here," Balvinder answers softly.

Zac runs a hand through his hair, a piece of it falling back across his forehead. "You can't tell me anything more?"

"Not now," is all Balvinder offers.

I study Zac from behind—his broad shoulders, lace-up boots and matching leather apron. His gait is easy, despite the look of concern etched across his brow each time I catch glimpse of it. Balvinder is only a couple of inches taller, but his stride is different. Unusually graceful. Closer to gliding.

Up ahead a clearing opens to a tiny, stone house with a thatched roof. Beds of flowers are planted against the sidewalls—tiny bursts of yellow against the grey. Zac works a key into the lock and swings the door open, gesturing for me to go through.

I cast him a glare on my way past that I hope conveys something like ... *I might be small, but if this is a trap—I'll fight you*. He seems to read the threat on my face and faint amusement crinkles at the corners of his eyes.

"Welcome," he says.

It doesn't take long to scan my surroundings—because there isn't much to them. In one corner I see a small bed, unmade, and in another, a table with three chairs. A narrow kitchen bench setup occupies the front, nearest the door, and at the back there's a blackened fireplace partially concealed by a threadbare couch.

Zac beckons for me to take a seat, and I do, hesitantly, as he pulls up two chairs from the table for himself and Balvinder.

"So," he says, his eyes searching the room. "She can hear you."

Balvinder touches Zac's shoulder as he moves past him to drop into one of the empty chairs. "She can see me too," he says.

Zac's attention cuts abruptly to me, and he angles his head like I'm some outlandish creature and he's not sure whether I should be allowed inside. "So the last has ..."

"Passed," Balvinder answers. He stares into the fireless fireplace. "She has passed."

"I'm sorry to hear it." Zac unties his apron, balling and tossing it into a corner before swinging his chair around to sit on it backwards. He grips the polished, wooden edges, looking at me again with that same uncertainty. His shirt, a muted navy blue, has a high collar pulled together loosely with drawstrings. A hint of his sharp collarbone shows through.

"What do you mean *she can see me too?*" I ask Balvinder. "Why wouldn't I be able to see you?"

He's silent a moment, still watching the fireplace. Then he cuts those sapphire blues to me. "You are the Melder," he says. "You possess certain abilities others don't. You can hear me. See me. Most can do neither."

I laugh, without much humour. "This gets better and better." The two of them just stare at me. I shift in my seat and clear my throat. "You're invisible, is that what you're saying?"

"Yes," Balvinder says, unflinchingly.

I open my mouth for a retort, but it freezes ajar—as a memory rushes forward like a stopper thrust into the frame of a door before it can slam shut.

The bar. The waitress at the bar. She looked totally confused every time she approached the table. She'd ignored Balvinder entirely, and given me odd looks whenever I gestured to him.

What if ... she couldn't see him at all?

"How is that possible?"

Balvinder leans forward, elbows coming to rest on his knees. "Abbey," he says, steadily. "Everything I have told you— can you claim without a single doubt that it is all impossible? That there is not the slimmest chance you really were transported elsewhere for a purpose? That the brooch you found is not an indication of it? That this world is not your own?"

I chew on my lip, considering, *really* considering for the first time. The likelihood of uncovering something completely and—for the most part—inexplicably new. A foreign world, a separate layer to the universe. A discovery with the potential to crush any possible summation of my understandings.

"Look, it's probably the last conclusion I'd reach," I say finally.

Zac grins—straight, white teeth framed by a lively, dimpled smile. "Well then, I keenly await your reaching it."

"Abbey wishes to return home," Balvinder says. "And I will take her."

"Take her?" Zac shakes his head as if to clear it. "I didn't know it was—"

"Will you accompany us?" Balvinder cuts in.

"To Amnoralas?"

"Yes."

"It's a long journey," Zac says, pulling at his chin.

"One you have taken many times before."

"And if she does enter the portal? What then? Another will appear to take her place?"

Balvinder pauses a beat. "Perhaps."

"Whoa!" I throw up my hands. "Let's just ... stop. For a second. The *portal*? *Amnoralas*?"

"Yes, your way home," Balvinder says. "Amnoralas is where the portal lies—the only passage from Ethra to Earth."

"This is crazy." I press against my temples with stiff, splayed fingers. "That woman, she told me the same things. I woke up in a room with this dead body ..."

"The Melder past," Balvinder interjects, his expression slipping under a shadow of sorrow.

"Uh, okay. Well I met this other lady—her name was Kayna—and she told me similar things. She said she could take me home. Do you know her?"

"Kayna?" Zac's face is blank. "I haven't heard of the name. But if she knew what we know, she must be—"

"Yes," Balvinder interrupts. "She ... she is."

"Is what?" I demand.

Zac glances Balvinder's way, as if requesting permission. But something has shifted in Balvinder's eyes. A milky veil slipping over the blue, turning it cloudy.

He slumps forward in his chair and I launch out to catch him, just as he falls forward. Zac jerks away from his chair while I struggle under the weight of a body twice as heavy as mine.

"Help," I croak.

With wide, searching eyes, Zac reaches out his hands until they find the material of Balvinder's shirt. He grabs at the man's shoulders, hauling him up from the chair. Balvinder's feet drag and his body shudders as Zac walks him across to the bed, laying him down gently.

"Balvinder?" Zac's tone is stiff. Alert. "Are you all right?" He runs his hand over Balvinder's shoulder to his face, his cheek, and holds it there as he twists around to me. "What happened?"

My throat closes up, but I force the words out. "I think he's unconscious. His eyes went all weird. The same thing happened when I first met him. Check his pulse."

Zac gives me an odd look. "His pulse is irrelevant."

"What? How?"

"It will never stop," he says, as if that's meant to make total sense. "But this is new. He leaves for weeks and now this ... something must have happened."

I watch Zac carefully, the way his eyes roam the mattress without latching onto anything. "You can't ..." I swallow hard, hardly believing I have it in me to speak such a bizarre question aloud. "You really can't see him?"

"No." Zac straightens and rakes a hand through his hair. "To me, Balvinder is just a voice."

✻

Another tremor ripples through Balvinder's body. I move forward instinctively. Reach out my hand without thinking. Touch his forehead, which is as freezing cold as the first time.

Just like he did then—he stills. His eyes flicker closed and I pull my hand away.

"What do you see?" Zac asks, carefully gauging my movements.

"He ... he's stopped shaking," I tell him. "If it's anything like last time, he'll be okay. Do you have a phone I could use?"

Zac looks at me blankly. "Okay. Never mind." That commune theory might still just hold up.

A heavy breath gushes from Zac as he stretches his arms above his head. "This isn't like him."

"Well people don't really *choose* to have seizures," I point out, but Zac is shaking his head.

"You don't understand." He casts me a brief glance, and adds, "Yet," before moving back to the chairs and dropping into one.

I turn to Balvinder once more—his complexion smooth again, unaffected. He looks asleep. The rise and fall of his chest is even, and his lashes rest like delicate snowflakes against his pale cheeks. They're a shade or so lighter than his silver hair, which cascades back over his neck and shoulders.

Staring at him is like appreciating something immense but frozen, like a snowy mountain or a glacier, centuries old. A static wonder.

"What a strange looking dude," I murmur. Speaking breaks my reverie, and I remember I'm not alone.

I perch on the armrest of the couch opposite Zac, folding my arms over my chest. He looks up at me. At Balvinder. Back to me. "What does he look like?" he asks, in a voice so low I barely catch it.

My heart picks up pace as I slip further into believing Zac might somehow be blind to the guy. That everyone might be, except me.

"He has silver hair," I say, carefully assessing Zac's reaction. "Not the kind you see from age. It sort of shimmers, like pale ash." I bring my voice to a whisper. "And his eyes are ... freaking weird. They're blue—this piercing shade I've never seen before."

Zac's expression is stiff. I can see muscles jumping in his jaw and the ball of his throat bobbing. It doesn't look like an act.

"Why ... why can't you see him?" I ask, the taste of the question unsettling in my mouth.

Straightening, Zac sets his hands over his knees and sucks in a deep breath. "I'm not sure you're ready for it."

"For what?"

"The truth."

"Look, I just want to get home," I tell him. "Are we even in Melbourne? Can you get me there? I'll know my way once I'm closer."

Zac's eyes stay on me, vaguely amused and mottled with mesmerizing dark and light specks of green. "I don't know *Melbourne*, but I can get you closer to home." He gestures to the bed, toward Balvinder. "We both can. I think."

A few short moments later, Zac declares that it's cold enough for a fire. Although the day was sweltering, he's right. It might as well be winter inside the house. Zac marches out the door, muttering about wood, and a freezing breeze sweeps through the room. I'm shivering by the time he returns with his arms full of logs.

Outside, the sky is dragging into an inky blue. The day is almost over. What must Mum have thought this morning—finding my bed empty? What's she doing about it now? Would she have called the police?

Sudden agitation has me springing to my feet. I start to pace as Zac busies himself with the wood, sparking a cluster of kindling with what seems to be a piece of flint.

No matches? Unsurprising I guess, considering the look on his face when I asked for a phone. I might as well have asked for a spaceship to fly me out of here.

I come up behind him and set my hands on my hips.

"I can tell you're not from here," Zac says without turning. He takes a rusted, metal poker from beside the hearth and pokes at the logs as the kindling ignites.

"How's that?"

He rests the poker over his shoulder and twists around, eyes dropping to my pants. I look too, feeling suddenly conspicuous. Despite the craziness of all this, I sort of find myself wishing I'd worn something else to bed last night.

But I keep my face frank. "What? You don't wear pants here?"

"The pictures," Zac says. "I've never seen anything like them."

"Winnie-the-Pooh?"

Zac's expression flickers between perplexity and amusement. He returns to the chair nearest the fire, arching a brow at me as he goes.

My cheeks growing hot, I perch again on the couch's arm and look to the door.

"You can sit, you know," Zac says. "Properly."

"Thanks," I shoot back, staying where I am.

The logs in the fireplace shift and Zac reaches across from his chair to nudge them again with the poker. "I've never met a Melder before," he says. "Balvinder has told me about them— vague details, at least—but I've never come face to face with anyone who can speak the truth with me."

I stare at him until he looks up again, and quickly cast my gaze into the fire before he can see the fear behind it.

"You know," he says slowly, "I understand the confusion. I found out when I was ten years old, and even then it took time to believe. To *really* believe."

I say nothing, but frayed nerves spin and pulse under my skin.

"If you don't understand now, you soon will," he goes on. "You'll have to."

"What I *have* to do is get back to Mum."

Zac's mouth twists. "That's what doesn't make sense to me. If you wish more than anything to return, then why did he send for you?"

"Who?"

"The Overseer."

"Ah, yes." I roll my eyes. "The Overseer."

A creak sounds from the corner and I spin to see Balvinder's pale form upright on the bed. His bright, blue eyes find me, and he smiles.

"What's the matter?" Zac inquires. "Is he awake?"

"He is awake," answers Balvinder. He rises and closes his eyes a moment before making his way over to the fire, moving with weightless elegance. "Before you ask questions, Zacharias, know that I am unable to answer them as I wish I could. But I will, when the time comes."

Zac's dark brows lift high. Then he seems to come to a conclusion that brings them back down, level. "I know," he says. "I trust you."

He speaks with the same boldness I hear calling from somewhere deep inside me whenever I look at Balvinder. Telling me to believe him. To trust him with everything I am. It makes no sense at all.

"Can you at least tell me how long it will take me to get home?" I ask them both.

Balvinder glances at Zac—who has started inspecting the end of the poker with a small smile.

"Amnoralas grows deep within the Petrified Forest," Balvinder says. "It will take days to reach it."

"*Days?*" I jerk up off the couch. "Are you serious?"

"Quite."

"What about that Kayna lady? She said she could get me home fast."

Balvinder flinches. "No," he says, his tone harder now. "We will take you."

I sigh and let myself flop down into the couch. It's possible, I guess, that I was brought somewhere far from home. That I was left unconscious for days, or drugged to forget the time passed. If I had to choose a travelling buddy, Kayna probably wouldn't be my first pick. There was something ominous about her. I mean, it isn't exactly reassuring that we met over a dead body.

The instinctive pull I feel toward Balvinder somehow feels like a pull away from Kayna. Like I can't trust both.

All I know is that I need to get back to Mum.

"All right then," I say. "But if you're trying to trick me somehow, I will hurt you."

Zac looks up, mild surprise caught in the frame of his eyes. It quickly draws into humour, and I look into the fire before I'm tempted to smile back.

SEVEN

AFTER MUCH STEADFAST INSISTENCE FROM Zac, I take his bed, while he rolls out blankets on the floor by the fire for himself and Balvinder. I turn onto my side, wedging my hand under a lumpy, circular pillow that smells like lemongrass soap and spices. I wonder if Zac smells the same.

Quickly, I realise how creepy the thought is and eradicate it. But then I picture him lying right here—his arms draped over the bed, hair mussed, his cheek pressed against this very pillow. It makes my heart skitter and pushes me further away from any slim chance I had of sleep.

The mattress is stiff and unforgiving under my back. I toss and turn, wondering what would happen if I snuck out. Searched for some way home myself, without their help.

A tap at the window has me bolting upright. Light but sharp, like nails against glass. Peering out into the dim night, dashed only by the silhouettes of trees, there's no obvious source.

I turn to the fire. Balvinder is awake, his eyes on the window too. They flit briefly to me before closing.

Sleep takes me in short bursts. I wake suddenly, each time surprised to find myself in an unfamiliar room. A rush of strange memories takes over my mind, again and again. All that I've heard—from Kayna and Balvinder and Zac—snakes through the logical paths in my brain and strains to slash new trails I don't recognise.

I dream of the brooch—touching it now and drawing into its shadowy spiral until I land in my own bed. Tyler appears, telling me to stop overthinking everything. He smiles his gap-toothed smile and says, "*Just go with the flow.*"

Go with the flow. Wherever I'm flown. Consider the possibility. Blaze trails into a new space, where new possibilities exist. Where just maybe, what I've been told could be true.

✳

I jolt awake at the sound of a door swinging on its hinges. Just as tall, pale, and ethereal as I remember him, Balvinder strides past the bed with a bundle in his arms. He's dressed in fresh clothes—the dirty, torn shirt I found him in replaced with a firm, grey tunic. He looks like a prince stepping right out of a fairytale book.

After laying his bundle down on the bench, he turns back to me. "Well-rested?"

I rub at my eyes and try to sit up. My stomach roils with the movement and the realisation that I'm still here. It's all still real. "Yeah," I lie.

Harsh morning light beams through the window and across my forearms like hot rods. A jumble of equipment is strewn across the floor at Balvinder's feet. Knives, rope, boots, pants, belts. But the boy from last night—he isn't here.

"Zacharias is procuring a few more supplies from the market," Balvinder says. I blink at him, wondering if the timing of the statement was just coincidence or whether I'm that easy to read.

I shrug and push back the tangle of sheets.

"Here." Balvinder holds up something round before throwing it over to me. A piece of fruit, the skin a deep-blue and lightly fuzzy under my fingertips. "You must be hungry."

I inspect the fruit more closely, turning and prodding it. Then I take a bite and juice runs down my chin. I hastily cup a hand underneath to catch the drops. It's intensely sweet, and when I pull it away I see that the flesh is vibrant yellow.

I *was* hungry, I realise, as the sick feeling in my gut begins to ease. "What is this?"

"A bolikon," Balvinder says, weaving a belt through the loops in his pants.

Bolikon pie—what he made me order yesterday. So it *is* a real thing.

I finish off the fruit and discover there isn't a central seed, only a few little ones. So I eat the entire thing, licking my fingers clean.

"Zacharias stores all this under the house," Balvinder says, gesturing over the bags and other bits and bobs. "But he is buying new gear for you. We weren't sure how much protection that ..." His gaze wanders to Winnie-the-Pooh. "... that material, will offer."

"Protection?" I repeat, my wariness growing.

"We will be journeying on foot most of the way," Balvinder says. "The terrain can be treacherous, particularly when unfamiliar."

I'm about to ask what terrain he means exactly, when the door swings open. It's Zac, carrying a wooden crate. He's wearing a dark shirt and a belt slung low over his hips. His eyes meet mine, and he offers one of those half-smiles, hooked up into a dimple on one side—the only feature that breaks the perfect symmetry of his face.

"See how they fit," he says, setting the crate at the end of the bed. "I can return them, if need be. Is Balvinder here?"

"Yes," comes his answer from the bench. I glance between them—still uncertain whether to believe Balvinder is really, wholly invisible to Zac. If it's all a trick, they play it well. And if it's true ... I don't know what to think.

I peer inside the crate and pull out a leather jacket, black pants, socks, and a belt looped around a pair of lace-up boots.

"You didn't have to buy all this," I say, pulling my hair back more firmly into its elastic.

Balvinder steps swiftly aside as Zac begins sorting the contents on the bench into piles.

"Well we certainly won't have you trekking through the mountains in those," Zac replies, glancing across at my pj's.

"The *mountains?*" Well that answers my terrain question.

"You should have seen Tarli's face when I bought the clothes," Zac says to Balvinder, ignoring my exclamation. "She asked who they were for and wouldn't let me leave until I was forced to invent a story about my distant cousin who is visiting from the northern continent. I don't think she believed it."

"Ah." Balvinder chuckles. "I have no doubt. She likes to keep one eye on you and the other on anyone who dares to show interest."

Zac unbuckles a small case, opening it to reveal a series of knives strapped against the material. "Well, she certainly didn't offer a fair price this time," he says with a sigh. "What should we take in the way of weapons?"

"*Weapons?*" I cut in. They both look to me.

"Of course," Zac says, pulling a curved knife out of its straps. He opens a drawer and picks out a scabbard to match before buckling it to his belt and sliding the blade into place. "How else will I hunt?"

I blink at him, wondering whether to laugh or not.

"Don't worry." He waves away my concern, which immediately resurfaces when he adds, "I can teach you."

✳

My search for a mirror leads me to a cupboard under the kitchen bench, where I find one no bigger than my face. It has a metal handle and the surface itself is dusty and looks unused. When you're as pretty as Zac, you mustn't need to check yourself regularly.

I lodge the mirror under the window and spin up and around and down to see as much of myself as the small square will allow. The moleskin pants sag, but with the belt I can draw them around my hips tightly enough. And the boots are only a touch too big for me, although I fix that too by pulling the laces in tight. The jacket—which I have on over my singlet—is my primary concern. I pinch at the leather. It's like a second skin, thick and stiff. The shoulders are capped in hard pads, which continue down my arms.

Sighing, I go to the window and rap at it to signal my readiness.

Zac comes inside, giving my potato sack pants and clown shoes a once-over. "Fits well enough?"

"Well ..." I cross my arms, feeling the leather tighten across them. "The jacket is firm."

The sun floods into the room as Balvinder steps through the doorway behind Zac. "It will loosen," he says. "That material is impenetrable."

I decide not to go on about it. Beggars can't be choosers, as they say. I unpin the brooch from my singlet and slide it through a softer flap on the outside of the jacket. Then I do up the buttons, which start at my left hip and rise right up to a high collar.

We have three packs ready to go—soft brown leather pulled together with ropey straps. My nerves didn't exactly ease as I watched Zac stuff them earlier with waterskins, thick blankets, bags of nuts and dried fruit and some sort of jerky. Not exactly luxury camping supplies.

I glance down at their boots—similar to mine with their thick soles and dark laces. Somehow they manage to look slick, whereas I feel totally ridiculous.

Zac grabs the packs, swinging one my way. I fumble and miss the catch. "Where?" he inquires, the other bag poised and ready.

"Here," Balvinder says, extending his hands. Zac throws it at him. "Is the boat ready?"

My eyes spring wide. "Boat? What boat?"

Zac grins and tugs a sleeveless hoodie over his shirt. He sweeps hair back from his face and picks up the last pack. "You can swim," he says, "if you would prefer."

Balvinder shoots him a wry smile before turning to me and explaining, "We must cross the lake to get to the mountains. Zac has a boat we can take."

Large bodies of water have never thrilled me. Even the beach and I don't tend to get along. Mum, who dives freely under waves and can lie for hours on the sand, can't understand why, and I try to explain—the sea is an endless abyss, and we haven't even discovered the half of it. Splashing around in such an unknown doesn't sit well with me. I'd rather appreciate it from afar. Which happens to reflect how I feel about boys, too.

Zac leads us out and around the house to a path between the trees. I notice now that their trunks are ashen, bark crusty. The branches bend a little toward the ground, drooping sickly pale leaves.

"The trees," I say. "Are they dying?"

"No." Balvinder turns to me with a strange smile. "They are waiting for the moonlight." He seems to deem that a sufficient explanation and walks on, leaving me with more questions than before. He and Zac pick up their pace before I can ask either of them. I hurry along behind, tugging the straps of my pack until it rests comfortably under my shoulder.

"We may stop at Preo," I hear Balvinder say. "Our supplies will need replenishing by then."

Zac's posture stiffens, but he continues to walk. "Oh?"

"It might be time, Zacharias. If you are ready. And if not, we can send Abbey down."

If Zac answers, I don't catch it. I'm tempted to ask where Preo is, since I might be *sent down* there, apparently, but something keeps me quiet.

Soon enough the trees become fewer, then clear entirely to reveal a still, glassy expanse. Zac leads the way across a bank of rocks that crunch and crumble under our feet. A long, wooden rowboat is tied to a post at the water's edge, two oars laid inside it.

Across the lake, a jagged, grey line marks the horizon— the spectral silhouette of a mountain range. I've never seen or heard of anything like it close to home. And so, there's no point in denying it now.

Home isn't just around the corner.

Zac nimbly unties the rope securing the boat, and Balvinder, now barefoot, pushes it out into ankle-deep water, swinging his boots into the bow.

"Abbey?" Zac extends a hand. I take it, my fingers meeting the warm, rough skin of his palm, and take a jump up into the end of the boat. I stumble inelegantly up to the front, sitting across one of the three, wooden beams and laying my pack at my feet.

My hand still pulses from where Zac held onto it.

He takes a leap from the bank and lands behind me as Balvinder pushes the boat further out.

At the last moment Balvinder climbs in too, and by that time Zac already has both oars slicing through the silky water, his sleeves pushed up to his elbows.

I grab for one of the oars but he jerks it back. "Let me help," I say. I'm not the most solidly built person, but these scrawny arms are deceiving. I can beat Tyler in an arm wrestle any day.

A fleeting smile crosses Zac's lips and he says, "I'll pass them on when I get tired." Judging by the muscles in his forearms, snagging my attention as they pump the oars, lean and strong, I have a feeling I'll be waiting a while.

As we glide smoothly across the lake, the rolling hills and farmland of Emba's heart appear behind the trees. Further down the bank, there's a stream of activity—a pier with an enormous barge and workers teeming to and fro. Crates and barrels are carried up onto the deck, some small and others requiring one person for each corner.

"We trade our produce for Preo's timber," explains Zac, clearly having noted my interest in the scene. "They send stone, too, from their quarries in the mountains."

I nod, trying not to let my confusion show. Preo—another unfamiliar place.

Two worlds exist in parallel, Balvinder had said back in that bar. *Earth—your homeland, and Ethra—where you now find yourself.*

The water's edge gradually shrinks, along with the barge and the people shifting from the pier to its deck. My sanity must be slipping further away too, because out on this lake—so unlike anything back home—it's becoming a fraction easier to believe Balvinder's story.

My focus meanders across the static mountains and then to the dark water over the boat's edge. Fear prickles at the periphery of my consciousness. We're nothing but a speck on a broad sheet of black glass. I feel suddenly small, like I could easily be stamped out or sucked down and no one would ever know.

"How long does this usually take?" I ask, the faintest trace of nausea rumbling in my gut.

"We will reach the mountains before dark," Balvinder says.

There's a lengthy silence—broken only by the sound of water sloshing against the oars.

"So." Balvinder clears his throat, and I turn at the decisive note in his voice. "I do believe we should know more about you, Abbey Shader," he says, "before we send you home again."

I shift one leg over the wooden beam until I'm sideways and can see him more clearly. "What do you want to know?" I try not to look at Zac, whose gaze I can sense.

"Do you have sisters or brothers?" Balvinder asks.

"Nope. Just me." Mum's face drifts to the forefront of my mind. "And Mum." I try to toss the thought aside, since dwelling on her won't get me home any faster.

"Do you have any siblings?" I ask him.

Balvinder inclines his head and hesitates. "In a sense," he says. I glance at Zac to see his lips caving in, as if suppressing laughter.

Not understanding the joke, if there is one, I throw the question his way. "What about you then?"

Zac shakes his head. "None."

"And your parents? Why don't you live with them?" He does seem young to be living out of home already.

The green in his eyes darkens with the reflection of the water as he turns sharply toward it. "They are gone," he says simply.

Balvinder gives me a wary look, as if to confirm that there's more to the story, but now isn't the time to ask for it.

The sun is huge, poised like a giant orb behind streaks of passing cloud. It's abnormal—the size of it. Almost three times the diameter of the sun on any other day.

"Tell us about your friends," Balvinder says, distracting me again. "I am sure you have many."

"Oh, well, not really. There are a few from school, but it's mostly Tyler." I hesitate. How much do I tell them?

Before I can draw the reins in on my personal information, it comes pouring out of me. "We met in Year Seven drama class, and after that we spent almost everyday together. He's a loose canon and I'm pretty much as safe as you can get—so we're a good combo. He helps me take risks and I help him minimize them. We balance each other out."

Zac's eyes lock with mine, and he inclines his head thoughtfully as he rows. "I like that," he says. "My closest friend is invisible. Is that as tragic as it sounds?"

I find myself nodding.

Balvinder chuckles and Zac twists his head around.

"You aren't supposed to agree."

"I didn't," Balvinder retorts, covering a smile.

Zac lifts the oars up high and splashes them down into the water with vigour. I catch sight of a pale mark on his chest, some formation of defined lines against his bronze skin. He shrugs his shirt back into place, concealing it. "Laughter is a form of agreement," he says. "The cruelest and most passive kind."

Balvinder rolls his eyes and grins freely at me. Something softens inside my chest, and I start to contemplate the reality of the situation again. The truth draws almost close enough to believe, but then flips on its head before I can grasp it fully.

"You say that I have been summoned from Earth," I say slowly. The pronouncement seems to take them by surprise, since both pairs of eyes, sky-blue and emerald-green, are abruptly intent and on me. "That I'm now in a place called Ethra, some parallel world. Right?"

Zac repeats, "Right," and Balvinder gives a sombre nod.

"Okay, let's say it's true. That there really is some sort of underlying bridge between the world I know and another I don't, and I've been transported across it somehow. What I'd want to know is—*why*?"

"Perhaps that is a question for the Overseer," Balvinder says. "Typically, those Melders who are sent for, stay. At least for the duration of their destined ruling."

"What would I be 'destined to rule' exactly?"

"The Essences," Zac answers, and the word springs back to me from yesterday. I still don't understand it.

"If you think I have some sort of ... *power* ... you've got the wrong girl."

Balvinder sighs. "There is power in your—"

The boat lurches suddenly. I'm flung forward into Zac, my ribcage colliding with one of the oars. There's a shudder and a slap as the front of the boat hits the water again. I skid back the other way, grabbing at the wooden beam I've been sitting on.

Zac's brow is furrowed as his eyes roam the rippling water. Balvinder looks stricken, which seems only to rattle my nerves further still.

I whirl around to inspect every square inch of the lake around us. The darkness of the surface makes it impossible to detect any shadows.

"What was that?" I breathe—right before a stronger force jolts the boat. I tumble into Zac again but this time I'm jerked sideways with a sudden second blow. My head smacks into wood and I fall.

EIGHT

I'M SUSPENDED. DAZED. I HEAR MY NAME called but it takes a moment to wrap awareness around the rest of my body.

I'm weightless. Freezing.

Instinctively I open my mouth to gasp and water rushes in. I bark out a cough, bubbles tickling my cheeks. Willing myself to stay calm, I squint around at the darkness until shards of glimmering light appear to my left. Then I snap into action— pushing toward them with all my might.

My heavy boots and clothes are like lead threatening to drag me the other way. Unhelpful flashes from all the B-grade horror films I've seen flood my mind. Dangling legs above dark abysses. Fast, slippery bodies poised to strike. Thank you mother, for introducing me to *Jaws* at the age of twelve.

I break the surface, spluttering and coughing up water. Once there's air in my lungs I spin to look for the boat. It's a few metres off. Balvinder is standing still, ghostly white. Zac is in a crouch beside him, an oar outstretched toward me.

"Abbey," I hear him say carefully. "*Swim.*" There's steadfast insistence in the word, verging on alarm.

My heart thrums as I start to paddle, craning my neck to keep my head above water. I lock my focus on Zac's eyes instead of the oar, following them as if they're the rescue rope pulling me in.

But then they shift upward.

A swell pushes me forward from behind, where Zac's gaze is now fixed. I turn—and a sharp breath catches in my throat. A grey, swollen mound is rising rapidly from the water. Bulbous eyes appear, round and pale with irregular pupils. The creature—something akin to an enormous, misshapen frog—gleams wet and slippery under the sun. Dread drops like a stone in my stomach.

"*Swim!*" Zac shouts.

I kick hard for the boat. Icy water fills my mouth and nose and I splutter through it. I don't dare waste time by turning back, even when the urge becomes unbearable.

Once I'm close enough, I lurch for the oar and grab hold of it. Zac drags me in so quickly I feel like I'm flying across the water. Balvinder yells something but I don't catch it. I look over my shoulder as a thick barb surges toward me.

Agony explodes across my back.

I collide with the side of the boat and feel Zac's hand, firm on my arm, right before everything goes numb.

The sky shrinks in, black at the edges of my vision.

I feel nothing, but see Zac and Balvinder's anxious faces hauling me in like a sodden rag. Behind them, the creature's head appears again. Terror grips me but all I can do is widen my eyes a little.

Zac spins and I catch a glimpse of iridescent steel. The barb—which I now see is a deadly tongue, snaking from the creature's wide, toothless mouth—lashes out again. There's a crack as Zac slams his dagger into the boat.

The creature writhes furiously, exposing a pale, bloated belly while it tries to free itself from the blade pinning its tongue. Zac jerks the curved knife out of the wood and the creature sinks back beneath the murky surface.

I try to sit up but I feel detached. Like the pathway from brain to body has been severed, any commands futile.

Darkness closes in.

"Can I—" Zac stops short. His voice sounds far off.

The sky starts to dim as Balvinder's face bends into my narrowed view, strands of silver hair so close I swear I can feel it against my cheeks. "She is hurt," he says. "We must." I'm vaguely aware of my jacket coming off, and then a sharp intake of breath.

"I was worse," Zac says urgently. "I was worse and you fixed me. You can fix this too."

Their voices slip away, along with my last glimpse of the sky.

✳

I wake to night studded with glittering stars. The moon is full and immense. Startlingly bright. I drag myself upright, feeling a band of pressure compress around my chest. The boat is beached on large pebbles at the still rim of the lake. Grey slabs of stone loom ahead like shadowy soldiers warding away intruders.

"The mountains," I breathe.

"Yes."

I jolt at the voice; Balvinder, resting idly against the boat behind me. He looks at me. Those shining eyes, in combination with his luminescent hair—could have him pass for a very wise, very old owl. *Old* only in the feeling he evokes. His complexion is just as smooth and youthful as Zac's.

Zac.

Memories from the lake flood over me. "What—what happened—" I stop, registering tightness as my breathing picks up. I'm wearing only my singlet, but underneath I prod at a thick bandage. I follow it under my arm and around my shoulder.

"You will begin to feel the pain throughout the night," Balvinder says. "There was only so much I could do about a wound inflicted by ... by an ordinary creature."

"*Ordinary?*" I try to stagger to standing but a sharp pain snags in my shoulder, urging me back down. "Nothing about that thing was ordinary," I breathe, gritting my teeth as I lower myself back into the boat.

Balvinder pushes smoothly off the ledge and steps across the rocks, stopping with his boots inches away from the lapping water. "Ordinary has many meanings, doesn't it?" he muses. "What seems ordinary to one might be quite extraordinary to another."

"No, no," I quickly retort, shaking my head. "If that giant frog thing didn't shock you ... seriously. Nothing about that was normal." Balvinder turns to me. Under the huge moon, every part of him seems to illuminate. "And that!" I point up to the sky. "When did the moon get so big? And the sun! Explain that." Slowly, Balvinder walks toward me. I start to tremble, my teeth clattering together. "I don't know what's going on. I don't know where I am. And Zac—where's Zac?"

"Slow your breathing, Abbey." Balvinder crouches beside the boat until his eyes are level with mine. "Zacharias went ahead to scope out a resting place. And as for your other questions—there is time. Time for answers and discovery. You will hear everything that must be heard before returning home, and you will be granted a choice at the end of it. It is the sum of all choices that has landed you here at all, you see."

"I don't see," I tell him, flatly.

Balvinder's mouth curves up gently at both sides. "In time."

A shape in my periphery seizes my attention. Zac is walking toward us from a narrow valley between the mountains. Steel flashes at his shoulder. It's his dagger—I see, as he gets closer—he's spinning and catching it by the handle, over and over.

I run my gaze over his rangy frame, wide at the shoulders and narrow through the hips down to his long legs. "Balvinder?

I found a fold where we—" Zac stops in his tracks, staring at me. "You're awake."

I lift a brow. "Disappointed?"

He huffs a laugh, and I can hear relief in it. "How does your shoulder feel now?"

I offer an unconvincing thumbs up, feeling a muscle twinge as if on cue. I hide it though, and force myself to my feet.

Balvinder is still crouched, but now he looks up at me, the angular planes of his face alight. "Already you intrigue me, Abbey Shader."

NINE

"I CAN TAKE IT, REALLY." I TRY TO SWIPE AT the pack, which Zac is swinging over his shoulder along with his.

"Stop," he says.

"I'm fine!"

"Don't be daft. You were paralyzed and unconscious all but a few moments ago," Zac retorts. "That doesn't sound like *fine* to me."

A little affronted, I trudge along behind him with Balvinder's chuckle resounding from the rear.

Zac's probably right. Despite my desire to show a fierce sense of resolve and resilience, the pain in my shoulder is intensifying with every step. Even bending my arms to get my jacket on wasn't easy.

The gap we're moving through is so narrow we're forced to march in single file. I'm glad it's night and the walls are difficult to see clearly. But even so, I imagine them creaking closer. Loose rocks plummeting down and trapping us between them.

A gust of cool air tousles my hair as we finally break free from the suffocating gap. I breathe it in, ignoring the throbbing in my shoulder long enough to fill my lungs. Zac leads us up a slope and then down into a small valley.

Ahead, the mountains go on as far as I can see. Their solemn, grey faces are so pale in the moonlight they almost look snow-capped.

Zac sets down our packs and starts pulling out blankets and bags of food. I didn't register my hunger until now. Any emptiness in my stomach has been filled with the sick feeling of unease or the panic of the lake.

I help Zac lay the beds out into a rough triangle formation, and then we split a crusty roll of bread. "No," Balvinder says when I offer him a piece. "Not for me."

"What do you mean?"

"I don't require it," he replies, settling back on his blanket. "The two of you do."

It's not a particularly convincing argument, but when I look to Zac he just shrugs. I'm not about to force-feed Balvinder, so I drop it and chew on my bread.

"I am deeply sorry for what happened," he says. "Some things are quite impossible to predict."

"Don't be." I sweep crumbs off my lap. "I was the one who fell in. Not exactly your fault."

The naturally kind incline of Balvinder's brow furrows into something steelier. "We will protect you, Abbey. It won't happen again."

"Well that's a relief," I say, attempting to keep my tone light. "There are only so many barbs a girl can take." I fight back the flaring memories—water gushing down my throat, my boots dragging me down into that endless darkness, the force of the creature's attack knocking me into the timber of the boat. I stare up at the moon, using it to anchor my mind on dry land.

"You are taking it well, considering," Zac comments, his head resting at an angle while he regards me.

I shrug and try not to react to the resultant muscle spasm in my shoulder. "Character building."

He blinks. "What?"

"My Mum goes on about it a lot," I tell him. "When something doesn't go to plan, you have two choices. Sulk in self-defeat or take it as an opportunity."

For instance, if my exam results were lower than I expected—character building. If I broke my arm and had to wear a cast for three months—character building. If my Dad was a self-centred arsehole who would rather work than see his own daughter—character building.

Making it through these things could be vital to making it through bigger things. That's the theory, anyway.

Zac arches a brow, a chilly breeze sweeping the gentle, dark waves of his hair into his eyes. He briskly brushes them aside and leans back on his elbows. "I still think we could have done without it."

"Well, yeah," I concur. "I'd say the *character building* mindset is mostly just a coping mechanism for when things get really shit."

"Your mother is wise," Balvinder says, smiling.

"Oh, the wisest." I let myself smile back. "After me of course."

Balvinder gives Zac a look, which Zac doesn't return. Supposedly, I remember, he isn't able to see him at all.

A few moments later Balvinder announces his drowsiness and tells Zac to wake him for night watch. He settles into the grass, pulling one of the red blankets over himself.

Zac taps his shoulder while glancing across at mine. "How does it feel now?"

I trace the bandage outline under my jacket and through my singlet. For the first time I realise that they must have undressed me to wrap it. My nerves flutter at the thought of Zac's hands on my bare skin.

"It's fine," I say rapidly—which isn't true. Even resting, the muscles around the wound burn and sting if I move so much as an inch. Judging by Zac's narrowing glare, he seems to see right through my nonchalance. "Giant frogs," I murmur, snorting to myself. "Who knew?"

A waver of amusement catches in the corner of his mouth. "Giant frogs?"

"That's what it looked like. Don't you think?"

"Verlom," Zac says. "That's what they're called. And they aren't typically so aggressive. They're funny creatures."

"Yeah, really hilarious."

He casts me a rueful smile. "You don't have anything like them on Earth?"

I frown, momentarily thrown by the word *Earth* spoken in such a removed sense. "Uh, none that I've seen." Despite the accumulating evidence, I still find it hard to believe this isn't the world I know. There must be some other sensible explanation.

Zac rifles through his pack and retrieves a bag of small, jelly-like cubes. He pops one in his mouth before offering the bag to me.

I take it and roll a few of the drops into my palm, thinking back to the conversations I've shared and heard to this point. "I need to ... get my head around some things," I start, wondering how I can ask the questions I need to ask without sounding like an escaped asylum patient. "Some things I don't understand. I mean, I'm trekking across lakes and mountains with you, blindly trusting that home is somewhere beyond it all, so I think it's about time I was given real answers. Satisfactory ones."

Zac rolls up the bag and sets it down. "All right." He leans forward, wrapping his arms around his legs. "Ask away."

For a split-second I'm too stricken by his gaze on me to remember what my questions were. I fall into the lines of his face, a delicate sort of nose and high cheekbones under bright, glistening eyes. Freaking hell. How am I supposed to function around a face like that?

"Well—" I glance away, focusing instead on the grass around my feet. I pluck at it, strand by strand. "Balvinder said I'm a *Melder*." I hesitate, waiting for some sort of reaction. Maybe a laugh. A dismissal. But Zac keeps quiet, so I ask, "Well what is that?"

"Do you remember what we told you at the house?" he inquires. "About the Essences?"

"Essences." I chew on my lip, thinking back. "That I'm here to *rule* them, or something?"

He gives a flourish of his hand as if all my answers have been provided.

"Okay—wait." I shift around to face him, wincing at the pain in the movement. "What *are* Essences exactly?"

Zac purses his lips, shooting a side-glance at Balvinder. "Is he asleep?" he mouths.

Peering over at Balvinder's peaceful form, I see the breath easing in and out of him smoothly, his lashes frosted crescents against his cheeks. I nod back at Zac.

"You spoke of character building earlier," he says, a new light sparking in his eyes. "Well, the Melder kind of does the same thing, but for others too, and quite literally."

I puzzle over his words. "I have no idea what you're talking about."

Zac shifts nearer the edge of his blanket, closer to me. "There is a process behind every living being that goes mostly unrecognized." He lowers his voice a touch. "It allows us to be free, free in spirit, so we can be who we are and compose our own characters."

Staring into Zac's steadfast expression, it's easy to take his words as unequivocal truths. But there's still too much missing for the story to resonate.

"There are Essences in the air we breathe," he continues. "Certain spheres are designed to sustain our bodies. But the Essences exist in an alternate layer unseen to the common eye—the *erodosphere*." He cuts the space between us with a hand. I've noticed he uses them a lot when he speaks, like they're telling stories of their own. I blink and attempt to draw my focus away from the elaborate tale of the hands and back to what he's actually saying.

"Everyone needs a spirit to exist, to truly exist, otherwise we would be nothing but empty shells," he says. "The erodosphere sustains our spirits. It's the metaphysical component of Earth and Ethra, just as essential as any other sphere."

"Wow." I look up at the sky, widening my eyes at the stars as if this erodosphere will reveal itself amongst them if I look hard enough. "That's quite the theory."

"It isn't a theory."

I try not to smile. Whether it's true or not, he certainly seems to believe it. And I don't want him to think I'm mocking him. "So you're saying that this invisible 'erodosphere' is composed of Essences that our spirits need to survive. Essences we breathe." The combination of words feels foreign on my tongue.

"*Yes.*" Zac grins, clearly under the misconception that I'm closer to understanding what he's saying. "Balvinder tells me there are two Major Essences—Good and Evil—and a number of Minor Essences, which can be used for either motivation."

Good and Evil? Is he serious?

"Uh ... so Balvinder is the one who told you all this?"

Zac nods, and I start to wonder if we might both be victims of some elaborate, cultish evangelism.

"How did you meet the guy, anyway?" I ask, again drawing my voice into a whisper. I wonder if their introduction was anything like mine and Balvinder's—involving dust and rope. I still don't know why I found him that way. Maybe Zac can tell me. "Who is he?"

With a sigh, Zac presses back onto his hands, arching his head back to the sky. "I'm not sure I can say."

I snort. "Really? After all that?"

He looks back to me, the edge of a smile crooked on his lips. Then he drags a hand through his hair. "We met ten years ago—I was ten at the time. Just a boy." For some reason, I make a mental note of it. That would make him twenty now. Three years older than me. "Balvinder raised me through a turbulent time."

"Raised you?" I shake my head. "He doesn't look much older than you himself."

"Doesn't he?" Zac's smirk returns. "I wouldn't know."

"Oh, right. Because you can't see him."

"Why do you say that like it isn't true?" There's some exasperation in his tone now. Maybe my skepticism is finally wearing him out. It's wearing me out a little too.

I extend a beseeching palm. "Because it's crazy!"

"There are other things we can't see," Zac says. "Like the wind."

"Yeah, because the wind is made up of air molecules."

"Then wouldn't you agree that there does exist more than our eyes are capable of seeing?"

I hold his gaze for a second or two, but the unyielding frankness of it has me averting my eyes.

"What, like Essences?" I pose. "Good and Evil?"

"Exactly," Zac says, either missing my sarcasm or choosing to ignore it. "Do you see Good or Evil?"

"I see the effect of it."

"All right. Where does it come from then?"

"It—I don't—the sum of our choices, I guess."

"Yes." Zac rolls his shoulders. "Because our spirits allow us to choose."

I squint at him. "You really believe all this?"

"With everything I am." He looks again toward Balvinder, and I consider the earnest edge to his voice and his gaze. If he's fibbing, he's fantastic at it.

"There's a reason I can't see him and you can," Zac explains, his expression wide open, insistent. "Balvinder is an Essence."

He rocks back, assessing my reaction. But I'm not sure how I feel, or how I'm supposed to feel. It's like he's speaking another language. He could have just told me Balvinder was a peanut and I'd probably feel much the same.

"Didn't you say the Essences existed in that erodosphere thing?"

Zac tilts his head side to side. "Yes, but they are represented by bodies too. Bodies only *you* can see, as the Melder. You have been called here to restore the balance." When I just stare, he breezes on. "I can't tell you which Essence Balvinder is, because he hasn't revealed as much to me. I gave up on questioning him long ago. His face is hard to read when you can't see it. And besides, he claims it's better that I don't know."

"Wow."

Zac sighs and reclines back on his blanket. I do the same, lowering myself onto my good shoulder.

"I can understand your confusion," he says. "But you were transported here by a brooch. If you can believe that, perhaps you can believe this."

I don't know how to respond, but my fingers go to the brooch pinned to my jacket, tracing its curved edges. I study the gentle frame of Zac's profile, lit by the moon, and the way his hair falls back from his ear to expose the line of his jaw.

"I still have questions," I finally say.

"Of course." He says it matter-of-factly, like more questions are inevitable. But that isn't particularly comforting, because it means he's prepared to defend his theory some more.

And if he manages to convince me, even the tiniest bit—what then?

There are no library books or internet connections out here to affirm or diminish its validity. No diagrams or charts to outline the theory. Just me and one beautiful boy convinced of this supposed truth.

I *should* need logical explanations and I *should* need evidence. Why is there a part of me that feels it doesn't need either to believe it?

TEN

MY SLEEP ISN'T SO MUCH A SLEEP AS IT IS A jarring switch between real, agonizing pain and a series of disturbing nightmares.

The gash in my back blazes throughout the night. It seems impossible to get comfortable in mind or body since both are plagued by the aftermath of the lake.

My final jerk into wakefulness leaves me momentarily disoriented. The mountains are on full display before the rising sun, and it takes me a few seconds to remember why I'm here at all. When I do, things don't exactly clear up.

I scan the area; the three packs beside me, Balvinder and Zac's blankets missing. They're standing a short distance away at the crest of a nearby mountain, facing the opposite direction.

Balvinder is a few feet behind Zac, a hand resting on his back.

Our conversation last night returns to me. The *erodosphere*, Zac had called it. An unseen layer of the world that feeds the spirit like the atmosphere feeds the body. It makes certain sense, that there would be things about the universe yet to be discovered. But why should I be the one to discover them?

Zac also said that Balvinder is an *Essence*, and I—being the *Melder*—am the only one with the ability to see him. If I choose to take his word for it, what exactly am I choosing to believe?

Balvinder turns and sees me watching him. I hastily sit up, groaning as pain shoots through my back. When I open my eyes he's crouching in front of me.

"Careful." His radiant gaze flickers to my shoulder. I consider then that it doesn't feel entirely impossible to believe Balvinder is something other than human. The colour of his eyes alone is alien compared to any I've seen before, and the frosted hair and clean-cut tunic only add to the effect.

Zac ambles over to us. I see that he's holding a dagger, but the hilt of his own knocks lightly against his hip. "Abbey," he says. "We've decided you should have this. Just in case."

He approaches Balvinder, who moves swiftly out of the way just as Zac claims the position in front of me. He hands me a dagger in a leather sheath, with a loop at its end. Pulling it from the casing, I inspect the faded red handle and the fine markings down the centre of the blade spread like the veins in a leaf.

"Comforting," I mutter.

"It will be," Zac says. "If you should need it."

I slide the dagger back into its sheath and reach down to buckle it to my belt. "You mean if I should stumble across another giant frog."

He offers a wry smile. "Hopefully the verlom are behind us."

"The verlom might be," Balvinder says, "though the terrain ahead will be rough. Might I inspect your wound before we go on, Abbey?"

"Uh, sure." I start unbuttoning my jacket, peeling it away with a wince.

Zac grabs two of the packs and starts walking, obviously deciding to offer some privacy. I don't feel uncomfortable pulling the strap of my singlet down for Balvinder. Something about him evokes an instinctive ease you usually gain around lifelong friends, or family.

He helps me unravel the bandage and then I rock forward over my knees while he prods at my shoulder. Though his fingertips are cool, I feel warmth spread from the touch. A buzzing, numbing feeling.

I look curiously over my shoulder as far as I can turn. "What are you doing?"

"It seems to be healing well," is all he says.

Once I'm dressed I roll up my blanket and tuck it under my arm. Zac has taken my pack, again. He's waiting for us at the base of a mountain ahead. The uneven rock is difficult to navigate with any degree of dignity. My clown boots nick on the scree and despite the fact that the pain in my shoulder has eased up—I still feel unsteady on my feet.

We trail up the slope together. By the time we near the top of it, I've fallen far behind their long strides. Balvinder and Zac stop to wait, and that's when I notice a distinct difference between them. From Zac's feet, the sun casts a long shadow across the rock that almost reaches mine. But Balvinder ... he has no shadow.

I'm breathless when I reach them, my brain reeling from the stark observation. I consider asking about it—but something stops me. Maybe I know, somewhere deep down, that the answer might validate Zac's theory. That Balvinder is different. A sort of *Essence*, as he claims. Maybe I don't want it confirmed.

"We can slow down," Zac says.

I shut my mouth and breathe in deeply through my nose as though I do this everyday and my lungs aren't burning from the effort. "No," I say. "The sooner I get home the better." A sea of grey peaks rise in frozen waves, taunting me. "How far do we have to go?"

"Well once we reach the edge of the mountains, it will take us a day to reach the Moonlit Woods," Zac says. "Then another two or so until we get to the Petrified Forest, and Amnoralas."

"Remind me again what Amnoralas is?" I ask, still catching my breath.

"The great tree," answers Balvinder. "Keeper of the portal."

"Right." I grab at my pack, which Zac is still carrying. He retreats a step but I hold on.

"Your shoulder—"

"I have another one," I tell him, tugging at the ropes to stuff my blanket inside. After a moment's hesitation, Zac shrugs off the pack and hands it over.

We go on without much conversation. The labour of our trek through the mountain pass zaps my will or ability to speak.

A few animals cross our path, which is more than a little startling since they're mostly small, furry creatures the same colour as the rock—camouflaged until they bolt suddenly out of hiding.

"How did the Melder pass?" Zac asks out of nowhere, along a relatively flat stretch of rock.

"It was peaceful," Balvinder says. "She left peacefully."

"You mean the body I saw when I arrived?" I inquire between panting breaths. The memory of the woman feels far off, even though it wasn't long ago that I saw her in that musty, stone room.

"Yes." Balvinder ducks his head. The sorrow in his voice has me glancing across at him, but his face is concealed behind a sweep of silver hair. "I wish, Abbey ..." he begins softly. "I wish I could—" The word hitches and his pack drops off his shoulder.

Zac spins around to us. "Balvinder?"

My senses, weary from the walk, barely register Balvinder's fall. I toss my bag and rush toward his crumpled form.

"He's down," I tell Zac, heaving Balvinder up against my knees. He shudders head to toe, as if charges of electricity are ripping through every bone in his body.

Zac crouches beside us, the pained look on his face a mild reflection of Balvinder's. "Is it the same as last time?"

I nod, pressing a hand to Balvinder's cheek. His skin is smooth and freezing cold. White foam boils in the corners of his mouth, hissing when it hits the rock.

Zac helps me support his towering frame as we stumble across to a shallow nook carved into a slope nearby. We lay Balvinder there on his side and Zac tells me to prop a blanket under his head. The convulsions cease but he remains unconscious.

Glancing up at Zac, I notice that the toggles of his shirt have been pulled loose, revealing more of his bronze chest. A shape there arrests my attention. I've caught a glimpse of it once before, on the boat—a mark on his skin. This time I can see most of it—a triangle dashed with a horizontal line across its centre. It's a symbol I recognise. The alchemical symbol for *air*.

I did a great deal of research on alchemy studies not so long ago. The whole field was relatively philosophical and even spiritual, an investigation of the world and nature and how we interact with it. But it wasn't all airy-fairy. Alchemy led to real and important discoveries in modern science. And it involved a heap of symbols, though the most notable to us were the Hellenic elements—fire, earth, water and air.

Without a doubt, I know the marking on Zac's chest to represent air. It's pale, almost pearl-white against his tanned skin.

I want to ask about it, but remind myself that there's a more important matter at hand. Deciding we should have

yesterday. Now that would just be embarrassing for the both of us.

I push with all my remaining energy. The beast shifts enough for my arms to escape from under it. Then I'm able to twist my legs out.

Every muscle aches—particularly the arm that took the force of the collision—and my singlet is coated in sticky, brown specks. The white of my forearms has flushed red and I'm soaked in sweat. I yank my buried dagger from the animal's fur, which results in another spray of blood that has me gagging.

Not quite able to wrap my head around what just happened, I stagger to my feet and stare at the vast beast on the ground in front of me. A shudder racks my body. I search absently for my pack, spotting it a short distance away. It must have fallen in the chase. I pick it up and drift back to the others on a cloud of shock.

When I catch sight of them, Zac is perched beside a now-conscious Balvinder, who is sitting upright and sipping at a waterskin. They turn to me as I approach. Judging by their expressions, I must look even worse than I feel.

"Abbey!" Balvinder exclaims. The waterskin in his hand slips forgotten to the ground.

"I found my pack," I say weakly, letting it slip from my shoulder before I start to sink down after it. Hands grip onto my shoulders. I wince at the pressure of Zac's hold but let him lower me steadily onto a folded blanket.

When I start running them through the encounter, my voice drifts away from me. I hear the words as if they aren't mine. Like the real me is sitting alongside the others, staring at this girl rattling on about some colossal wolf, wondering whether she made the entire thing up.

"Oh, Abbey," Balvinder murmurs, a heartbreaking tenderness to his tone. He curls his fingers around his ears, slipping strands of silver hair behind them. "If I hadn't—"

"It isn't your fault," Zac breaks in, resting his hand over his mouth and speaking through his fingers. "I shouldn't have let her go alone."

A breeze sweeps over us, chilling the coating of sweat on my skin. I flinch as I draw my knees in. "Stop," I say. "It's dead. I'm fine."

They're silent—Balvinder watching me carefully and Zac looking away, kneading his temples. "Is this just bad luck?" I ask no one in particular. "Why is this happening to me? Two attacks in two days. What's with that?"

"We must be more careful," Balvinder says, his expression grave. "I am sorry I wasn't there."

I want to point out that despite his absence, I still managed to kill a freaking monster—but I resist. It was, after all, a last ditch effort.

Zac exhales sharply. "I want to see it." He charges past me without a backwards glance.

"Be careful," Balvinder calls after him. Then his eyes flit to me, glazed with curiosity. "You were brave," he says.

I blink away, drawing my attention to the rises and dips of the mountains and the patches of crusted grass baking under the sun. His words resonate deep inside me, for a reason I can't quite pinpoint.

You were brave.

Somehow, they feel like a charge of energy, restoring strength to my muscles and lessening the terror of the memory. The feeling is foreign. It makes me suddenly wary and I say nothing more until Zac returns.

"It's dead." He sits right beside me and rakes his hair back. "You killed it. One strike through the heart."

I glance at him—his expression one of incredulity crossed with bemusement. He looks like he might even laugh. Unexpectedly, I'm the one that does.

"Through the heart," I repeat, nodding slowly. Abbey Shader—Wolf Hunter. Who would've thought? Someone should start a TV series around that. Then they could cast someone who actually looks like they could kill a wolf. It would be a hit.

Zac reaches over for my arm. It takes me a moment to realise what he's going for. The dagger. I'm still gripping it tightly in my right hand. Have I been holding onto it this whole time? My knuckles are all blotchy and white, the skin pulled taut.

"I'm impressed," Zac says, peeling my stiff fingers from the worn, red handle and straightening them out. "Very impressed."

If only he could see how unimpressive the ordeal really was. Perhaps it's best I leave him thinking it was a heroic and expertly timed attack rather than a feeble *I'm about to die so let me just wave my dagger out here and que sera sera.*

My hand lingers in the curl of his palm and I wish it hadn't turned numb because some small part of me wants to feel his skin against mine. "I often impress myself," I say, mostly to lighten the mood.

Zac lays the dagger—still coated in sticky crimson—aside. His hands work their way up my forearm, turning it gently. Despite his care, I wince at the pain. Then I jerk away.

"It's just bruising," I tell him. "It's fine."

"*Fine,*" he breathes, humourlessly. "You wield that word like a well-acquainted weapon—too instinctively."

"Well, it's true."

Zac's eyes narrow, but a dimple flickers to life above one corner of his mouth. "There is no victory in stubbornness."

"What are you talking about?" I crinkle my nose at him. "There's *only* victory in stubbornness. It means you're never wrong."

There's a low chuckle. Balvinder is resting back against the mountain wall, his eyes shut but his mouth upturned in a smile.

"And if we are both stubborn?" poses Zac, quirking an eyebrow. "Who is wrong then?"

"You," I say. "Always you."

He bites his lower lip, as though catching a grin before it can show. Clearly he sees the irony, which triggers a smile from me too.

When I'm sure he isn't looking, I peer casually down at the damage. My right arm—which took the brunt of the wolf's impact—is the worst. The redness has bloomed into blue and purple blotches, aching from my shoulder to my wrist. It looks far from fine.

✳

We don't go much further. Although I try to walk with an ease I don't feel, eventually I can't hide the fact that it's a struggle. At the base of a particularly steep slope, Balvinder announces that we should set up for the night, even though the sun hasn't fully set.

Zac offers me more bread and a handful of nuts, which I have to force myself to eat slowly, before taking the first watch. Balvinder falls asleep quickly, but I take longer. I face Zac, squinting through my lashes to watch the cool breeze mussing his hair.

I want to know more. More about him, more about Balvinder, more about their erodosphere theory. I want to know *how* I'm here, and whether there's any truth to what they're telling me. The further we trek through this place, the less I can believe it's familiar to me. Everything about it feels unearthly—even the gleam of Zac's green-gold eyes, and Balvinder's piercing blue. And they are as real as anything.

"Hey," I whisper.

Zac turns to me, his brows arching in surprise.

I swallow and prepare myself for what I'm about to say. "What if you're right?"

Silence holds as he gazes down at me. Without having to ask what I mean—he answers, "Then everything will change for you.

TWELVE

"COME." THE WHISPER COMES FROM ALL around. *"Follow me. I will take you." It fills me from the inside, spilling out in currents of smoke. "I will take you now."*

I gasp for air but find none, only the whisper. The words. "Follow me."

"Abbey." Another voice. Sharp and gentle all at once. It beckons. Urges.

"Abbey."

I stir into waking. The sky is pastel pink, the vast sun rising behind strings of fairy-floss cloud. Balvinder's form takes shape over me. His hand rests lightly on my arm. "We should move on," he says.

"Yeah, okay." I rub at my eyes before taking in the mountains. The dawn tints the rock a chalky white. Mist settles into the valleys, softening the rough terrain. I spot Zac a few yards away. He's standing with his legs apart, drawing his hand forward and back in an arch. Only when he lurches forward do I register the flash of his dagger.

There's a loud crack. I scan the area, my eyes catching on a small tree that would have to be at least fifty metres from where he's standing. The hilt of the dagger protrudes from its trunk, and Zac strides over to collect it.

I'm too stunned to comment on the distance or the accuracy. Balvinder seems to register my shock anyway. "Never misses," he says.

"Never?"

"Never," Balvinder repeats, his eyes wide as he watches Zac reposition himself to throw again. "You have seen how treacherous this journey can be, and Zacharias has tackled it many times before. As a boy it was impossible for him to cover the cost of weapons training at any station in Emba. So he taught himself. Daggers, slingshots, crossbows—anything he could find. Missing wasn't an option."

I watch as Zac hurls the dagger again. "Why?" I ask as the wood snaps, the top half of the tree lolling back, broken. "Why come out here if it's so dangerous?"

Balvinder looks at me, sadness etched around those pale brows. He opens his mouth to answer—just as Zac calls out. "Ready?"

✳

We take more breaks today, sipping at our waterskins and sharing dried fruit around. According to Zac, we're drawing near to where the mountains join the plateau.

Having refused his offer to carry my pack, I heave it and myself up a particularly steep and nasty section of crumbled

hand, totally enamoured by the fact that her Daddy trusts her with them. I feel so sorry for her. Like I'm cringing into a moment that was never mine.

I want to take the scissors and tell her that the power she feels now will soon be stripped away, and she shouldn't waste her excitement on things that will only make her sad to remember later.

I want to warn her, tell her to draw away from her father while she can, before he leaves and it hurts and she's left feeling that maybe it wasn't *actually* the best hair cut he'd ever had, maybe he just said that because he thought it was what she wanted to hear, and maybe he never really cared much about her at all.

Zac's hands are clasped together with his face to the roof of the cave, as if in prayer.

"Oh relax," I say, and hack at the hair with more vigour.

Breathing myself away from the memory of Dad, I finish the cut, leaving the top a little longer than the sides.

I face Zac front on, crouching in front of him to assess my efforts. The line of his jaw is more distinct with the cut. His green eyes stare back at me, wider than usual and awaiting my evaluation. It's as though there are opposing magnets in mine, like I can't look directly into his for too long before they skim away.

"Finished?" Zac asks.

"Yep." I slide a finger across the flat side of the blade, removing any cut, static hair. "All done."

Zac twists the ends of his hair between his fingers, a smirk forming. "How does it look?"

"Wonderful," Balvinder says from behind me. I jolt, having almost forgotten he was there. "Might I request a cut too?"

I turn to him in surprise, eyeing the silvery waves by either side of his angular face. "Uh, I guess so. I don't want to—" I stop, unsure how to express my discomfort about tampering with it. How it would feel like chiselling a piece of intricate stone masonry from a gothic cathedral. Changing what should be left unchanged.

"It's quite all right," Balvinder says, swinging himself around. "I trust you."

"You hardly know me," I remind him.

He brushes his hair back over his broad shoulders. "So you seem to think."

"Okay, only a few days ago we were strangers," I say, feeling an unreasonable degree of agitation growing inside me. "Why do you act like we've known each other longer?" *And why do I feel it too?*—I almost add, but stop myself.

"Trust isn't always earned," Balvinder says. "Between us, it simply exists."

I scoff. "Well that's a presumptuous call." As I say it, that small, unfamiliar voice in me throws a shade of doubt over my words. Can trust be instinctive? Is it more natural to trust or to distrust? Which is more worthwhile?

"It isn't a presumption," he says. "It just is."

I shake my head and approach Balvinder on my knees, Zac's dagger in hand. I hesitate before taking a sweep of silky hair between two fingers. "I don't know what to think anymore."

"Ah." Balvinder laughs softly. "Then you are a step closer to understanding."

Zac scoots forward and extends his legs beside me, leaning back on his elbows. "You must have more questions for us, Abbey," he says. "When Balvinder first told me about the Essences, I swore to secrecy, before rushing out to confide in my closest friend at the time—Terrance. I needed someone else to know. Though, when I told him about the disembodied voice that kept me company most days, our friendship abruptly ended."

I slice through Balvinder's hair, only taking an inch or two. "Unsurprising," I murmur. "When you told me, I didn't particularly want to be your friend either."

I catch Zac's grin in my periphery and cast him a small smile back.

"Where does that leave you, then?" he inquires. "Since you can hear *and* see what others can't."

"Either insane, or dreaming," I say. "That's where."

"If you were truly insane, would you still be able to question your sanity?" Zac counters.

"Hm." I mull it over as more of Balvinder's hair falls loosely to the cave floor like a spray of stardust. "Maybe."

"And how could this still feel like a dream?" presses Zac. "You can't really believe that's all it is, can you?"

I look at him again, his hair now curling neatly around his temples, and my first instinct is—yes. Everything feels surreal, from the weight of that wolf against me, the ache in my shoulder and the heat of the sun on my skin, to the way my nerves spin when Zac's gaze holds mine. It's all so extraordinary— how can it be real?

"I don't know," I say honestly. Then I follow up with a less intimidating but probably equally important question. "So is every animal out here freaking ginormous?"

Balvinder laughs. "Ethra is filled with impressive creations, large and small."

"The folorians," Zac says, pulling out his blanket.

"Great," I murmur. "What are folorians?"

"Nothing to worry about," Balvinder reassures me. I move around to his side to trim the hair around his face, receiving a side look from the corner of his sky-blue eye. "They are beautiful creatures. Winged, with shimmering, golden-brown coats."

I raise a dubious brow. "They probably want to kill me too."

"I doubt that very much," Balvinder says. "The folorians possess a greater deal of wisdom than most humans do."

Humans. A shiver goes through me. He spoke the word like he spoke of the folorians—in a way that alluded to another species entirely.

Balvinder is an Essence, Zac said.

He's right. I do have more questions. But maybe they're not for him to answer. Maybe they're for Balvinder.

"Done," I say, handing the dagger back over to Zac.

I haven't cut much length off—just enough that the longest pieces fall to Balvinder's jaw rather than his shoulders.

"Short hair is becoming on you," Zac says, dropping his head to the side to look our way.

"You can't see me," Balvinder answers with a wry smile.

"True." Zac tosses his dagger a metre or so in the air and catches it on the descent, an inch from his nose. "I just have that much faith in Abbey's ability."

Balvinder nods, and then his expression shifts a fraction into something a little more sombre. "Me too," he says.

A short while later, Balvinder tells us to get some sleep.

I rest my eyes and imagine I'm in my bedroom; the rock of the cave, hard underneath me, is my plump mattress, and the smell of dirt is the smell of yellow roses at our door and Mum burning her toast in the morning. She always toasts it twice for extra crunch and forgets to press stop the second time around. So nearly every time there's a black chunk of charcoaled bread in the rubbish.

I can hear Zac breathing steadily beside me. For some reason I let myself match his rhythm before falling into sleep.

THIRTEEN

WHEN I OPEN MY EYES THE CAVE IS STILL shrouded in darkness. Balvinder is awake though. He seems to gleam amidst the black, just across from Zac's still frame. His hands are clasped between crossed legs, exuding an alert sort of calm.

Just before my eyes shrink to closing, I see Balvinder's head snap sharply toward the cave's opening. The line of his back straightens swiftly, a movement reminiscent of some sleek animal jolted to life by the sound of its prey.

And then I hear what he seemed to sense before it came. A gushing wind. It whistles by the cave until a cold draught reaches my cheeks. The suddenness of the change sets my teeth on edge, and not just because of the chill.

I lift my head and Balvinder turns to me. "What's happening?" I hiss.

He looks back into the circle of night at the tunnel's end without a word. I'm about to ask again, assuming he didn't hear me over the wind, when he finally answers—"This is Ethra," he says. "A land of extremes. Where the heat scorches, the cold can freeze in all but a few seconds. It is different to the world you know."

As if on cue, the wind ceases.

Balvinder gets to his feet, approaching the cave's mouth. I push my blanket back and follow, careful to step over Zac without waking him.

My jacket, however dubious I was about it initially, keeps me toasty warm, even as I step out of the cave and into the chill. Balvinder's hair gleams under the moon's full light. But beyond that I can't distinguish much, only the jagged outcrop of the mountains biting into the night sky.

"Do you like it here?" His voice is gentle, like a remnant of the wind already passed. I glance at him but he's not looking at me. His gaze is set ahead.

"Uh ..." I think for a moment. "Apart from the frog and wolf attacks and all the hiking? Yeah. It's ..." I look up at the brilliant moon and run my eyes over the shadowed craters, so close it's as though I'm wedged in the end of a telescope, at risk of becoming a part of the sky myself if I took two steps closer. "It's fascinating."

Balvinder says nothing, and when I look across at him I see his mouth curved at the sides.

"I need to get home, though," I say. "Orient myself. Figure out what happened."

"There are wonderful things to see here," Balvinder muses. "Though your welcome has been—" a glance at my shoulder

"—less than amicable, I can assure you that Ethra is worth exploring."

"I'm sure," I say, nodding my feigned agreement. "But Mum will be scared shitless already. I can't stick around for the sake of my own curiosity while she's still wondering where I went."

Balvinder's eyes flutter shut. "These sacrifices always seem impossible. Much does, until you jump."

We stand in silence for a time. I cast my eyes along the line of the craggy mountains—until they snag on a shadow atop the tallest peak that seems out of place. Narrow, and flickering. A dark figure.

In a blink it's gone.

I stare at the space—that piece of dull sky left behind—still seeing the dark outline. I turn my eyes on Balvinder and see that his brow is furrowed. It's only a mild expression of concern but it throws me off nonetheless, considering his usual, composed state.

"Did you see—"

"It's almost morning," he interjects, guiding me away from the cave's mouth with a gentle hand on my arm. "You should rest."

I don't resist, but once I'm set up under my blanket I take a moment to peer out at that peak again. Still no shadow—just the level crest of the mountain.

Balvinder doesn't return to sitting. He stands straight-backed, with his legs braced at the entrance of our shallow cave. I grow tired again and drift easily into dreams, Balvinder's unassailable form seeming to shield me even there.

✳

The next day, I decide to plough into the hardest questions. Those pressing most heavily on me.

We can see the edge of the plateau ahead now—an umber line that disappears and reappears as we climb down and up the remaining slopes.

I ask about the brooch. I ask about the position they claim I've been summoned to fill—the *Melder*. I ask more about Ethra. And all along I try to open my mind wide in order to gain the fullest picture I can before deciding how much of it makes sense.

Balvinder tells me that the odd piece of jewellery pinned to my jacket is the Melder's brooch, handed down to every successor, which is apparently why I now have it. Its purpose was to bring me here, but the power behind the call came from the Overseer. I'll meet him at Amnoralas, supposedly, before I return home through a *portal*.

Parts of the spiel I remember from what Balvinder told me back in the village. It wasn't long ago, but I don't have the same panicky feeling I did then. The problem is—the story is holding.

My mad attempt to connect the seemingly isolated dots is shaping into a complex picture, still unfamiliar to me but clearly alluding to some sort of intended design. It's also consistent with everything Zac told me. And although there are still holes and grey areas, each question answered patches a small section of my doubt.

Instead of disbelief, a sense of dread now churns in my gut. Fear of what it could mean if it were true.

Zac keeps quiet most of the time. He seems to be listening intently, which makes me wonder whether some of Balvinder's answers he's hearing for the first time too.

My suspicion is confirmed when he chimes in—"Why must the Overseer meet with the Melders at Amnoralas? You speak of him as though he exists everywhere. Anywhere. Why bring them to the portal?"

I shrug my pack further up my shoulder and watch Balvinder carefully as he seems to consider Zac's question. "It's a symbolic meeting place," he says at last. "A point of connection."

"I don't understand it," Zac murmurs.

"Thank you!" I give him a nod. "I was feeling pretty alone over here in my lack of understanding things."

His emerald eyes are a subdued green under the cloudy sky, but when he smiles they seem to light up, causing my heart to accelerate into uncharted territory.

"As for your questions about Ethra," Balvinder goes on, "yes, there is far more to it—multiple continents, small towns and sprawling cities, all vastly unique. Though there is only one portal, you see."

"Well that seems inconvenient," I say, and then hastily add, "if true."

Balvinder laughs. "For some, perhaps."

At last, the grey of the mountains becomes a dusty, flat expanse dotted with pale-green shrubbery. The sight of it expels a sigh of relief from every despondent muscle in me. One mountain more and I might have dropped on the spot.

"The Moonlit Woods are ahead," Balvinder says, and then he looks to Zac. "Do you feel ready?"

"Ready for what?" I ask, letting my heavy breath disguise my nerves. Ready to leave the mountains behind? Ready for the hike to follow? The question wasn't for me, though. Balvinder awaits Zac's response and I instinctively retreat a step.

I can see the muscles in Zac's neck pulled taut, his jaw stiffening. "No," he says finally. "I'm not." Hesitating only briefly, Balvinder nods and sets off across the plateau. "Perhaps it's best I never go back," Zac murmurs, looking to the space Balvinder left from.

He thinks he's still there—I realise. I move forward and stop right beside him, watching the intensity of Zac's gaze snap into recognition over me. "He's gone," I say, gesturing ahead.

"Oh." Zac yanks his pack nearer his neck. "Shall we, then?"

He starts marching across the dirt and I skip to catch up. Every joint and muscle twinges from the effort. Hopefully we're due for another rest stop soon.

"What were you talking about?" I ask Zac, once I've matched his pace. "Did you mean you're never going back to Emba? Your hometown?"

He glances at me, adjusting the toggles of his shirt. "It wasn't always." His tone is so void of feeling that it sounds too flat, too cold—uncharacteristic of the boy who has smiled easily throughout our mountain trek. "I lived in Preo until I was ten. It's a village in the Moonlit Woods. Balvinder was simply asking if I wanted to return, for supplies."

I turn his clipped words over in my mind, wondering what stem of emotion they're attached to. I know the voice, because I use it when people ask about Dad.

I see him occasionally. Occasionally is enough for me.

There aren't any hard feelings between us.

Things are actually better this way, with just me and Mum at home.

Every statement around the topic has to be drained of feeling, because already the questioner has pity dancing in their eyes, and the last thing you want to do is drag that out into conversation.

Zac is withholding something. But I don't press him. Forcing information out of someone is never a clever idea and generally unearths things that would be better left buried.

As the minutes go by, a heavy fog comes to rest across the plateau in sporadic clouds. It sweeps across the land on a current of brisk wind. Balvinder's silvery form fades in and out of visibility ahead of us—until finally he stops, allowing us to catch up.

I almost crumble to the ground when he suggests we take a breather. Chewing on a few hard, dried berries from my pack, I peer ahead through the mist. A border of trees can be seen now. The *Moonlit Woods*, I'm assuming. We're getting closer. Closer to home. Maybe the *portal* they keep speaking about is some metaphorical waking point for me. An escape from this dream.

But no, as much as I want to believe it is, this can't be a dream. I would have awoken a long way back if it were.

People commit their entire lives to religions based around the unseen. And there are scientifically validated aspects to the universe that are unseen—that can't be denied. Gravity, for example. We feel it in a real way. But we feel other things too. Pain, love, hatred, bitterness ... who's to say they aren't constructed from a system we're yet to identify?

Zac's spiel about Essences and spirits—I can't write it off without admitting to myself that I'm applying limitations to the vastness of possibility.

To be fair, the concept of a spirit isn't an unfamiliar one. I've watched plenty of philosophical videos over the years, for school and just for fun. It seems everyone has a different opinion on the subject of human emotion and how it came to be.

Evolutionists go on about communication strategies of the brain and fight or flight responses and natural selection and all these other mundane explanations for it all. I find them interesting to study, but if I'm being honest, it's never felt that black and white. It takes faith to believe there's no purpose to things, just as it takes faith to believe there is.

This isn't a textbook I can shut, or a video I can exit on my laptop. I'm living this theory, somehow. Living it firsthand in a place I don't recognise in the slightest. I was home, and now I'm far from it, wearing a brooch that somehow brought me here.

As terrifying as the notion is, I can't deny anymore that there could be some truth to all this. I'm cynical, but I'm not an idiot. Credit where credit is due, and truth where truth is due. Holding onto my baseline skepticism is starting to feel like holding onto a rope that's slipping rapidly out of my grasp, out of my control. What am I trying to prove? That I know everything there is to know?

Balvinder tells us to sleep an hour or two.

"What about you?" I ask him, frowning as I throw my blanket over me. "You've barely rested at all."

"I don't always require it," he replies with a soft smile.

"Ah, right." I give a breathless sort of laugh. And then, feeling dizzy from all the frantic, improbable thoughts streaming around in my head, I lay my head down on my pack and switch off almost instantly.

FOURTEEN

I WAKE TO THE SOUND OF A DEEP, MELODIC hum. It's resonant but delicate, like a ripple on the surface of an endless sea.

Balvinder's eyes are shut and he's sitting cross-legged. Though when I shift up onto my elbows, the humming ceases and he turns to me, blue eyes luminous against the earthy palette of the plateau. "You can sleep on through the night," he says. "If you wish."

I still feel groggy, and maybe that's why I dare to say, "Zac told me something about you," without thinking better of it.

Balvinder inclines his head, an unsurprised, considering look.

"He told me you're—" I stop, and it's as though I have to hunt for the word along an unfamiliar track in my mind. "An *Essence.*"

A shroud of mist comes between us, freezing my cheeks and nose. It seems to shock me back to sense too, because I instantly feel like a complete whack job for bringing it up. I'm not even sure why I felt the compulsion.

"Do you believe that is what I am?" he poses.

I rest my head back down on my pack, forcing myself to regard him with as much ease as he's regarding me. "I think you're something."

"Oh, good," he says through a gentle chuckle.

"Something different," I amend.

There's a pause, not awkward or tense—just placid silence. Zac's snores rip through it. I stifle laughter and Balvinder's expression brightens too, before the weight of our conversation sinks down over us again.

"For some reason, Zac can't *see* you. And neither could the people back in that town. Emba. And then there's your shadow, or, lack of." I'm speaking in a fast whisper, so as to avoid waking Zac, but angst blooms in my chest. "It doesn't make sense, I know it doesn't. But against all my better judgment, I feel like I can believe you. Like I can trust you."

The mist clears to reveal Balvinder's eyes still on me, unwavering. "You can," he says. "Because I am what Zacharias claims I am. And though you cannot trust every Essence, you certainly know every one of us already."

"How?"

"We are the unseen components that together, feed a spirit. When you breathe, you take us in, and your spirit casts us into the mold it desires."

I swallow hard and take a moment to close my eyes. "You're sitting right in front of me." I slant a narrow look at him. "You're a person, not a floating entity I can breathe."

Balvinder raises his hands, palms up, inspecting them as though they fascinate him. "Our bodies are gifts from the Overseer who created us," he says. "A culmination of the quality we offer. But in Essence form, we exist in all places."

I'm struck by a memory then, as though Balvinder's words have drawn a veil from it. Gilded clouds. A stream of blue descending. The career counsellor, staring blankly into the sky where I was convinced I saw something out of the ordinary.

The sapphire intensity of the colour had struck me then, and it strikes me now—glowing brightly in Balvinder's eyes.

"What are you?" I breathe.

"A lot of things."

"Well, Zac said there are Minor and Major Essences. *Which* are you?"

"You will see," he says. "In good time."

I turn my face to the sky and wonder, just for a few seconds, what the erodosphere might look like. An array of distinct colours, or a smoggy mixture, filling my lungs and shaping my personality.

"So what you mean is, who I am—my character—is dictated by forces or *Essences* outside myself?"

"The exact opposite," Balvinder says. "Your spirit dictates who you are, and which Essences you will choose. The Overseer created *us* to allow you that freedom of will."

I gnaw on my bottom lip, thinking it through. If Balvinder's claim is true, that he's a physical embodiment of a certain human quality, which is he? How many are there?

Zac said Good and Evil are the Major Essences, but he didn't elaborate on the Minor ones.

It feels so beyond me that I can't bring myself to press him further, for fear of stranding myself on an isle of irreversible bewilderment with no way back.

*

There's no escaping them. The scratching whispers swarm in, flooding my throat and demanding silence. I can only listen from where I'm hidden, barricaded inside myself by a darkness blacker than night.

"Where are you?" It's the only intelligible sound—Mum's voice, broken. I try to cry out but the shadows have filled every crevice of me.

"Where?" The question is more an exclamation of raw panic. "She was here last night, yes, she was here. Tyler visited right before I—yes. I went to bed and Tyler was here. I heard them talking."

I can't see her, only blackness. But I hear her distress rising. "I don't know! Aren't you listening to me? I was asleep and I—I didn't hear anything! I just woke up and she was gone!"

I wrench myself away from the shadows—

—and wake with a scream. Thick smoke surrounds me. I gasp and cut a hand through it. Wispy, black tendrils coil around my wrist, hissing like snakes. They draw in tight, jerking me to standing.

The movement is so quick and sure that for a split-second, I feel my boots lose contact with the ground. I kick and struggle until I come slamming back down into the dirt. Whirling in a circle, I can't see any trace of the others. Just my blanket, a twisted clump beside me.

I'm awake. Fully awake. But the shadows from my dream have woken with me. They're real and alive, and even as I watch them they shift with intention.

Soon I'm caught in a cylinder of black vapour receding into curved walls. Still no sign of Balvinder, or Zac, but above me I can see the moon peeping through a high opening in the cloud.

Panic has me jumping to all sorts of conclusions. If I was really transported to this place, Ethra, maybe it's happening again. Or maybe I'm about to be transported home.

But we haven't reached the portal, and the others ... they would have said goodbye if this was the end.

Totally dumbfounded, I stare into the wavering smog—and a path opens in its midst. The ground is gradually uncovered like the passage of a winding river, veering left up ahead. I inch forward. There must be an end to this, whatever *this* is. Balvinder and Zac can't be far.

The vapour has changed, its translucent texture taking on a glossy sheen. I press a tentative hand out into it.

A yelp escapes me as the substance seizes my skin.

I yank my arm away, watching as what appears to be black tar stretches with it like glue. My heart pounds fast. I stumble toward the only visible path out of here, the clutches of the wall peeling away from my skin as I do, as though allowing me the escape.

Moving quickly now, I make my way through the passage. The hair along my freed forearm stands on end, prickling sharply as I march further.

I keep my arms close to my body, for fear of the walls clinging to me. My pulse is a wild flutter as I round a corner of the gleaming black corridor.

Another passage extends before me. I run along it this time, keeping my gaze set ahead. The next corner leads me right. I take it swiftly and stumble over my feet. My elbow dips into the wall and I feel that same, awful sticking sensation as I rip it away and press on.

Up ahead there's an opening in the darkness where I can see the moonlight shining on the plateau, illuminating a shrub or two beyond. A way out.

But as I make for it, something appears there. I stop abruptly, my chest heaving. Materialised from nowhere, a dark figure outlined in ghostly light now stands still and statuesque at the exit point. The face is indistinguishable. I wonder optimistically if it could be one of the boys.

"Balvinder?" I call out. "Zac?"

No response. No movement.

A suction sound spins me around. The black smog is caving in behind me. It narrows. Pushes closer. The only way is forward, towards that figure.

I take a quick, steadying breath before charging ahead—just as a sudden burst of blue light splits the walls.

Its force alone blinds me before a powerful wind knocks me clean off my feet. The impact of the fall back to the earth leaves me momentarily winded. All I see is white.

A few seconds later it fades, and I sit up with a groan. The black walls are gone. The plateau is just the same as it was before, an expanse of bare land lit an ashy-grey by the moon.

Just as I begin to consider that perhaps I was still caught up in a nightmare, and only now am I waking up—I feel a hand on my shoulder.

I leap away in fright.

But Balvinder is there, staring down at me with the moon framing his broad shoulders and lean torso like a luminous cape.

"It's all right," he says softly.

I whirl around. Our camp setup is a long way off. Zac is still there, asleep under his blanket.

Instinct has me grabbing at Balvinder's arm. My grip on him is tight but shaky. "What—did you see—?"

Balvinder pulls my hand away and covers it with both of his. I turn still inside the safety of his cool, slender fingers.

Without a word, he helps me stand and leads me back toward Zac.

"Was I—was it a dream?" I ask, shaking my head. "Was I sleepwalking?"

Remnants of a prickling sort of fear shift under my skin, the feeling of being surrounded by those dreaded walls.

"Perhaps," Balvinder replies.

The moon leads us through the dark. Beads of light glint as we go, small creatures stalking by. I can't work out if they're threatening or simply curious, but either way I stick close to Balvinder, turning stiff every time I spot a pair. "You are safe now," he says. "They mean you no harm."

I relax a little. It was just a dream.

Once we're settled near Zac, Balvinder offers me his waterskin. I gulp down a mouthful. "It felt real," I whisper as I twist the lid and pass it back.

"Strange," Balvinder murmurs, "how the dream realm can often seem more tangible than reality itself."

I let my gaze wander across the plateau, considering the sentiment. "You're full of gems, aren't you," I say. "I'll have to jot that one down and pin it to my corkboard when I get home."

Balvinder chuckles and I want to smile back, but I can't quite muster it with that terrible dream still weighing over me.

A soft thud sounds to my left, loud in the silence of the night. I turn and a sharp breath catches in my throat.

Standing only a few yards away—is a tall, unfamiliar man. He's staring right at us. His slicked, dark hair gleams in the moonlight and, I note with another jolt of terror, he's clutching a crossbow.

✳

"Who are you?" I demand.

The stranger takes a step forward, and I scramble back. He is clad in a tailored, double-breasted coat with a high collar and large, gleaming buttons, and his face is clearer now—wildly angular planes, hair to his shoulders and thick brows pinched tight.

He's striking, in every unnerving sense of the word.

The man inclines his head. "Who am I?" There's a deep belligerence to the tone, which seems to say that the answer should be obvious.

I glance again at his crossbow, before feeling a cool hand on my shoulder. "It's all right, Abbey," Balvinder says, and then to the man, "Thorne—how did you find us?"

They *know* each other?

There's movement under Zac's blanket as he stirs in his sleep. This *Thorne* character notices it too, and his whole face contorts into a snarl.

"What is this?" he snaps. "Zacharias Nellerwood? And the girl—" His glare simmers as it returns to me. "She sees us. That must mean—"

"Yes." I turn to Balvinder as he nods. "The Melder has passed on."

Without a word, Thorne crosses the distance between us. I instinctively spring to my feet and he stops a foot or so away, stealing my breath as his dark eyes scrutinize every inch of my face. There's an odd appeal about him, but it's minimized by a dominant nose and jutting chin and the heaviness of those brows.

"What's the matter?" It's Zac—now awake and alert. I don't turn from Thorne, though. I hold his gaze as levelly as I can, considering him as he considers me. For some reason I'm nervous to turn my back, even for a second.

"What is she doing?" I hear Zac whisper, and Balvinder answers, "It's Thorne."

"Who?"

I can hear the smile in Balvinder's voice as he replies almost flippantly, "Thorne is an Essence, like me," the same way he could've told us that Thorne is six foot, or Thorne has dark hair.

"Like you?" Thorne snorts. "Hardly."

Zac moves to my side and I glance at him, hair mussed from sleep and his shirt askew, exposing a line of that mysterious, silver mark. His right hand is hovering over the hilt of his dagger.

"So this is your dear Zacharias," Thorne says, with no small amount of venom. "Forever involved in truth beyond his understanding."

A fleeting look of bewilderment crosses Zac's face, but then his jaw stiffens and he answers stiffly, "I understand enough."

Thorne gives a short bark of laughter. Zac jolts at the sound, and I watch as his gaze traces the space it came from, restless and searching.

"You can't see him either?" I inquire, a little hesitantly.

Zac shakes his head.

"Of course he can't," Thorne growls. The muscles in his neck stand at attention and his words are terse, slipping through a locked jaw. "The very fact that he can hear me is troubling enough."

Balvinder appears beside the man and reaches for his shoulder. They're almost the same height, but Balvinder has a few centimetres on him. "I am certainly glad to see you my friend," he says.

Thorne's eyes are still on me. "A new Melder. So young ... and entrusted with so much."

On an impulse, I grip the brooch on my jacket and quip, "Age doesn't necessarily equate to capability."

Thorne's huge brows lift high. "Age equates to experience," he says. "Experience is knowledge and knowledge is intelligence. Something you would do well to uphold, dear heart."

An unexplainable rush of boldness comes over me, and I'm suddenly intent on proving him wrong. "Okay. Experience is knowledge, yeah, but intelligence isn't a result of knowledge," I parry. "Intelligence is how you act upon what you know."

I'm not even sure why I'm bothering to argue with this stranger, but there's something thoroughly irritating about his demeanour that makes it all too tempting.

Thorne's lips pull together, like he might be about to spit. Then he turns sharply to Balvinder. "What—might I ask—is this petulant child of a Melder doing in the middle of the plateau? Have you not taken her to the Overseer?"

"We are on our way to Amnoralas," Balvinder says. "Abbey arrived in Emba, but she wishes to take the portal home."

Thorne blinks, a flicker of bemusement sparking in his gaze. "Home?"

"Yes." Balvinder gives a sure nod. "The Overseer can speak with her before she returns."

Thorne takes a step back from me and throws the crossbow over his huge shoulder. I catch Zac flinching as wood and metal clatter. "You have journeyed from Emba?" Thorne inquires, cutting a look at Zac. "On foot?"

Another nod from Balvinder, which bends Thorne's mouth into wolfish amusement. "How interesting," he mutters. "Well, allow me to accompany you on this little ramble through the woods."

I look from Thorne to Balvinder, hoping Balvinder will jump in and send this dude away. But he doesn't. In fact he seems pleased with this turn of events.

Zac, on the other hand, doesn't appear so thrilled. He and I exchange a look and I can see my unease mirrored in his face. If I feel anxious, I can't imagine how he must feel about the prospect of hiking through the bush with a girl who can't keep up and two disembodied voices.

If any part of this was starting to make sense, Thorne's appearance has shaken it all up again—mostly because having another person validate Balvinder and Zac's theories makes holding onto my skepticism seem pointless. Unhelpful, even. But despite everything, my end goal remains.

Home.

I need to get back. And if it will take three literally out-of-this-world men to get me there, each with elaborate stories to keep me entertained along the way—so be it.

FIFTEEN

MY FINGERS HAVE LOST ALL SENSATION. EVEN my toes, in socks and boots, have turned numb. I tuck my fingers under my armpits and stagger on.

The wind claws at my face, flecked with ice. Frost clings to my lashes and forces my line of vision into narrow slits.

It happened so quickly. There was a crisp chill to the air before, but this is something else. The storm swept across the plateau like some sort of grey, smoky demon and now we're completely consumed. My muscles throb from pressing against the onslaught and I feel that even if I gave up and fell forward, the wind wouldn't let me.

"The woods will protect us," Balvinder had said, just as the storm started up. "Let's move as fast as we can." And I'm trying. But shrouded in a sea of stirring, white mist, I feel like I've been walking on the same spot for an hour.

I'm vaguely aware of the two figures ahead—Balvinder's outline pale and Thorne's dark and easier to discern—and Zac lumbering alongside me. A weight presses against my back. With the wind freezing my senses it takes me a while to re-alise that Zac is holding me, urging me onward. Despite the torrential storm and potential hypothermia, I find myself quite content with his closeness.

Zac lets me go, returning a moment later with a twisted piece of material—which I soon realise is the hooded vest he has been wearing until now. He stops me to wrap it around my neck and under my chin.

I squint at him through the frost as he tucks the jumper securely into the collar of my jacket like a sort of neck warmer, and then procures his blanket to drape around my shoulders.

I want to tell him not to worry, that I'm *fine*, but my teeth are clamped tight against the cold and the words won't come. It would be a lie, anyway. So I let Zac cocoon me, his face so close I can see flecks of ice melting on his lips.

Again he holds my body against his, and I shut my eyes as we go on, trusting him to guide me in the right direction.

✳

When the warmth comes the change is immediate, just like the wind on the plateau. My teeth are still chattering as frost melts and tracks down my face. We've walked straight into a forest of tall, still trees, their thick branches entwined above and roots growing amongst brilliant green undergrowth. Sunlight pierces through to dapple it white and gold.

The storm lifted like a veil the moment we reached the border, chaos replaced with stillness in an instant. My body buzzes with gratitude as I start to thaw.

"Much better," Thorne says with a huff, patting down his coat.

Balvinder turns to me, the icy particles in his hair turning to liquid before my eyes. "Are you all right?"

I nod and forcibly unclench my teeth. "That was *crazy*."

"Quite," he concurs.

Zac is ruffling his hair, water droplets flying. I shrug off the blanket he set over my shoulders and pull his jumper from around my neck. "Here," I say, holding both out to him. "Thank you—you didn't have to."

Zac says nothing, just rakes his hair back and smiles at me. It fades the moment Thorne pipes up with, "I do believe you very nearly froze our new little Melder solid. You know there is no need—"

"It was the only way," Balvinder interjects, casting Thorne a pointed look I can't decipher.

We take a few sips from our waterskins. "How is this not empty by now?" I ask, shaking my waterskin and hearing a slosh sound from inside.

"A little help from Balvinder," Zac says, his gaze wandering around us as if seeking him out.

I frown as Thorne barks, "This is absurd." He stalks up to Balvinder, and then points a finger back at Zac. "The boy should know *nothing* of the truth, and here you are exposing your abilities without a single care. He has no part in this at all—meeting with the Melder, escorting her to the

"We thought you—you—" She's interrupted by her own shuddering breath.

With a glance back at me, Zac draws Rylah back by her shoulders. She looks small in his grip, but her expression is as severe as her black braid, drawn tightly away from her face.

"This is Abbey," Zac says, and Rylah's eyes follow his to land on me, momentarily blank.

I try to smile, but it feels more like a baring of teeth.

"Abbey," she murmurs. "Where is she from?"

Why she deems it necessary to speak about me in the third person, I have no idea.

Zac ducks a nod and gives me a pointed look. "Emba," he says, and I suppose I'm meant to go along with it.

Don't say a word about us, Thorne had said, *or what you are.*

"Yes, Emba," I repeat, doing my best to make my face as convincing as my words. The girl's expression doesn't soften. "Nice to meet you," I add, somewhat insincerely. But before I even finish speaking, she has turned back to Zac, cupping his face in her hands.

Who does she think she is? It's a good question. Who actually is she? And why is that sinking feeling in my chest starting to rise into my throat, a nervous lump I have to swallow back?

The reality is—I don't know everything about Zac. In fact, I know very little about him. It shouldn't surprise me that he's accounted for.

I shift my attention to a mound of fruit nearby, scanning their swollen surfaces and dull colours, some still smeared with dirt as if they've been freshly plucked from the ground.

"What happened to you?" I hear Rylah ask.

In my periphery I catch Zac squeezing her shoulders as he replies, "Wait here a moment."

He pulls a small satchel from his pack and throws our items on the counter. I watch him count out coins—a jolt of surprise running through me as I realise that the currency is unfamiliar to me. Silver. Gold. Copper. I'm too far away to inspect the engravings, but I crane my neck to get a closer look. The man behind the counter wipes his hands on his apron and fires, "That'll be seven great," receiving Zac's change and obscuring my view.

"Emba," Rylah's voice, cool and distant, sounds behind me. I hesitate before turning to face her, though her eyes remain steadfast on Zac. "How long has he been there?" It takes me a moment to register that the question is for me, since her gaze is elsewhere.

"Oh, uh ... a while," I answer, vaguely.

I glance warily back at Zac. He's starting to pack the food into his bag as the shop assistant counts out the coins.

"You know Zac from ... from when he lived here?" I ask Rylah, and her eyes finally cut to me.

"Zacharias is my cousin," she says. I'm hit with a sudden surge of relief. Perhaps I was a little premature in my judgment.

"It's been ten years—" Rylah falters, a tremble seizing her bottom lip. "We thought he was dead."

My relief dissipates. "Dead?"

Zac joins us before she can say more. He hands me a few neatly wrapped parcels, which I shove into my pack, willing him to look me in the eye and explain what's going on. But he doesn't, and I can tell it's an intentional evasion.

"Mother will want to see you," Rylah says to him, her expression sombre.

He sighs and straightens. "Not now."

Rylah recoils as though she's been slapped. Her cheeks flush red with rage. "All these years—" She chokes, pausing. "You are alive, Zacharias. You didn't bother to tell us. The least you can do is see her now."

Zac raises his hood over his head and guides Rylah out from the stalls. I blunder along behind them, still mystified by the whole scenario. He casts me a short, stoic smile, which I struggle to return.

We move with the crowd until he makes a sudden left, pressing through the traffic of busy customers. Rylah's frame is tiny under Zac's, her shoulders slumped and trembling. She thought he was *dead*? Why?

Zac leads us to a side tunnel, stopping once we're concealed by the inner wall. The passage is empty. Lamps hang from a chain that runs along the ceiling, casting licks of orange and gold against the rocky walls.

"I don't understand." Rylah's voice has lost some of its bite now, more a twist of anguish and confusion so profound I almost want to reach out and comfort her myself. "We found their bodies. Everyone assumed you were dead too."

Their bodies. Zac's parents? I recall our conversation on the boat leaving Emba—he had said they were *gone*. He hadn't elaborated. But it would make sense, given that he lives alone.

The realisation has me stepping away to separate myself from the conversation. Zac's tension is palpable, even in the stiff lines of his back.

"I fled," he says.

"Evidently," Rylah hisses, anger rippling dangerously in the word.

"I'm sorry." The muscles in Zac's jaw harden. "Coming home, to everything here, without them ... it would have been—" he stops. "I couldn't."

"We were here."

Zac says nothing, and the pair regard each other in silence for a long moment.

"I would have come with you," Rylah finally says. "Neason would have too."

With the time and space to study Rylah more acutely—I do spot the family resemblance. Initially I hadn't noticed the familiar curve of Rylah's nose and how it matches Zac's. Their eyes are similarly wide and sparky, though his feel warmer, and his skin is darker where hers is ghostly white. Most of the people we've seen down here so far have had skin like hers—unlike

the farmers and villagers in Emba who shone like burnished bronze.

"I could never have asked that of you," Zac says in a hush.

Rylah rocks forward to rest her head on his shoulder. I avert my eyes and lean against the tunnel wall, realizing I probably feel more out of place here than I did when I first landed in that stone room beside the unfamiliar, lifeless body of the previous Melder.

"We are journeying back to Emba." Zac rests a hand on Rylah. "That's where I have been all these years."

Back to Emba? Hell no. I'm going home.

Zac seems to sense my unease, casting me a fleeting—*go with it*—glance.

Rylah draws away to narrow her eyes at him. "Why so suddenly?"

"I *will* return." Zac squares his shoulders, like he's readying himself to follow through with the promise.

Rylah clutches his arm until her knuckles lose colour. "Zacharias, there was a time you never lied to me."

"And I'm not lying now," Zac says, and then he sighs. He looks her straight in the eye and repeats, "I'm not lying," in a way that has me wondering if he really meant it the first time.

Rylah glowers back, before giving a single, begrudging nod. Her attention shifts to me as if she's seeing me for the first time, and then her eyes drift downward. For a moment I wonder why she is so unashamedly staring at my chest, before she points out the state of my clothes. I inspect my once white singlet, which is now a grimy shade of brown. I must look horrendous.

Rylah offers to supply us with fresh gear, and we agree, following her back to the stalls and then up a nearby stairwell. It meets the level of narrow walkways suspended in the air, unnervingly high above the ground.

There are ropes on either side, which I latch onto as we walk, studying the motion of the busy crowd dancing beneath our feet. Zac leaves us at the entrance of an interwoven net of hanging, tree roots that form an unexpectedly large room.

The roots gleam faintly, like the hollow of the tree we entered from. There are two single beds on one side, and a closet on the other. Rylah pulls its doors open and retrieves three plain shirts. She lays them on the closest bed and beckons for me to approach.

"Whichever you like," she says, sweeping a hand across them.

I glance at the relatively sparse closet. "Are you sure?"

"Yes. Zac can bring it back when he returns." A fleeting look of indignation crosses her face. Evidently, she must remain dubious about his coming back. Or about me.

After scanning the shirts laid out on the bed—grey, burnt-orange, and green—I choose the green.

Rylah leaves me to change and I shove my filthy singlet down to the bottom of my pack, brooch and all, not sorry to be rid of it. The bandage around shoulder is scratchy, edges frayed and brittle with sweat. I remove it and crane my neck to get a glimpse of the injury. I can't quite see it, but my fingertips identify a long, crusty scab. Super sexy.

I pull the green shirt over my head. Rylah is smaller than me, but the shirt is still a relatively comfortable size, with toggles to pull it tighter or looser at the neck.

Once I'm fully dressed, I move for the door. I hesitate there, tuning into Rylah and Zac's quiet murmurs outside.

"... not ideal," Rylah is saying. "It's quite different."

"What do you mean?"

"Pacer Toryn is as good as gone," she replies, so softly I find myself leaning in to hear the rest. "They say he is ill ..."

There's a pause, before Zac speaks. "From what I remember, he never particularly associated with villagers aside from the Gage."

"No." Rylah huffs. "And it may be time we find someone who will."

When I step out, Rylah snaps her mouth shut.

"It's all right," Zac says, as she glances warily between us. "We were discussing Pacer Toryn," he tells me. "He oversees Preo—or at least, he's supposed to."

"Either he is highly unsociable of late, or too ill to leave his quarters at all," Rylah explains, although she's still glaring at me, like she isn't sure whether I'm to be trusted.

I nod along, not entirely sure what they're talking about but glad to be included in the loop.

"What's Pacer Aubrin like?" Rylah asks.

"Involved," Zac says, "I see her nearly every day—overseeing the farming, speaking with the villagers, leading assemblies ..."

"Hm." Rylah sighs. "How it should be. A Pacer can't lead blindly. They must be as much a part of the body as they are the head."

I listen to the conversation continue on but find myself drifting in and out of understanding. The existence of Pacers—I can't deny it. I met Pacer Aubrin in the flesh, after all, and she introduced herself as such. You don't see many politicians back home overseeing the work of farmers in their fields, or on the other hand, remaining as aloof as Rylah describes Toryn to be, never showing their faces. Politicians love the spotlight.

As much as it freaks me the hell out to admit, this foreign governing system is only further confirmation of my predicament. My displacement—a world away from home.

I draw back to Rylah's rant just as Zac announces that we need to leave. Reluctantly and without another word, she brings us to the tree we entered from. She embraces Zac stiffly, staring at me over his shoulder. I avert my eyes.

"I'm ready," says Zac, as he releases her. "I will explain everything when I return."

Rylah says nothing, but a look of immense sorrow passes over her face. She quickly masks it with a flat smile.

We turn to leave—just as Rylah's hand shoots out to grasp Zac's. Her eyes burn into his. I expect her to speak but she doesn't, she just looks, until Zac nods and moves into the luminous hollow of the tree without a glance back.

As we ascend the stairs, I dwell on the multitude of questions I want to ask him, stacked one upon the other—about his parents, their death, why Rylah thought he had died too, why he left and why he's ready to return. I don't ask any of it though. I just feel through the gloom until I find his arm. I brush it, lightly, just to let him know that I'm still here.

My chest lurches as Zac's hand reaches down to grip mine. His skin is rough and warm. We stay connected all the way to the top step, but when we step out into the light—Zac drops my hand, leaving the moment behind in the darkness of the hollow.

EIGHTEEN

"FINALLY," THORNE DRONES WHEN WE APPEAR. He and Balvinder are sitting either side of a nearby tree. They look like two opposing, wild creatures forced into the same enclosure, a stark contrast of silver and ebony.

Balvinder swiftly rises and moves toward us. "All went well?"

Zac doesn't so much as glance Balvinder's way. His eyes are hazy, his mouth bent to one side.

"All good," I answer for him, smiling awkwardly. Encountering Rylah isn't my story to tell, and I'm not sure Zac will want to tell it anyway. Not in front of Thorne.

My voice seems to break Zac out of his reverie. He blinks back to focus with a start. "Yes, of course. Yes." A broad smile replaces his distant expression, and he glances around as if searching for Balvinder beyond the apparent veil between him and the Essences. "We got what we needed."

"New clothing," Thorne loudly observes, striding across to the three of us. He gestures to the green shirt I'm wearing of Rylah's. "I see you took the time to update your wardrobe while we sat in wait."

I glance at Zac, who's ruffling in his bag to rearrange our new supplies.

"It's for the best," I say. "As fantastic as I am at working the grimy, smelly, sweaty look ..."

Thorne considers me. "You are all in urgent need of a wash," he says candidly. "Though you would be wise not to waste anymore of our time, little Melder. If you really are to leave us, you must at least first discuss the matter with the Overseer who summoned you, without further delay. Dress-ups are a low priority."

"Can you not show even one glimmer of respect?" Zac demands, glaring in Thorne's direction. I look around in surprise at the sharp-edged bitterness to his voice. "Is your tongue so twisted beyond repair?" I open my mouth to tell Zac that it's okay—I'm not overly affected by Thorne's snide comments, but he ploughs on. "This is all new to Abbey, but she is the Melder, your Melder, even if only for now, so please drop the gratuitous snobbery."

Thorne stares at Zac, frozen, and I get a terrible sense of the eerie calm before a storm. "How *dare*—"

There's a sharp crack. We all look in the direction of the sound. Balvinder has broken a low-hanging branch—a metre or so long—from a tree a little way off. The end has snapped fairly cleanly, a series of fine rings displayed at its centre. But that isn't the strangest part. Shrugging aside the rising tension between Zac and Thorne, I move in for a closer look.

A glow emanates from the flat, inner timber of the branch in Balvinder's grasp, just like the hollow of the tree leading down into Preo. Zac was right. The trees glow. Perhaps I should start believing what he tells me.

My gaze wanders to the tree Balvinder took the branch from, and the luminous circle left behind at the bough. It makes no sense at all, but it's there. I can't dispute what I can see. Can I?

"Strip the bark," Balvinder says.

"What?"

"We will need its light."

I glance back—Thorne is watching Zac like a hawk, but Zac is now watching me, smiling a little. Perplexed, I return to the branch and tuck my fingernails under the crisp shell of the bark from the point Balvinder broke it. Quite easily, it falls away. I gasp at the fluorescent surface left behind.

"Splendid," Balvinder whispers, holding it by the smaller end like a torch. "It will fade, but not anytime soon. Now we can move on." He ventures further into the woods and the rest of us hesitate.

Zac seemed off the moment we left Rylah behind. Shaken, and then easily triggered by Thorne's rudeness. Obviously there's a story to his parent's death and what came after. I sensed it before, from the impassive way he spoke of his time growing up in Preo. Rylah thought he was dead, like his parents, which would imply he hasn't been back to his hometown in the ten years they've been gone. No wonder he was so hesitant.

I'm brought back to attention as Thorne thrusts his shoulder into Zac—who looks suitably startled—glowering at me on his way past.

"Thorne's Essence ..." Zac murmurs as we follow on. "What do you think it is?"

I chew on my lower lip and mull it over. Eventually I admit, "I don't know if I have this Essence thing figured out enough to even wager a guess."

If Essences are supposedly the physical embodiment of a single quality, how many are there? How should I know what they are? I would just be taking a stab in the dark.

"Perhaps he is the Essence of Merriment," Zac says. I glance across at his stoic expression, which is soon broken by a crooked smile.

Thorne strides ahead of us, his powerful gait knocking the crossbow against his burly shoulder with a light, continuous *clank*. "Is there such a thing?" I ask. "Like, an Essence of Joy? Or Hate? Love? Etcetera?"

Zac runs his fingers through his hair. The lean muscles in his arms swell with the movement, and I glance away. "The way I understand it," he begins, "is that the two Major Essences of Good and Evil possess many qualities between them, those that are purely Good, and purely Evil. But the Minor Essences can be either. They swing from one side of that moral compass to the other, like pendulums. All qualities stem from an Essence of some sort."

I force myself to stop biting on my lip, which has become chapped from the cold and the sudden heat of the woods. "And how does the Melder fit into all that, then?"

"Well, the Melder—" he looks pointedly at me, "—breathes in a combination of the Essences like the rest of us. The difference is, that it's a combination required to restore balance to the erodosphere as a whole."

I shudder at the scale of his words, but at the same time an intense curiosity pulsates through me, sending my mind into a whirl. "This just gets weirder and weirder."

Zac casts me a weary smile, that signature dimple appearing ever so faintly under his cheekbone. "There's a process called the Breathing, during which the Melder re-establishes the balance. Balvinder has spoken of it, but only obscurely. I'm not sure I can offer you much more on it."

"He likes speaking obscurely, doesn't he?"

Zac laughs—a full, warm sound that instantly makes me want to think of ways to hear it again. "You have no idea," he mutters.

✳

As night descends, the woods come alive. Fine cracks start to appear in the bark of the trees, meandering across their trunks to reveal the luminescent bodies beneath. Small animals rustle in the grass, occasionally scampering across our path. I can't see them properly in the dark, but here and there I catch a curling tail or a sharp-tipped set of ears.

Balvinder's makeshift torch has led our way, but eventually the light of the branch stops ahead with him. Zac and I catch up, arriving at the edge of a coursing river. Streaks of foam flash silver within the current. Thorne dips a hand into it, gulping a mouthful down.

My breath catches at the sight of the trees opposite—emerging from the dirt like ominous, grey statues under the moon, skeletal and disfigured. Unlike the Moonlit Woods behind us, there isn't one degree of movement amongst them. No bend in the canopy and no leaves wavering in the breeze. No breeze at all—only a bleak sort of stillness. A shudder goes through me.

"The border of the Petrified Forest," Balvinder says. "Our oases lie within, but most villagers avoid it."

"I can't imagine why," I comment, wincing with the realisation that we're about to venture right into that dark web of stone. "What do you mean by oases? You don't live in there do you?"

"Oh, yes." Balvinder smiles widely. "Every Essence is granted an oasis. An area we can call our own, removed from prying eyes."

"I live on the coast," Thorne declares. He raises his chin and those dark eyes flit from me to Zac. He might as well carry around an—*applaud now*—sign.

With a start, I notice something about the river I failed to register before. Half the water—the side closest to us—is totally still. The farthest half is turbulent. It froths against jagged rocks and churns with an unnatural degree of force. There is an invisible line where the two bodies of water meet and don't cross.

The scene makes about as much sense as the glowing trees at my back. Inside my mind, I feel cogs spring to life, dormant parts of me forced into understanding by the evidence before my eyes.

"What is this?" I say carefully.

Balvinder paces his way along the water's edge. "Ethra reflects the nature of Good and Evil in ways that may be unfamiliar to you," he says. "Two opposing forces obliged to exist side by side." He pauses as a spray shoots across at us from the turbulent half, falling against the calm side and vanishing without a ripple.

There is a splash, and I turn abruptly to see Thorne waist-deep in the water. "After you Balvinder," he says, throwing his crossbow and quiver to the other side.

Balvinder steps in, beckoning for us to do the same. Zac takes my pack and casts it across to the opposite bank with his. I sigh to myself and wonder how hard it would've been to bring along a floating device of some sort. Not super convenient, I guess, but worthwhile.

"Is there another way?" I try hard to phrase it like I'm casually curious rather than a spoiled princess.

Thorne barks a laugh. "Well ..." He looks to Balvinder, the pair of them immersed in the water just before the turbulence.

Balvinder shakes his head. "We must go through it," he says.

Zac plunges into the river and extends his hand out to me. "I'm fine," I tell him as I swing my legs into the cool water. The drop is further than I expected, the river almost reaching my shoulders. My shock must have shown, because Zac starts to laugh. I flick water at him.

Balvinder is the first to cross the centre divide. He moves easily, striding across the uneven riverbed with an elegance I try and fail to match. When he passes into the choppy water—it stills around him.

I shiver as we follow his path, sticking to the trail of calm in his wake.

With a deft leap Balvinder springs from the river and onto the bank. Thorne is close behind, dragging his body up over the rocks and rolling to his feet. The water Balvinder stilled swirls back into motion just as Zac and I scramble up the bank.

I wring out my shirt and shake my head feverishly. "How the hell did you just—?" I hesitate, not particularly sure I know what the question should be. How did he control the water? It sounds ridiculous. But then not sounding ridiculous is a ship that sailed long ago.

Thorne marches forward, shaking off his clothes as he goes. Balvinder's radiant, blue eyes shine as they meet mine, somehow telling me—*there is more where that came from.*

NINETEEN

THE FURTHER BEHIND WE LEAVE THE
Moonlit Woods, its webbed light receding like a distant gal-
axy of stars, the greater the dread that swells in my chest.

The Petrified Forest is silent; the only sound our breath
and the padding of our boots against the hard dirt. Above us,
a thick canopy knots branches into tangles. Dimness settles at
the forest floor, like the moonlight has decided it would rather not reach down here. I don't blame it.

If Balvinder is right, and Good and Evil exist side by side
in Ethra, I'm fairly certain which we're leaving behind.

It takes me a while to realise that Zac is no longer following behind me. I turn, spotting him stopped further back.
He's standing very still, palm pressed against the hilt of his
dagger. After a quick glance at Balvinder and Thorne, who are
still walking ahead under the light of that glowing branch, I
go to him.

"Zac—what's wrong?"

He looks at me sharply, a crease disturbing his brow.
"It's—nothing." I receive a smile that falls short of his eyes.
"It's all right."

Before I can question him further, he presses a hand to my back and guides me onward.

I haven't known Zac long, but I can sense that something changed in him after our Preo stop. He has retreated— shrunk back from his surface, below what I can see.

✳

Every December, Mum and I take a trip along the Great Ocean Road, just the two of us. We dedicate a week to reading our books, walking along the beach and breathing in the fresh, salty air around the Twelve Apostles—stacks of limestone jutting from the water like giant chess pieces marching out into the ocean.

Just last week Mum was telling me about this new hotel that opened up down there—with rooftop spas and in-room massages—that we could try at the end of the year. She said it's pricey, but since I'll be graduating this year we can consider it a celebration. Book in somewhere extra special.

Whenever I'm away with her, I always get this sense that if everybody else in the world faded into oblivion and only we were left, I'd be perfectly content. Okay well, I'll take Tyler too, in this post-apocalyptic scenario.

I don't need much, but I do need them.

Tyler listens, but he also isn't afraid to smack me back to earth with his ever-harsh truths. And Mum, she's a master of channelling strength until nothing is too much, and she makes me laugh every single day—no matter how dreary things might seem.

Right now, I would kill for a minute alone with either of them. Just one conversation to make sense of all that's happened. To ask what *they* would do, or if they'd be inclined to believe that this alien world, *Ethra*, really exists, as everyone here keeps telling me.

Even in the company of Zac and Balvinder and Thorne, a buzz of loneliness creeps into my gut.

The moon is beaming down in pieces, broken by the shadows of the branches. We pass a cluster of thick trees, their roots mangled into a complex lattice above the dirt. It's Balvinder who suggests we take a rest stop. When he says it, the exhaustion I've been ignoring by reminiscing on things back home sets in.

I can't think too much about the portal, or Amnoralas, or this creepy forest, otherwise I might just sink into the ground and never come out.

We set up our blankets against the tightly knitted roots and sit in a rough circle. Zac starts distributing the food we bought from Preo, and Balvinder takes some this time. He said in the mountains that he wasn't *required* to eat ... I assume that's another Essence attributable feature. No shadow. No hunger.

In one of the parcels Zac put in my bag earlier, I find strips of what seems to be jerky, assuming they're not dog treats. Skeptically, I take a whiff of one. A surprisingly sweet scent fills my nostrils, urging me to take a bite. If it's meat, it doesn't taste like it. The flavour is spicy and warm on my tongue.

"We've come so far," Balvinder says chirpily, taking a piece that I offer him. "Perhaps it's time for a hearty meal."

Zac snaps a piece of jerky with his teeth and chews at it while springing to his feet. "Shall I?"

I stare at him. "Shall you what?"

"Hunt," Thorne supplies, with an arched brow. "Though if you really desire substantial meat, you should send me out, not the Nellerwood boy. I never miss. Harlie will attest to it."

I don't know who Harlie is, but asking her to attest to Thorne's hunting abilities doesn't factor high on my current, to-do list.

Balvinder passes me the glowing branch, our only source of light aside from the moon. "Go with him," he says with a smile.

I hesitate before accepting the branch. "You don't need this?" Thorne scoffs and Balvinder just shrugs. "Do Essences like the dark?" I inquire, nudging Balvinder's shoulder with the end of the branch. "Does it make you feel more mysterious?"

Balvinder's smile widens across a set of pristine-white teeth. "We are plenty mysterious already," he says.

✳

I direct the branch's light into the dim forest as Zac and I pick our way through the trees, the mutterings of Balvinder and Thorne receding behind us.

Acutely aware of the fact that I'm very much alone with Zac, and might not get to be again, I decide to seize the opportunity to ask some of my stickier questions. "You've been out this way before?"

I see him glance at me, but keep my gaze set ahead. "Yes."

"How often?"

"Quite regularly, for a time."

"Why?" I ask, trying not to let my bewilderment show. "I mean—it's a serious trek." *Too serious for it to be aimless*, I'm tempted to add.

The swift sound of scraping steel makes me turn. Zac has stopped to pull out his dagger. He rotates it between his fingers, looking off into the trees. "You're probably wondering why I never returned home," he says. "Why Rylah thought me to be dead."

I clamp my bottom lip between my teeth, commanding myself to wait for Zac to guide the conversation.

"I was ten when my parents were killed," he says, his voice soft and careful. "I couldn't face the rest of my family. My desire to see them was always outweighed by ... guilt."

I search around for a way to ask about the deaths. Why they should evoke any sense of guilt unless he had something to do with it ...

Suddenly, Zac's attention snaps left. At first I think he's staring at me, but then I follow the line of his gaze and swing my branch into the darkness with it. All I see is the pale, shimmering reflection of my light across the dirt and the layers of roots, static and ghostly—like a sea of stony snakes.

A soft thud spins Zac into motion.

Swoosh.

I catch the flash of his dagger just before it disappears into the cloak of night.

Thump.

Zac strides past me while I stand stock-still, clutching the branch close. A moment later he returns with a furry, grey body slung over his shoulder. A rabbit—judging by the long ears.

I try to hide my shock by gluing my lips together. But my eyes are wide and I can't stop staring at the animal. One throw in pitch black. *How?*

Zac raises his brows at me as he sheathes the dagger. "Need I remind you that you killed a wolf twice your size?"

"Fluke," I tell him. "And in broad daylight."

"There is no trick to it," Zac says. "It's just to do with listening, that's all. And of course practice. I was throwing daggers from the moment I could walk."

"Well that sounds dangerous."

"You would pick it up quickly," he says, repositioning the rabbit further over his shoulder like it's nothing more than a bag of groceries. "You are the Melder, after all. I would be surprised if that didn't grant you some sort of superhuman aptitude, be it around strength or accuracy or speed."

I let out a short laugh. "If it does, I don't feel it coming on yet." I reach for the Melder's brooch before remembering I kept it pinned to the singlet buried in my pack. "Maybe all the power is in that brooch, and I have to unlock it somehow."

I'm totally messing around, but Zac's eyes go wide.

"Perhaps," he murmurs, stroking the rabbit thoughtfully.

"Oh, come on." I throw up my hands. "You're willing to believe anything! So long as it's completely improbable. Where's your healthy degree of cynicism?" It comes out more harshly than I intended it, but to his credit, Zac doesn't seem perturbed.

"Cynicism is more trouble than it's worth," he says simply. "And that brooch—it brought you here, Abbey, from an entire world away. Soon enough you'll have to accept that truth runs far more deeply than what we can see."

TWENTY

ZAC LEADS US BACK TO THE OTHERS, navigating his way through the dark with the same innate sense of direction that earned him the rabbit over his shoulder. Watch the roots—he tells me—and the way they bend into defining shapes. "There's a story in them, one that can take you anywhere and back again if you follow it closely."

He must sense my skepticism, because then he starts pointing things out. The knobby root surrounded by finer tangles—a baby wrapped in a blanket. The splay of circular lines etched into the base of a trunk—a sunset. Mangled roots curved into an arch—a bridge.

Then he tells me the story he formulated of a woman crossing a bridge at sunset, hearing cries and discovering a baby underneath it. As we continue on, it becomes so elaborate and ridiculous that I start to snort with laughter.

"And here," Zac says, pointing at two roots crossed over, "the woman passed by a man in a boat, who was rowing furiously in the opposite direction. Could he be the one who left the child? He looked suspicious, because there—" Another gesture toward a random cluster of roots. "The man only had one eye."

"How did you get *one eye* from *that*?" I try to stifle my giggles, but they burst out of me defiantly.

"Look, they're twisted into a single line—a number one—one eye," Zac explains frankly, as if I really should've seen it too. When he looks back to my baffled expression, he grins freely. I shove him with my elbow, surprising myself a little with the familiarity of the gesture. The warmth of his skin on mine lingers well after we part.

✳

We return to find Balvinder and Thorne by a flaming, shallow pit in the dirt beside the network of roots supporting our packs. If it weren't for the heat, I'd wonder if it was a fire at all with the flames so electrically blue, spilling out from the pit in radiant waves.

I let the branch drop to the ground. "What the hell is that?"

"What?" Zac inquires, staring at me and then casting his lost gaze around.

Thorne's head droops back and he sighs loudly into the night sky. "Isn't it funny how the scale of her fascination seems to have no limitations," he comments, to nobody in particular. "A moment ago she couldn't believe the branch shed light." With what appears to be concerted effort he draws his face back to me. "Really, little Melder, please in future attempt to moderate your shock. For all our sakes."

"Oh shut it," I say, shifting closer to the fire. The hard planes of Thorne's face draw in stiffly and he gets to his feet. With a swift swipe, he snatches the rabbit from Zac's shoulder.

Zac whirls and catches Thorne's wrist.

"It's only me, boy!" Thorne hisses through his teeth, jerking his arm from Zac's grip. He straightens his coat and stalks back to the roots, where he sits and lays the rabbit over his knees. "Surely you are familiar with disembodied voices by now, having spent most of your life in Balvinder's company."

Zac glares Thorne's way. "Balvinder doesn't ordinarily rush at me out of nowhere," he says.

"Hey." I beckon for Zac to sit beside me on the edge of a large, smooth root, partially to distract him from Thorne but mostly because I want to know—"can you see the flames?"

He drops down and considers the space before us. I know the answer already, from his darting gaze.

"No. What am I missing?"

The blue of the flames spirals toward us, licking the edge of my boot. Above them, Balvinder smiles at me. "I think it's Balvinder's version of a bonfire," I tell him, a little breathless with disbelief. "You really can't see it?"

"Fancy that," Thorne cuts in, proceeding to skin the rabbit with a knife he whips out from his jacket. "Zacharias can't see the flames—yet another cause for mighty shock." I look on in horror as he lops off the head and tail. "It's not like he hasn't been able to see Balvinder his whole life. Or any of the Essences for that matter. But the flames—dear me—it's a wonder he can't see them, isn't it?" Thorne removes the rabbit's front feet and legs at the joints before peeling the entire hide down over the body, as if turning down a sock.

Balvinder winces and raises a placating hand, but his expression is resigned, like he knows he'd have more success ordering a raging bull not to run at a red flag.

"So," I say, turning right away from Thorne and resting my head in my hands so I'm fully facing Zac. "If you can't see the Essences, can you see what they do? What they touch?"

"Sometimes." He nods in Thorne's direction. "To my eyes, all that appears to be cutting that rabbit into pieces is thin air."

"I simply love it when I'm referred to as thin air," murmurs Thorne, tossing the rabbit hide against a tree and glowering at Zac.

Balvinder crosses his legs and sets his eyes on the wispy, blue flames. "I find it difficult to witness the skinning of animals," he comments, his voice oddly removed.

"Careful Balvinder." Thorne flashes me a wolfish grin. "You'll spoil the surprise."

I narrow my eyes at him. "What surprise?"

Thorne sniggers, pulling a knife out from some hidden fold in his jacket. "His Essence. He hopes you will figure it out without hearing it from us. Though, at this rate he is bound to give it away himself." With a steady hand, Thorne makes a cut down the full length of the now ambiguous rabbit's underside, groin to breastbone.

"Freaking hell—" I duck my head toward Zac, feeling my cheek brush the hard curve of his shoulder. He laughs softly and touches my temple with his fingers as if encouraging me to remain close, away from the rabbit butchery. His scent—a combination of natural musk and earth—fills my nose and head. The moment feels suddenly more intimate than I think either of us intended, and so I pull my face away to break it, my eyes catching on Balvinder's over the roiling fire.

✳

It doesn't take long for the rabbit to cook. Thorne manages to secure it to our branch torch and the blue flames quickly turn the meat crisp. We dig into our portions without much conversation, and after however many nights of bread, jerky and nuts—it's luxury.

I've never tried rabbit before. Probably due to my tendency to avoid consuming animals I consider cute. I once expressed this to Tyler, and he made me feel like a horrible person, claiming that according to this philosophy, I—"*only eat the ugly ones.*"

For now, though, I'm breaking my rule. Because this tastes glorious. Maybe I've been missing out. The cuter, the tastier. I shake my head to eradicate the mildly psychopathic thought.

"So," I say to the group collectively, once I'm finished. "I want to know more about Ethra."

Balvinder's face lights up behind the licks of blue flame, and for a moment I find myself considering how tragic it is that Zac has never seen him—because Zac's face has broken into a smile too, mirroring Balvinder's. They seem connected, but not in the way most people are. It's more subconscious and instinctive, an indiscernible cord between them. Zac's words from before spring back to mind—*you'll have to accept that truth runs far more deeply than what we can see*. I feel like whatever he shares with Balvinder might too.

"What do you want to know?" Thorne asks gruffly, tossing a bone over his shoulder.

"I guess ... where I am? Where Ethra *is*, exactly. And how it exists in relation to ... home?"

Balvinder clasps his hands together and leans toward the fire, silvery strands of hair falling by his face. I still remember how it felt to cut—softer than silk. "Think of it this way," he says, "the Essences of the erodosphere, although very much present—are invisible on Earth. In Ethra, we are more tangible. This is a dual dimension, created by the Overseer to establish a system of sustenance for spirits in both worlds."

His words seep through my mind like water, running through the gaps in my understanding and collecting in an unfamiliar space somewhere inside of me. I've heard similar things before during conversations with Zac, but a new chord is struck in Balvinder's voice, the resonance of it demanding that I believe every word.

"There is an interconnection," Thorne supplies. "Our worlds coexist, conjoined by the erodosphere, but it is here that the system Balvinder speaks of is implemented. Here that we are granted bodies that the Melder is able to see."

"Okay." I swallow back the remnants of my cynicism. "I think I kind of get it."

"It was about time you kind of got it," Zac chimes. I whip my head toward him, startled by the jab. His mouth tugs up on one side.

When I look back to Thorne, I see that he has shifted closer to Balvinder, muttering rapidly into his ear.

Zac seems to register our exclusion from the whisperings, because he sighs resignedly and inclines his head my way again. "Now you know a little about Ethra," he says, "tell me more about you." The reflection of the fire makes his emerald irises glisten brightly—although, the rings of colour are narrow and the pupils dilated, as if absorbed by the darkness.

It's only further confirmation of the fact that he can't see the fire—that the only light perceivable to him radiates from the branch torch speared into the dirt in front of us. The thought of two fields of vision, perfectly aligned and yet somehow different, makes me somewhat uneasy. But at the same time … there's a sense of safety in knowing he can't see me as clearly as I can see him. I feel as though I can look him in the eye without flinching.

I smile, freely. "There's not much to me. I'm in my final year of school, without much idea of what to do next. Maybe something science-related. I have one best friend and basically one parent, but I love them both more than anything." I feel a pang and glance away from him, stretching my hands out toward the blue flames until my fingers prickle from their warmth. "That just about sums me up."

Zac waits for a long while, Balvinder's and Thorne's murmurs rippling away in the background. "Your father," he says finally. "May I ask what happened to him?"

"My father," I repeat, with a breathy laugh. "He comes and goes. He's been coming and going for as long as I can remember. So when he left for good, it was more of a relief than anything. Anyway—tell me about *you*. I'd say your life is far more interesting."

Zac shrugs, sweeping a curl of dark hair out of his eyes. "I'm not sure interesting is the word."

Of course it isn't. His parents *died*. I have no doubt that what I've had to deal with wouldn't even compare to what he has endured. I bite down on my lip, berating myself for the thoughtless comment. "Sorry," I say. "Your parents, I'm sure they cared dearly for you, and that's worth something. But I can't imagine what you've been through. I don't see my Dad, but he's not ..."

Zac inclines a brow at me. "Dead?"

"Sorry," I say again. This is why you shouldn't talk about feelings with people you don't know well enough. Disaster is inevitable.

Although, a quick glance at Zac shows me a gentle smile curved into that pretty, elusive dimple of his. "Well, you're right," he says.

"About what?"

"That they cared. And that it's worth something."

TWENTY-ONE

"WE SHOULD BE CAREFUL IN THESE PARTS,"
Balvinder says, evening out an area of dirt with his foot and
laying down his blanket. "Stay close and alert."

Thorne, who offered to keep watch for the first part of the
night, empties a packet of nuts into his mouth and chomps on
them loudly. "Why? Rest assured the apparitions won't show."

Balvinder hesitates, his lips pressed firmly together as if to
hold something back—before he drops to the ground without
a word. The blue fire fades within seconds, leaving only the
glow of our broken branch.

"Disgusting creatures," Thorne goes on, grabbing my
pack. "I wasn't sorry to see them go." He ruffles around and
pulls out my blanket, settling back into a nook of the nearest
tree and yanking it over his legs.

I glance at Zac, who seems to have understood what happened if his look of contempt is anything to go by. He must
have seen the bag snatched, just like he could see the rabbit
skinned—if not the snatcher or the skinner.

I'm about to berate Thorne for taking my stuff when Zac
throws his blanket over both of us. It takes me a moment to

decide whether I'll accept the offer, or tug-of-war my blanket from Thorne.

But when Zac sidles down—the heat of him so near, barely a foot away—I find myself doing the same. I kick off my boots and snatch my bag from beside Thorne's feet to rest my head on. Then I lie on my back and look up at the canopy, counting the stars glittering through it.

Thorne's mention of *apparitions* drifts back to my awareness. I don't like the sound of them. *Disgusting* creatures, he said. I think I've had enough of those for one week—Thorne included.

"Awake?" Zac whispers. There's a certain intimacy to the word, or maybe in how he says it—hushed, so only I can hear. I turn my head to see him on his side, facing me, his pack pillowed under his head like mine.

"I find it hard to switch off," I tell him, and tap a finger to my temple. "There's a lot going on in here."

His chin grazes the dirt as he nods. "I found it hard too, for a long time."

"Not anymore?"

"No."

"What changed?"

Zac shifts his head closer to mine and my insides seem to contract all at once. "I realised that sleep isn't intended to drag you toward your fears—more to draw you away from them."

"Interesting." I turn my gaze away from his as a swell of nervous energy seizes my chest. "Like an escape."

"A temporary escape. Just enough."

"How do you explain nightmares then?" I parry. "Wouldn't you say they usually play on our biggest fears?"

"Sometimes they find a way in," Zac concedes. "But even then, you don't experience pain in the same way. It's muted, removed. More bearable."

I ponder the concept in silence until Zac asks, "What do you dream about?"

I cast a quick glance over at Thorne. He's inspecting one of his arrows, running his fingers across its feathered end—and doesn't appear to be listening. Nevertheless, I lower my voice further as I pull back to Zac. "Home," I say, turning on my side to face him. "Recently, home. But I've had these other weird dreams ... there's this black smoke, and it swallows me whole. I either choke on it or get lost in it."

Zac shifts a hand under his pack, regarding me curiously. We look at each other for what feels like a long time, longer than we've ever looked at each other before, and it's Zac who breaks the silence again. "Tell me about your home. What is it like?"

It takes a few seconds for me to conjure a picture of my house, and when I do see the little red brick, rose-adorned entryway, the image warms me from the inside.

"It's nothing grand," I say. "Relatively ordinary, but I love it anyway. Our front door has this cool arch over it, which is kind of nice." I draw the shape of the arch in the dirt between us. "And there are ..." Zac's fingers meet mine, brushing them softly. The whisper of a touch. I try to ignore it and rush on. "There are roses, climbing roses, on the front wall. They're this bright yellow, really bright. I've always loved that. Whenever I see them growing other places I think of home—" My voice wavers on the last word and I break off suddenly. Zac probably thinks the hitch was emotional, rather than a nervous reaction to his touch. Embarrassing—but, I guess, the lesser of two evils.

Zac's fingers trace my knuckles, skirting around them to wrap over my hand. Every square millimetre of his skin on mine seems to flare up and burn through to some part of me that can't work out if it should panic or reciprocate. Or both.

He runs his thumb lightly across my index finger. My heart pulses madly through me, right down to my toes and fingertips.

A light breeze eases over us, traces of it creeping under our blanket. The first sign of wind in this god-forsaken forest. I'm grateful for it, but it also makes the hairs rise all over my arms. I pull the blanket up under my chin with my free hand and then close my eyes. If I were watching Zac, I don't think I'd be able to muster the courage to turn my palm and interlace our fingers. Which I do, albeit shakily.

We stay that way for quite some time, hands locked between us. It feels wild and strange. Like two pieces of two different puzzles somehow fitting together. A picture that shouldn't work but does. Perfectly.

"You snore, you know," Zac says at last.

I spring my gaze on him, frowning. "I do not."

"It's all right." He smiles. "I still think you're lovely."

Lovely.

Lovely.

Lovely.

The word sets itself to repeat, spinning around and around in my head and clouding any articulate response. I force it away with some effort, focusing instead on the comment that preceded it. "*You* snore, Zacharias."

He cocks an eyebrow. "Zacharias?"

"Uh-huh, it's true. The first time I heard it I thought you were dying."

Zac snorts, which elicits a ridiculous giggle from me.

"You know, we're taking this break for the two of you, mostly," Thorne drawls from his tree post. "Stop wasting time and go to *sleep*."

I give Zac a pointed look and he grins. Dragging my hand out of his, I reposition my pack and shut my eyes tight, even though sleep is the last thing on my mind.

A moment later, I open one eye to check if he's asleep. But he is looking at me, still. A sliver of light from the moon casts his cheekbone and the tip of his nose into white gold. His smile is gentle now and flips my heart onto its head.

I try and fail to bend my mouth into a sensible, straight line. "Goodnight."

"It was," says Zac, his words following me into a deep, *lovely* sleep.

TWENTY-TWO

"THIS IS PERFECT!" TYLER CRIES, TOSSING HIS *dark hair and throwing a pillow at me. "Exactly what you needed. A mega hottie to sweep you off your feet and get you out of this rut."*

"I'm perfectly happy on my feet," I retort. "Tyler ... he's lovely, but—"

"No Abbey, he's more than lovely." Tyler's expression turns suddenly serious. "Have you seen that dimple? A literal point in his favour, if ever I saw one."

"The dimple is ridiculous, I know, but—"

"Then what's the hesitation?"

I laugh, flopping back onto my bed with the pillow to my chest. "Well, he's got ... a tricky past. I think. And he could be from another world altogether, so there's that."

Tyler spreads his arms. "And?" He raises a finger. "Tricky past—don't we all? Another world—do you not have a romantic bone in your body?"

I sigh. "I'm leaving. Soon."

"So make the most of it!" Tyler cries. He gets up and makes for the beanbag in the corner. With a full smile that reveals the gap between his front teeth, he sinks into it—and disappears.

The bag begins to expand into currents of velvet, drawing my room into a spiralling black hole. I'm yanked off my bed by the force of it and dragged screaming across the carpet, which ripples under me before slipping into the darkness too.

I jolt upright with a start. Enough time has passed that the forest is just a little brighter, nearing dawn. To my left, Zac is sound asleep with his back to me. Balvinder appears to be asleep too. But Thorne is still awake. He's watching me, his dark eyes gleaming.

"Bad dream, little Melder?" He plucks at the bowstring of his crossbow, which is set over his knees.

I shrug. Sweat has glued hair to my face and I hastily wipe it aside.

Thorne gestures to a tree nearby, its roots frozen into gentle curves. "Come here. Speak with me."

After a lengthy hesitation, I decide that even a conversation with Thorne would be better than entering back into that dream. And so I slip out from the blanket, doubling it over Zac.

I shuffle into the nook provided by the roots opposite him, tucking my knees up to my chest. "What did you want to talk about?"

Thorne lets loose a jaded sigh. "You and Harlie are not unlike each other," he says. "Never bothering with preamble—always right to the point."

"I wouldn't say that," I retort. "I can be quite the preambler. And who's Harlie?"

"*Preambler* isn't a word," Thorne says with a reluctant smirk.

"It is now." I let my head flop back against the tree. The stone is harder than I anticipated, and I fiercely rub where it hit. "If this really is some other world, how can I understand you? Wouldn't Ethra have a language of its own if it were so separate from ... Earth?"

"It isn't so separate, and you are not the first to arrive from Earth," Thorne says, his usual air of irritation having slipped into a conversation verging on civil, even good-humored. "There are commonalities. Our connection to Earth goes back further than you could possibly imagine."

"Huh." I chew on my lip and look back to Zac and Balvinder.

Thorne follows the line of my gaze. "Balvinder doesn't ordinarily require this amount of rest. None of us do." His brows incline, considering. "I haven't seen him of late, but something feels different."

I think of Balvinder's seizures. Would Thorne know about them? I'll have to mention it before I go, so that he can help Balvinder, if he can.

I'm about to bring it up when Thorne slides closer to me. He tosses his crossbow and settles back, his burly shoulder pressing into mine.

"Little Melder," he begins, looking out at the forest, "Balvinder tells me that you are determined to leave Ethra."

I blink at him. "Well, of course. Even if there's any truth to what you've told me ... I don't see how I can hang around. Mum will freak the hell out."

Thorne shakes his head. "No part of you possesses a desire to learn more of our world? Or why you have been summoned?"

I roll my head to face him before realising how close we are and turning away. "I don't know. Maybe."

"*Maybe*," Thorne repeats with a huff. "I sense a disagreeable degree of Peirce in you."

"Who is—"

"Ethra has much to offer," interjects Thorne. "Beyond the confines of your narrow imagination."

I frown. "My imagination is perfectly unconfined, thank you."

Thorne reaches over, and I jump as his fingers glide across my cheek. They're slender and cold. "Allow me to expand it," he says in a hush. And then he curls his hand around my neck and leans in.

I jerk away, but the roots at my other side bar my escape. Thorne grabs my waist and draws me closer. I find myself pinned between his huge body and the tree behind me as his thin lips collide with mine, hard and vigorous.

In a moment of relatively thoughtless inspiration, I yank my head away and rapidly swing it forward. There's a sharp *clunk*.

I watch Thorne rear back, clutching at his forehead. A throbbing pain pulses in my own head, but I'm too relieved to be rid of him to care.

"What was *that?*" he hisses.

Heart racing, I cast a glance at the others, still motionless. "I might ask you the same question," I snap, scrambling to my feet. "Please *never* do that again."

Thorne stares at me with wide eyes—a look of genuine surprise. "What are you talking about?"

"I'm not interested," I say, pressing my lips tightly together.

He lowers his hand and opens his mouth to speak, then shuts it. His shock turns into a sneer. "I don't believe you." And then he's on his feet, reaching for me again—but I push at him. Hard.

Thorne is strong and sturdy, but the impact still has him staggering backwards.

"How *dare* you," he jeers. "Is it the Nellerwood boy? It is, isn't it?"

"What?"

His expression turns frosty. "You prefer him over me?"

"Prefer him over you?" I repeat, almost laughing. "You're not—you didn't even—" I can't settle on the right words. Everything sounds ridiculous. How in *hell* did Thorne get the impression I wanted him this way?

"You will see one day." He snarls. "You will come to see what you have denied yourself. From Ethra, and from me."

With that, he whirls around and stalks into the forest, leaving me gaping after him.

＊

It seems completely out of character. To this point, I'd concluded that Thorne couldn't give a hoot about me. In fact, I'd have said he actively despised me. So now I'm thoroughly confused and shaken. It makes no sense.

Unless … unless it makes perfect sense. If he is an *Essence*—the embodiment of a certain quality—as they say, then his nature would revolve around one thing.

Whatever that one thing is, it makes him forceful, bold, snarky and rude. It dictates everything he does and says. The nasty remarks. The attempt to kiss me. The expectation I would kiss back.

I rack my brain but can't think of one singular word to define it all. Sleaze? I doubt the Essence of *Sleaze* exists. But if it does, I can think of no better candidate for the title.

Conscious of the fact that I'm suddenly the only person awake in a dark and extraordinarily creepy forest, I drag my dagger from its sheath.

Gently, I press it against my open palm. The fine leaf-like markings along the blade are clotted with bits of dry, crusty blood—from the wolf attack. I scrape at it with a fingernail, shuddering at the memory of the wolf chasing me, lunging out with its teeth bared. And then I'm thinking of Thorne, who did close to the same thing.

I can't imagine Zac—or Balvinder for that matter—would be pleased to know about it.

My eye catches a flash of movement behind the camp. I freeze, blinking into the gloomy forest. "Thorne?" I murmur softly, so as not to wake the others.

No answer.

Tightening my dagger grip, I edge forward, past Zac and Balvinder and a little way through the trees. But I see nothing. Just a grey sea of dirt, stagnant roots and towering trunks. The morning creeps in through gaps in the close-knitted canopy, dotting the ground with spots of light.

I run my gaze over every inch of the landscape, every tree and space between—stopping at a dark shadow. It juts out from behind a narrow tree a few metres away. "Thorne?" I say again, finding myself hoping it really is him. Whoever or whatever it is behind the tree doesn't seem perturbed by my presence enough to run, or provoked enough to confront me.

I steel myself, and then move in.

Every nerve in my body stands at attention. I hold onto a breath, brandishing my dagger as though I might know what to do with it if the need should arise.

The shadow moves, a head appearing around the tree. I fix my eyes to the features ... and stop dead. The face looking right back at me—is mine.

TWENTY-THREE

MY CLONE APPEARS JUST AS I AM, ONLY ITS eyes are black pits. I'm already retreating as it steps out from behind the tree with an aberrant smoothness of motion, like its joints are elastic, stretching a little further than they should.

The apparitions. Thorne's comments from last night draw back to me. *Disgusting creatures.* But he also said they wouldn't bother us. That we could rest assured that they were gone.

"Shader," the creature croaks, and my skin prickles all over at the sound of my name. It slinks forward.

I back up further, keeping my dagger firmly extended. The creature pauses and with a strange snap of its neck, tilts its head at me like a bird inspecting its dinner before it swoops. The motion is enough to shoot a pulse of terror through me.

"Follow," it says. "Follow us."

"Who?" I scan the area and see no one else. "Why?"

The apparition's eyes freeze, though I can't be sure it's looking at me, since the whole of them are black and lifeless. "She summons you."

"She?" I frown, my skin coming alive with that prickling sensation. There's a beat of terse silence—before the apparition lurches forward.

Sudden terror propels me into a run. I yell as I go to wake the others. A slippery dragging sound follows behind.

It was a split-second decision that killed the wolf. Granted it was a semi-fluke—is it one that could work for me again?

Ahead, I see Zac bolt upright and whirl around to me. Some instinct kicks in and makes me spin to face the apparition. Unlike the wolf, which barrelled straight into my weapon, this creature isn't fooled.

Its advance slows, and to my horror, its mouth drops open—revealing a jagged set of teeth and a piercing screech. The tips of the teeth are impossibly long for the mouth, as if its skin too is pliable for devouring its prey.

The apparition springs forward and disarms me with a rapid blow. It claws at my collar with fingers that are now pronged talons, pulling it tight around my throat.

"Zac—" I choke, but the word is smothered as the apparition's grip tightens. The empty, black eyes are an inch from my own, and suddenly I draw a stark connection.

The woman I first met in Emba—Kayna. Her eyes were much the same, swallowing all traces of light with a gaze that made my skin crawl.

Follow us. She summons you.

The creature shrieks in my face and I turn my nose at the foulness of its breath. There's a noise behind me. The apparition jerks back and I gasp for air as it lets me go.

A dagger handle protrudes from the creature's shoulder. I turn to see Zac a few metres away, eyes wide and alert. He charges over to the creature as it crumples to the ground at our feet.

Its eyes glaze a milky grey colour. The clothes it wore, identical to my own, dissolve like ash. As does the hair. Its skin withers, turning grey, and what's left is a bald, emaciated foetus. I feel as though I've just watched a time-lapse of my end days from death to decomposition. And it's not pleasant.

Zac's nostrils flare as he sucks in a tight breath. "What was it?"

"I think it was an apparition," I say. "It looked like me. Until ..." Until it didn't.

"Is it dead?" he inquires, frowning fiercely.

I stare at him, momentarily confused. It looks fairly dead to me. Surely he can tell as much too. But then I realise—"you can't see it!"

Zac shakes his head, bending to retrieve the dagger.

"But—how then—how did you know? How could you know where to throw?"

"I sensed the direction of the attack," Zac says, swiping his blade across his trousers. I don't have too much time to be impressed or shocked that he threw a knife an inch from my face with nothing but a sense to go on, because Balvinder and Thorne join us and my gaze falls back to the shrivelled creature at my feet.

"That thing—" I stop, adjusting my collar and taking another long inhale. "What did it want from me?"

Thorne wrinkles his nose at the sight of the dead apparition. "Fear," he says. "Which you seem to give readily at every turn."

"No," I snap, feeling thoroughly irritated by him. Not only for the jab, but for his earlier advances too, which are rapidly returning to mind. "It told me to follow. *Follow us*, it said. And then it told me *she summons* me."

Balvinder and Thorne exchange a worried glance. "The apparitions are under Kayna's control," Thorne says, and then his brow furrows deeply. "Though, they don't ordinarily show nowadays. Not since her confinement."

"Kayna! You know her? She had something to do with this?" I glance at Zac but he only shrugs, apparently just as perplexed as I am. "And what confinement?"

"Of course I know Kayna." Thorne's eyes close in an exasperated flutter. "She isn't permitted to roam freely like the rest of us. Not anymore. Evil tends to refuse the reins of authoritative power, and besides, in excess it's just a nuisance."

"Evil?" Hysteria crumples the word as I speak it, and I recall the eyes of the apparition—the black depth of them, so reminiscent of Kayna.

"Keep up, little Melder," Thorne says.

"Kayna is ... Evil? An Essence of Evil? That woman I met back in Emba?" I turn to Balvinder, who has heard me speak of her before. But he doesn't look at me.

Thorne steps closer, swinging a hand behind him to rest on his crossbow. "You have encountered her already?"

I nod. "As soon as I got here. She was a weird girl. I felt ... strange, around her."

Thorne turns his head slowly to Balvinder, who is now looking up through the branches of the trees, a familiar veil over his eyes.

I see my uncertainty mirrored in Zac's face, which is some comfort, at least.

"Kayna is still secured, isn't she?" asks Thorne. When Balvinder doesn't answer, he cuts his attention back to me. "What did she say to you?"

"She told me she could get me home. That she had something to do first, but then she would take me." I strain to remember our conversation. It seems an age ago now. "The great tree, she said. The great tree would be my way home."

"Well I'll be damned." Thorne's broad jaw has stiffened, his chest rapidly puffing up. "She must have escaped somehow, the snake. Do you know anything about this, Balvinder?"

We all look to him, but he is still wearing that same vacant look.

"Balvinder?" Thorne presses. "What is the matter with you?"

A memory strikes me then—my nightmare on the plateau. Waking to a dark fog. Walls forming passages that prompted me away from Balvinder and Zac. It felt real at the time, before I dismissed it as a dream. But maybe my gut was right to begin with.

With a grim shudder, I recall the shadowy figure at the end of the passage. Waiting. If Kayna wants to take me home, it could be that she was trying to separate me from the others even then.

It wasn't the only time I've seen that shadow. I saw it in the mountains, too. Dread washes over me as I remember the figure standing on the peak, gone in a blink.

She summons you.

"It doesn't make sense," I burst out. "If this woman is the literal embodiment of Evil, as you claim, why would she want to help me find my way home?"

Thorne rolls his eyes. "Is it so hard to believe that not everybody wants you here, sweetheart?" I have to bite back a retort about his contrary behaviour a few hours ago. "But it's semantics," he breezes on, as if realising the direction of my thoughts. "Kayna won't kill you. Neither will her apparitions. Nor Balvinder, nor *I*." His eyes flare wide with a smirk. "Tell her Balvinder. The Melder cannot be slain by the hand of an Essence, and neither can one Essence kill another. Isn't it so?"

Balvinder doesn't look at us, he's still staring off at that same, far away place I suspect only he can see.

"Anyway," Thorne says, scowling Balvinder's way. "The only one of us in any real danger is the Nellerwood boy. He isn't protected by the same magic."

Zac grimaces in Thorne's vicinity. "I can fend for myself," he replies, tersely.

I jump as my hand is squeezed. Balvinder is holding it. He meets my puzzled gaze with a tranquil sort of calm crossed with weariness.

"No more games Balvinder," growls Thorne. "Tell her who Kayna is. Tell her who *you* are. It's about time she learnt something useful. Guesswork for the sake of guesswork is meaningless."

Balvinder's eyes remain on me and his mouth moves without words. A dark cloud draws over his face. I lurch out to grab him just as his knees buckle.

Zac immediately and impressively seems to realise what's going on. He reaches out to help and as we've done before, we lower his trembling body to the ground together, onto its side.

Zac finds Balvinder's cheek with his hand. "He is cold," he says, with some urgency. "Colder than last time."

I reach out myself and the chill repels my touch.

"What is going on?" Thorne barks.

I look up, having forgotten about him entirely. "Have you ever seen him do this?" I ask, and he shakes his head with an air of irritation, as if it bothers him to admit he knows less than I do. "It has happened a few times before," I explain. "He falls unconscious for a while, or ... unresponsive, at least. But then he seems okay when he wakes up."

Balvinder's shudders lessen and his limbs slump to the ground. His eyelids quiver before springing open. They're frozen, the blue veiled in milky white.

"I have known Balvinder far longer than *either* of you," Thorne pronounces, oozing haughty condescension. "That's right, even you Zacharias. I have never seen him behave like this. Not once. Not ever."

"He came to visit me a month or so back," Zac says, rubbing his chin. "Then I didn't hear from him until he returned with Abbey. Normally he returns every few days. Not to mention Abbey found him tied up with rope, and he wouldn't tell either of us why."

Thorne pouts, and I have a rather unpleasant flashback to our intimate moment last night. "Kayna," he mutters. "If her apparitions are roaming about, she is too. Perhaps, somehow, she swapped her confinement for Balvinder's, and—"

Thorne is interrupted by a sudden coughing fit. Balvinder's long body curls inward from the force of the coughs, and I squat down to pat his back until it eases. He presses himself up onto his knees and says, "I'm fine," peering at me with watery eyes.

I hear Zac sigh loudly and I can't help but laugh. "Only I'm allowed to say that and not mean it," I tell him.

Balvinder chuckles too, which leads to more coughing. When it's over, Thorne fires a barrage of questions his way, all of which are batted away with nondescript responses, as per usual. Of course this doesn't surprise me, or Zac, but it enrages Thorne.

"I will enlighten you when the time is right," Balvinder says.

Thorne snaps back—"If Kayna is running amuck again, we *must* know."

Balvinder's lips curl in, revealing nothing more. Thorne whirls around, dropping the subject but not without a snarl for good measure.

I watch the space between Balvinder's brows where fine lines mar his pale skin, intruding on his smooth complexion. I feel anger rise in me, but I can't say why, or where it comes from exactly.

What I can say now—is that I trust Balvinder. Against all my cynical inclinations, I trust that there's a reason he hasn't told us more. I trust that there is a right time, and that it isn't now.

TWENTY-FOUR

I CAN'T REMEMBER THE LAST NOVEL I READ, apart from those assigned in English classes. As a kid I loved the fantasy worlds of fiction, but growing older—I started to prefer real stories. Non-fiction. Information-based books. They never feel like a waste to me, because the knowledge always impacts me somehow. It becomes a platform to stand on and view the world from, every new book or piece of information adding another layer—lifting me higher so that I can see more.

But right now, Ethra is stranger than fiction. And I find myself wishing I'd read more of it, so that maybe I would be more prepared for the leap off my platform and onto another.

Darkness has descended like a thick curtain to the forest floor. We are set up on a grassy patch amidst the dirt and stone, which was unexpected to find considering how lifeless and dreary the rest of the forest has been.

Nothing should surprise me anymore, though. I just had an apparition try to attack me, after all, presumably sent by Kayna—the Essence of Evil herself. Things are either clearing up and making a new kind of sense, or I'm officially a lunatic. I'm not sure which conclusion I'd rather reach.

And then there's Zac. We held hands last night. *Held hands.* And he called me lovely. But nothing particularly notable has happened since, and I'd been telling him about home, so maybe it was just a supportive gesture. A handhold of solidarity. An—*I've got your back, buddy*—sort of thing.

I sit beside him now, running my fingers through the tangles in my hair while he rifles through our bags of food and sporadically passes me fruit or nuts. A little shampoo and conditioner wouldn't go astray. Not sure if the natural, greasy look is one to win hearts.

Balvinder and Thorne are immersed in a hushed conversation behind us. I can hear Thorne dropping names I've never heard before.

Colt. Gwin. Asha.

He mutters about Kayna mostly, her newfound freedom, how she's likely to come back, how she usually steers away from the Melder between Breathings so what is she up to now? Balvinder doesn't offer much on that, and so I tune them out.

Zac is looking up into the patches of yellow sky above the lattice of branches. "It will rain tomorrow," he declares.

"Oh?" I yank at a particularly difficult knot. "How do you know?"

He shrugs and smiles across at me. "I sense it."

"You and your senses ..." I shake my head before pulling my hair up into its elastic. "You threw a dagger at me on a *sense*."

"But it hit the apparition, didn't it?"

"Lucky for you," I reply grimly, curling loose strands around my ears. Now that I'm tuned into Zac's rain prediction, I do detect a strange scent to the air. Fresh and vaguely sweet.

Listening to the quiet chatter of the Essences behind us, I get thinking about the erodosphere. If it does exist around us, unseen, what would it look like if I *could* see it? That streak of blue I noticed in the sky back home—how much more is there?

Balvinder practically said Essences are omnipresent—everywhere and anywhere there are people who need them. But they have bodies too, like Thorne's and Balvinder's, which operate in a more *normal* sense ... apart from the lack of shadow and sleep and Balvinder's ability to conjure flames and water from nothing.

I imagine wispy threads of colour swimming around me. Inhaling them like smoke from a cigarette, feeling them curl inside an inner sanctum of me that supposedly desires some unique portion of each Essence. Suddenly I feel like I might choke.

I clear my throat and nudge Zac with my knee. "Hey."

"Mmm?" He turns to me, eyes still wide from taking in the sky. Now they glide smoothly over my features, like he's looking at me with the same captivated lens he used to look up. Like the words I haven't spoken yet are stars hidden behind clouds. I lower my gaze and pretend to fiddle with my shoelaces.

"Do you ever feel sort of helpless?" I ask him.

"Helpless?"

"Yeah. I mean, if we really do unconsciously rely so completely on this erodosphere, and the Essences, and some process outside ourselves to define us, isn't it all out of our hands?"

"That's not really how I see it," Zac says, inclining his head thoughtfully. "I'm not sure I have everything entirely clear myself, but a spirit is not a separate entity. It's bound to your subconscious, yes, but it's no less you than the *you* you know."

"That's a lot of you's."

"Like I said before, it's your spirit that draws from the erodosphere," he says. "But ultimately, you are in control. And you need to trust yourself—even the parts you can't access so easily."

"Huh." I finally look at Zac in full. His keen, green eyes. Fractionally parted lips. There's a childish excitement in the way he speaks about all this, but an aged sort of insight too. I'm sure his past—dealing with the death of his parents as such a little boy—has a lot to do with the unusual combination of youth and maturity he shifts between, exuding one and then the other in the beat of a breath.

"I have doubted, in the past," Zac says. "There is some blind trust required, but it's hard to argue with the system when you have a disembodied Essence personally narrating it to you along the way."

A thunderous roar sounds above us and I jump about a foot in the air.

"Folorians!" Balvinder calls. He points upward, his pale face radiating with delight. I follow his finger and blink a few times, then trace a path around the branches and the gaps between them. I see them at the same time I remember why the word *folorian* rings a bell—from a conversation we had back in the mountains when I asked what other creatures reside around here.

Glistening shapes cut across the buttery sky, disappearing and reappearing amid the shadows of the branches and streaks of cloud.

Two. Three. Four.

Their silhouettes are immense—wings and bodies extended wide. There's another rumbling cry, like nothing I've ever heard. A cross between the roar of a lion and the shrill screech of a bird.

"Folorians are new to you," Thorne remarks behind me. I'm not sure if it's a question, but I nod my head. The creatures have passed now, their cries fading with distance.

Balvinder's blue eyes are gleaming. "Astonishing animals, aren't they?"

"They are," I admit, grinning at him. "I just wish they'd slowed down so I could get a better look."

"Yes." Thorne chuckles, and I'm shocked to hear genuine amusement in it. "I'm sure if you had asked nicely they would have *slowed down* to indulge your curiosity."

Beside me I hear Zac stifle a laugh and wheel around, even more surprised by his input in anything Thorne has to say. He bites down on his lip, obviously restraining a smile.

"I have never taken much interest in florians," Thorne adds gruffly, now void of humour. Has he ever taken much interest in anything but himself?

＊

My house stands alone at the end of a long, unfamiliar road. I walk toward it, my shadow stretching out in front of me. My favourite yellow roses cover the wall around the door, but when I get close—the thorns grow. They turn into rows of gnashing teeth. Deadly needles. "Follow us," they say.

I dive for the door. The thorns launch toward me.

I wake in a mess of tears and sweat. After a short moment of utter disorientation, I remember where I am and hurriedly compose myself.

Peering around, I see Thorne asleep and Balvinder awake beside him. Zac is gone.

A faint, warm radiance has settled amongst the trees. The air is crisp with morning coolness, but there is still that same strange, sweetened quality to it that I can't quite distinguish.

I look back to Zac's abandoned blanket.

"He went that way," Balvinder offers. I turn to face him as he points into the trees. "He was looking for a better view."

"Of what?"

Balvinder smiles and gestures again, as if the answer is with Zac. Frowning, I straighten my shirt and retie my hair before moving in the direction he indicated.

It isn't long before the trees open to a small clearing where Zac stands, looking up to a display of rose-pink cloud blooming across the sky.

His attention snaps to me abruptly. "It's about to rain." Something about the way he's standing, waiting, hair mussed from sleep and giddy about the possibility of rainfall—makes me smile.

As I approach his smile grows too, reaching his eyes. I stop beside him and squint up at the sky. "Are we just going to wait here until—" A cold drop on my forehead startles me into silence.

Zac wipes it away with his thumb, absently, his touch seeming to spark against my skin. His thumb comes away shimmering in gold, but I barely have time to contemplate the abnormality of the fact, because Zac is brushing my face again, this time with purpose. My breath hitches.

And then the rain falls.

It's as sudden and forceful as the storm across the plateau, slapping against me. Ruthless. Without my jacket offering some layer of protection, it might even hurt. My mouth hangs open in shock, which water quickly rushes to fill. I splutter it out between my lips like a wild horse.

Zac's face is twisted too, his nose crinkled and his mouth wide as he struggles for air and then chokes on the rain. I erupt into wet, hysterical laughter. The cool shower envelopes us, leaving no room for escape.

I blink down at my arms and notice in full what I dismissed before. The droplets are golden. Literally, *gold*— a million, tiny shards plummeting from the sky.

"What *is* this?" I shriek.

Zac cups his hands around his eyes to look at me, rain falling in sheets from the edges of his palms. "Welcome to Ethra!" he yells back.

We stand together, frozen and drenched, but it's too late to really care. Eventually the rain eases a little, enough for us to look at each other more clearly through it.

Zac's green eyes are bright and shining from the reflection of the cascade. I laugh again and he grins back. There's a warm touch under my chin—his fingers, lifting my face to his.

A thousand thoughts barrel through my mind all at once, with the abruptness of the rain itself. As Zac edges closer, some internal gate of me unlocks and I step out. Closer to him.

I'm leaving this place. There isn't enough time. When we get to the portal, I'll have to go. There will be questions left unanswered already, things I'll have to leave behind. It would take a long time, longer than I have, to learn everything I want to learn about this world and what its existence means.

If anything more happens with Zac ... how much harder will it be?

The twinkling raindrops dissolve all traces of the thought—until I see only him. My body defies what's left of my resistance and presses in. Anything else feels impossible, or suddenly illogical.

My chest meets Zac's, my heart hammering hard and fast. I bring my hands to his waist, drawing them around to the hard planes of his lower back.

I shouldn't have done that. It's wrong. Pointless, in the end. But I did it. Because I want him. I want him so badly that I'm shaking all over.

Zac trails his fingers down my spine, pressing me so close I can feel the swelling of each breath he takes. His forehead drops to mine and luminous, gold raindrops slip from his hair to his nose and then the tip of mine.

A smile tugs at the corner of his mouth. "You're afraid?" The drumming of the rain on the ground seems to enclose us in the question, or the observation, demanding an honest answer from me.

I reply under my breath, a word that's barely there but the truest I know to say. "Yes." Zac holds my face and kisses my cheek. His mouth lingers, moving softly against my skin. Nervous electricity buzzes through me, turning my knees heavy and leaden.

He draws away again and studies me. My chin. Lips. Nose. Eyes. "Why?" he asks.

It takes me a moment to remember what preceded the question, since the nearness of him clouds everything else that might matter. "Oh. Why am I afraid?"

He nods, and waits.

Because I like you. I like you a lot. But it will be over as soon as it begins.

"I don't know," I groan instead. It's an ambiguous and unhelpful response, but I can't bring myself to tell Zac how I really feel. So I close my eyes and tilt my face into the pattering rain. It eases any remaining tension and drenches my concerns with certainty of only one thing.

I rise to my tiptoes and press my lips to Zac's. I feel his surprise—a split-second hesitation and beat of stillness—before he wraps me up in his arms and melts into the kiss.

For what could never feel like long enough, we hold each other under the golden rain. His lips are full and smooth and warm. Raindrops merge into the kiss, turning it soft and indulgent.

Something stirs inside me. A shift. Maybe a break. Whatever it is, it's unfamiliar. Wonderfully unfamiliar. Terrifyingly unfamiliar. A part of me relenting, shrinking, making room for a part of him.

This won't last.

I try to banish the thought from my mind, but as the raindrops lessen it becomes harder to ignore.

I'll leave. I'll leave Ethra and it will all end. For nothing. It will hurt. That part of me that has started moving aside to let him in—it will take time for it to fall back into place. I've seen it with Mum, on a much larger scale. For a long time she didn't know who she was when Dad left. I can't open myself up to Zac only to tear myself away. I can't do it to myself, or to him.

With an effort I pull back, pressing my hands flat against Zac's chest. His brow furrows. Sodden, shimmering hair hangs at his temples, dripping down the sides of his face. I resist the urge to reach out and bury myself into him, to join bodies again like I think it's all okay. Or like I don't care if it isn't. But what good would that do?

"Zac—we can't." I force the words out in a hoarse whisper. "Not now."

The muscles in his jaw tense up, but he steps back too, letting my hands drop between us. "I know," he says softly.

My eyes dart away from his. Away from the comfort of his arms, I feel exposed. Defenseless.

I gesture back through the trees. "The others will be wondering—we should probably go—" I awkwardly turn and start to navigate through the trees.

I don't think I could have made a less romantic exit if I tried. But maybe that's a good thing. Romance will only perpetuate this—whatever *this* is—which will inevitably lead to loss. I didn't come here to lose anything. I didn't choose to be here at all.

"Abbey," Balvinder says when I return. "You saw the rain?" He's standing beside a disgruntled-looking Thorne, who is tipping water from one of his boots. Both men are saturated in a sparkly, wet coating.

"Nah," I reply, managing sarcasm with a smile. "I missed it."

"Awful, isn't it?" Thorne huffs, shoving his foot squeakily into the now waterless shoe.

"The blankets are dry," Balvinder says. "We hid them in our packs when—oh, Zac. You were right about the rain, after all."

"I was," Zac replies. I can't bring myself to look up, but in my periphery I see him go to collect his pack without a glance in my direction.

I feel a pang in my gut. And as we prepare to set off again, I can't shake the feeling that things will be different now, whether I like it or not.

TWENTY-FIVE

THE EARTH IS DAMP UNDERFOOT, STILL
twinkling in patches from the rainfall. Zac and I have barely
spoken since the kiss, but the others haven't seemed to notice.

Well, there's a chance Balvinder might have, but it's not
like any of us could get a word in anyway with Thorne jab-
bering on about the grandeur of his home and his matchless
hunting skills.

I wonder what Thorne would say if he knew what happened between Zac and me. Only last night he expressed his
suspicion of my interest in Zac, that is ... right after he made
an advance on me himself. The literal knockback seemed to
bother him more than it should have, given I've only known
him a couple of days.

Although, I highly doubt Thorne's move had anything to
do with true feelings. It seemed more of a spontaneous, spur
of the moment decision. Still, I'd given no indication that it
was what I wanted, and there's no adequate justification for
that sort of arrogance.

With Zac ... it was different. Even in the way he held my
hand, a question in the brush of his fingers, a pause before

leaning in to kiss me. Every move he makes is a suggestion rather than a demand. And so I feel worse about walking away from him than I do about almost cracking Thorne's skull. I'm more responsible for what happened with Zac. I've reciprocated. It's on me.

Tyler would be shaking his head right about now, telling me I'm overthinking it all and I should just take a leap. My dream from last night returns to mind—Tyler in my velvet beanbag talking me through his thoughts on Zac. Of course, he was only a fabrication of my imagination. But it was still lovely to see him again.

"What are you smiling about?" Thorne demands.

"Nothing," I say quickly.

Thorne narrows his eyes. "As I was saying, you must aim for the cold days. The hide of a rabbit serves as poor insulation, so they're forced to take shelter." I'm not sure who he's talking to, but Zac, who is walking ahead of me, kindly nods his head in response.

I've been preoccupied with watching the soles of his boots for the past few hours, thinking about how it felt to have his arms around me, his hands on my face and his lips against mine.

"Go for it," Tyler would say. *"It's about time. Seriously, don't be a pussy, Abbey. If you don't do it I will."* He might as well be speaking straight into my ear.

I've kissed a few guys. Three, to be exact. I even had a boyfriend once. It was fleeting, but contrary to Tyler's belief, it still counts.

His name was Jeremy. We met up three times—our dates consisting of drawn silences and tentative, sweaty handholding. It ended because he moved schools for Year Eight and you know, long distance just doesn't work, even when you have something as beautiful as we did. Ah Jeremy. How I've missed you.

Being involved in anything *serious* has never really featured on my radar. Mum tells me that when you're alone, you should always feel enough. Like you don't *need* anything. More than what you are is just a bonus. It's not definitive.

Trusting one person so explicitly and wholeheartedly is a risk, at best. Zac has never given me reason to doubt him. In fact he's kind of saved my life a couple of times. But I've only known him a week, and maybe I'm falling for him for that very reason—we've been through a heck of a lot together in such a short span of time.

They say relationships are strengthened by experiences. Well, it stands to reason then that a giant frog incident, a hulking wolf attack, an ice storm and a deranged apparition confrontation could drastically draw two people together. Survival mode—maybe that's all it is.

But staying in Ethra isn't a possibility. Is it? If I did delay my leaving to find out more about this place and why I'm here, it wouldn't be for Zac. It couldn't be. I'd have to step into the role of the Melder ... whatever the hell that means. I guess I'd find out.

Seizing a pause in Thorne's anecdotes, I ask, "Has anyone before me rejected the Melder role?"

"Every Melder serves their time," Thorne answers, casting me a wary side-glance.

"What about their homes? Their families?"

He laughs loudly, but it's cold and unsympathetic. "Priorities, sweetheart."

"Yeah, exactly," I say, despite knowing we're on entirely different pages.

Balvinder, striding alongside Zac, turns to me. The glowing branch rests across his shoulders, still bright where I stripped the bark. "Abbey, the Overseer can see further than we are able," he explains. "Melders do not always remain here for their lifetime, you see. The system revolves as it is supposed to, when it is supposed to."

I say nothing, but think back to the woman I came across upon arriving here—the Melder before me, so they say. I remember her vividly. Ashen hair spread in silken waves. Her skin—pallid, features framed with kind lines. I daresay *she* spent a lifetime here.

"And what's the basis of the Overseer's selection?" I pose. "What about me was so fitting for this Melder role, particularly considering I'm not going to pursue it?"

Thorne and Balvinder exchange a glance. "It will become clear," Balvinder says.

"Ah, ambiguity," I mutter. "How unusual."

I hear Zac laugh, but he doesn't turn. There has been an unspoken tension between us ever since the rainfall. It's strained enough that when Zac goes to hunt at our next rest stop—I stay behind and listen to Thorne's story about the time he "slaughtered a beast" with his "bare hands".

When he finally concludes the excessive spiel, I'm startled to see a wavering blue fire before us, just like last night's. It made no sound, and I didn't even see it spring to life. I turn to Balvinder in question, but he only regards me with the same degree of confusion. I squint at him suspiciously, which finally elicits a small smile.

Zac soon returns, swinging two squirrel-like creatures in one hand.

"You couldn't find any bigger game?" Thorne grumps, snatching the animals and slicing into one. I wince as blood sprays.

"Options are limited out here," Zac replies shortly. He gestures to Thorne's crossbow lying disregarded beside him. "But please do venture out and see how you fare. You are quite the hunter, after all."

Thorne nods, failing to detect Zac's disdain, or just ignoring it. "That's true," he says. "I am."

The meat is cooked above the translucent fire around a set-up of stone branches Thorne fashions into a makeshift grate. My plan to evade one-on-one conversation with Zac turns pear-shaped when Thorne decides to strike up another secret, whispered meeting with Balvinder.

I try to look thoroughly occupied as I nibble on my portion of meat. Between bites I watch Balvinder and Thorne, and start to realise how unusual the pair are; Balvinder with his gentle nature, Thorne brusquely dismissing nearly everything he says. And yet, they seem to get along, even *enjoy* each other's company.

"What do you think of it?" Zac asks suddenly, breaking our silence and a ton of ice too.

"Sorry?"

"The meat."

"Oh!" I swallow my last mouthful, choking on it as I try to speak too soon. "Good," I manage between coughs. He asks me if I'm all right. I wave away his concern with a flippant hand.

We say nothing for another long while—until I decide this is totally ridiculous. We're not twelve-years-old. There are mature resolutions to be made, and no point in tiptoeing on eggshells for the rest of this trek home. Speaking up can't make things any worse than they are now.

I gather my courage and turn to him. The moment he looks across at me, I know that he can see the panic I'm working to conceal. "I'm sorry for before," I mutter quickly, with a glance at the others. They don't seem to be listening.

Zac holds my gaze. I can't quite pick the expression. Is it humour glinting in his eyes? Nerves? He throws his bone and draws his knees up toward himself, loosely draping his arms around them and linking two fingers. "You're sorry?" He inclines his head. "Why?"

I hesitate, tossing around a myriad of responses before settling on, "Just—I—you know ..." Nice.

Zac regards me with the slightest bend of a wry smile. "I'm not sorry."

"Neither am I."

"You just said—"

"Argh, I don't know why I said that," I tell him, shaking my head to clear it. "I guess I just meant—I'm sorry I left you there. Without explaining ..."

"You don't have to," Zac says. The sapphire light of the flames casts long shadows under his cheekbones. He opens his mouth to continue on, but as I do, seems to then register that conversation has ceased between Balvinder and Thorne. They're both looking at us.

"We are thinking of visiting our friend Gwin," Balvinder says.

Thorne's head rolls dramatically along with his eyes. "*Your* friend Gwin," he clarifies.

Balvinder ignores the aside. "She would like to see us. Her oasis crosses our path to Amnoralas—so we can stop there for a meal."

I remember back to what Balvinder said about the oases. That every Essence is granted an area that is solely theirs—away from regular people.

"Kayna," I murmur. "Does Kayna live—does she have an oasis?"

"Indeed," Thorne says, with a sweeping look at Balvinder. "Though she tends to prefer roaming. Ironically, the Nellerwood boy will be far safer at Gwin's oasis than he will be in the forest. Kayna's Evil is barred from crossing the borders of any oasis."

Balvinder looks to the fire as he begins to say, "Minor Essences cannot be—"

"*Minor* Essences?" Thorne spits at the ground, like a vile taste has been left in his mouth. "Please, Balvinder. You know I loathe the word."

"Why can't Kayna cross your borders?" I persist, eager to hear more. "How does that work?"

Balvinder rests his hand palm up over one knee, his fingers splayed. "The Overseer designed it that way, so we could live in peace."

"Relative peace," Thorne corrects. "Living peacefully amongst the Essences is not a simple feat, let me tell you ..." He trails off and crosses his arms as if waiting for me to beg him to tell me. God he's irritating. Despite my curiosity, I don't ask.

In the corner of my eye I catch Balvinder clenching his fingers into a fist—and at the same moment, the blue flames extinguish.

✳

The next day brings with it an influx of woodland creatures. We see rabbits and squirrels and other little animals I can't recognise or name. They scale the stone trees and scurry across the dirt, leaving frantic prints and pellets behind. There is grass too—not in patches but in extended stretches. Thorne announces that we're approaching water, and that Gwin's oasis isn't far beyond it.

Sure enough, we soon come to a babbling creek. Zac tosses his pack to the ground. "We should wash up," he says, and I just about throw my arms around him at the suggestion. It's been almost a week without a shower—other than that rainfall, which I'm sure left me looking more dishevelled than presentable.

Thorne swiftly drops his pants. Pale, muscled thighs bulge out at me, along with a few other things I don't need to see. To my horror, before I can avert my eyes—he *winks*.

I whirl, my cheeks burning. Zac inclines his head at me in question. But I can't bring myself to tell him Thorne's totally naked, so instead I say, "We'll let Thorne go first."

Zac nods and gestures to the trees nearby. "Shall we wait over here?"

"I'll check on Gwin," Balvinder says, "and return to fetch you."

Without a glance back at Thorne, I hurry after Zac. He stops against a tree and I settle my shoulders against it too, right beside him. It's the most alone we've been since the rain.

"Have you met Gwin before?" I ask him.

Zac shakes his head. "Balvinder has said that the Essences know of me, but I've never met them—heard them, I mean." So Gwin is an Essence too. Zac bends to pick up a broken piece of petrified wood from the dirt, turning it in his fingers. "I'm not entirely sure why he's allowing us to meet now. Unless ..." He hesitates, causing me to look up at him.

"What?"

"Unless it has something to do with you."

I frown. "What could it have to do with me?"

"Well, it does seem oddly coincidental, doesn't it? That Balvinder keeps me well away from all this, but the moment you appear as the Melder—I am suddenly escorting you to Amnoralas and able to meet the Essences I've never met before."

"I guess." I glance away from him. Seems like I'm not the only person asking the question *why me?* Or *why now?*

Zac makes it sound like Balvinder's actions to this point have been somewhat premeditated, even Zac's involvement. The thought leaves me feeling a little unsettled.

"There was a time I felt I could question Balvinder," Zac begins carefully, "but so much has happened since then. He has earned my complete trust, far more than I can tell you or even articulate to myself. I almost feel that now—to question him would be to doubt him. And I don't doubt him. I can't."

I think it over, unbuttoning my jacket in preparation for the creek. I fold it over my arm. "I don't get you two," I say, candidly.

Zac smiles. "I doubt many people would."

"Have you ever asked him what Essence he is?"

"Yes."

"And?"

"His answers are vague."

"Surprise, surprise."

"I suppose he tries to maintain some degree of discretion, since the Essences remain unseen to most."

I sigh and press off from the tree. My gaze absently wanders, and I catch a flash of Thorne's bare skin at the creek. I glance away sharply.

"Besides," Zac goes on, unexpectedly jabbing me in the ribs. "*You* are the Melder. If you stayed on, you'd be privy to all this. No guesswork. Everything would be revealed in full. Every Essence." His mouth twists in a playful grin. "And then you could pass it on to me."

"Zacharias," I say seriously, and with a note of whimsy. "You ask too much of me. If I tell you, I expect something in return."

His smile turns lopsided and he steps forward, crossing his arms as he regards me. "What do you ask of me?"

My throat closes up. Something about the way he phrases the question tells me the conversation could go one of two ways. One—flirty banter. Two—extremely flirty banter. The butterflies in my chest explode into a frenzy.

"Maybe you—"

"Come out, little Melder!" Thorne calls, and thank God, because I'm not sure where I was about to take that sentence.

Zac seems to be fighting to hide his grin, his nose crinkling a little as he rakes a hand through his hair. I leave him behind the tree and march toward the creek. Thorne has disappeared, along with his clothes. At least he's wearing them now.

Once I'm sure Zac is out of sight, I strip down—pulling Rylah's green shirt over my head with care so I don't aggravate my shoulder injury. The scabby line has shrunk somewhat, but I still wish I had a mirror to inspect it properly.

The stones in the creek are smooth and slick with slime. I carefully find my footing and lower myself into the water. It's cool enough to make me shiver, but warm enough for my body to adjust quickly.

I clean away the accumulated layers of sweat and dirt from my skin, and then attack my bird's nest hair. Once the knots are untangled I lie back and relish the rippling of the creek a moment longer.

We had a bath at our first house and I used it all the time. I don't like the beach, but I like controlled bodies of water void of creatures and sand. Steaming hot was my preferred temperature. I'd drop my head and feel the surface creep up my scalp until only my nose stuck out above. There was something comforting about the feeling, like the water was a warm blanket wrapped snuggly around every part of me. A space set up exclusively for my place in it.

The creek is different. It moves in wild swirls around me, carving its own path and sending my dirt far away from where I can see it.

I kick myself upright off the stones and let out a sharp squeal. On the riverbank, staring right at me in all my naked glory—is a girl, wide-eyed and fixated.

"Hello," she says, as I huddle over myself to cover all my exposed bits.

"Uh ..." I edge toward my clothes, keeping my hands firmly planted over top and bottom. "Gwin?"

The girl tilts her head. Short, sandy hair cut into a clean line drops over one shoulder. "No. I'm Harlie."

Harlie? I don't recall mention of a Harlie. "I'm uh—I'm Abbey." I clamber out of the water and seize my clothes at the speed of light, pressing them to my body.

"I don't recognise you," Harlie says.

Everything about her is long and narrow—tall legs in fitted pants and a cream shirt draped low over sharp collarbones—so slim she almost looks like a paper cutout. Her nose is distinct and aquiline, and equally striking are her eyes, which are a bright, yellowish green.

At last, I settle on, "I don't recognise you either."

The girl squares her shoulders and a smile crosses her features, as fleeting and light as the touch of a butterfly's wing. "I'm the Essence of Honesty," she says. "You must be the new Melder."

TWENTY-SIX

A MIX OF NERVOUS DELIGHT AND FEAR JOLTS through me—just as Zac calls my name from the trees.

"Don't! Don't come out!" I yell back, a frenzy ensuing as I attempt to dress myself without flashing Harlie. *Honesty.* There's an Essence of Honesty. And she's standing right in front of me. I try not to think too deeply about it as I wiggle into my pants.

She watches me unashamedly, her back stiff and arms folded neatly. Even in clothes, I feel stark naked under her scrutiny.

"Zacharias Nellerwood," she mutters. "Balvinder's Zacharias?"

"Uh, yeah."

Harlie hesitates, a slender finger to her lips. It trails an arc toward me. "You are fond of him."

"What? No. Well *fond*, yes. I guess I—"

"It's quite clear. You have me written all over you. Though you have taken my Essence in the language of the body, as opposed to the mouth." Harlie's lips thin in the faintest of smiles. "Don't be shy, Melder. Shyness is a severe waste of time."

"My name's Abbey," I tell her, grabbing my hair to wring the water out of it. "Zac! Come on out!" I yell—a plea for help more than anything.

He spins out from behind the tree, approaching the opposite side of the river with a look of mild mystification. "Is Balvinder back?" he asks. "I heard voices—"

"Harlie," the girl beside me announces. "Or Honesty. Whichever you prefer."

Zac freezes on the spot, blinking rapidly across at us. "How very ..." He sets his hands on his hips. "Odd."

I'm glad someone else thinks so.

"He really does hear us," Harlie muses. "But why has Balvinder allowed him to—"

"Well hello." I spin at the sound of Thorne's voice. He slicks his wet hair back as he strides toward Harlie, coming to a stop a few feet away from her.

"You," she says. "Will you explain what I'm seeing? A new Melder wandering through the Petrified Forest with Zacharias *Nellerwood* ... how did this come to be?"

"Good question," Thorne mutters, flashing Zac a dark look he can't see.

"We are taking Abbey to meet with the Overseer." It's Balvinder that spoke. He strolls toward us, but he isn't alone. A plump girl trots in tow wearing the brightest pink dress I've ever seen. Her hair is white-blonde—a shade more gold than Balvinder's—elaborately braided and interwoven with strings of flowers.

"I wasn't aware you were here Harlie," Balvinder says cheerfully. "Have you all been introduced?"

"Kind of," I murmur.

"Well—Abbey and Zacharias, this is Gwin."

The tiny woman stops in her tracks and looks at us. Then, to my bewilderment, she releases an earsplitting shriek at the sky before rushing for me and seizing my hands in hers.

"*You* are Abbey Shader, yes? Out with the old, in with the new! Balvinder told me everything," she gushes. "Our exquisite new Melder! The weight of the world is in your hands my sweet, indeed it is. And what fun we'll have!" She beams at me with a smile that looks as though it might just burst her round cheeks.

"Don't be hasty Gwin," Thorne drawls. "Abbey knows very little. I wouldn't grow too attached if I were you."

I pin a glare on him, but he sets his chin and looks away before he can see it. Doubly infuriating.

"She will learn, she will learn," says Gwin, now jiggling my hands with such vigour that the rest of me jiggles with them. "How can she understand if she hasn't yet been given a chance?"

Thorne grimaces and moves off in the direction they came. I like Gwin already.

"Oh and Zacharias Nellerwood!" She grins. "What an honour it is to finally meet you." With a contented sigh, she links her arm through mine. "Let us retire to the house. There is *much* to discuss."

Zac, still standing on the opposite side of the creek, remains very still, although his eyes dart all around. The poor guy. His count on disembodied voices just grew drastically. I imagine one was strange enough, let alone *four*.

As Gwin drags me away, I hear Zac telling Balvinder that he'll follow after us once he has washed up. She pulls me forward by the elbow, but not before Zac lifts his shirt and I catch a glimpse of his flat, tanned torso.

"Fine young man," Gwin whispers, ducking her head into my shoulder to giggle. I can't resist smiling, because I'd have to agree.

✳

The trees surrounding Gwin's oasis are very much alive, like those back in the Moonlit Woods, only here the leaves are thicker, heavy and lush. Her house is nestled amongst bent trunks and meandering roots. It's a simple, two-storey cottage that looks like it might fall in on itself it you were to breath on it. The grass here is long, unkempt. Brightly coloured buds dash the greenery like hidden gemstones.

"Aren't they just adorable?" Gwin sighs as we approach. It takes me a second to realise she's referring to the flowers themselves. "My little sweets don't require watering, they grow all by themselves. Boy do they grow. And they happen to make for divine hairpieces! Would you like one?"

"I—"

"Tell me your favourite colour. I'll bet anything it's red."

I'm not sure what that implies about me, but I just nod and smile. "Sure."

Gwin squeaks and finally releases my arm—then springs like a kitten into the grass. Balvinder, Thorne and Harlie have already disappeared through the front door, but I hang back to wait for Gwin. The train of her pink dress catches in the grass, the edge of it matted and discoloured. This doesn't seem to bother her as she plucks a number of red buds and skips back to me with a wink.

I'm led into a cluttered room. A quick scan reveals two couches hidden under masses of vibrant material, half-unravelled balls of wool tossed across the floor, small bouquets dried and tied with ribbon, a narrow hallway ahead, and a rickety staircase leading to the upper level.

Gwin scurries toward the stairs and beckons for me to follow. We step out onto an open rooftop where Thorne, Balvinder and Harlie sit around a circular table. The floorboards are coated in leaves clearly trodden on over many years—the bottom layer appears almost imprinted whilst the top is decorated in a freshly-fallen smattering that feels like carpet underfoot.

"How wonderful to see you all here like this," Gwin says, stepping back to take in the scene. "Almost every single one of us, and between Breathings too! It warms my heart. I must say—if Kayna were free to roam, I would almost invite her to complete the picture! Isolation is a tragedy for any soul, even one as black as hers."

"Black indeed," Thorne mutters. "You may have your wish granted, Gwin." He hesitates, glancing at Balvinder. "We believe Kayna may have escaped."

Harlie's fair brows soar. "Escaped?"

"We encountered an apparition," Thorne says. "Well, Abbey did."

"An apparition!" Gwin shrieks, and then she bursts out laughing. "What a welcome party." She's not wrong. I haven't even told her about the giant frog and the wolf and oh, meeting the Essence of Evil herself.

Harlie purses her lips. Her wide eyes are a brilliant green in the afternoon light, like fresh limes. "They are rather unpleasant creatures."

"It seems that Kayna wishes to escort our newest little Melder to the Overseer," Thorne goes on. "Though I presume she hasn't overtly revealed herself for fear of us locking her up again."

"And lock her up we would," Harlie says, her expression still only one of mild surprise. "How did she get past your restraints, Balvinder?"

He opens his mouth but doesn't get to answer, because footsteps ascend the stairs behind me and everyone turns to see Zac appear, his hair damp and his expression more than a little cautious. I offer him a slightly dazed smile before Gwin grabs both our arms and directs us to a small, cushioned stool by the table. She insists that we sit, but then wedges herself between us so that I topple sideways.

"Plenty of room!" she declares, while I shift half a cheek back onto the seat.

"If by plenty you mean none at all, then you are quite right," Harlie says, eliciting a chuckle from Thorne. He then takes the opportunity to inform the table that at his home, there is more than enough furniture to sit on. The insult seems to pass right over the top of Gwin's head though, because she beams a smile at him with the force of a thousand suns and starts going on about how she would love to visit his place in the near future.

I feel a tap on my back. Zac is leaning in behind Gwin, gesturing for me to get closer. He whispers, "I'm hearing four voices now. Still want to be my friend?"

I press my lips into a considering line—then give a decisive shake of my head.

Zac nods as though he's regretful but understands.

We tune back into the table conversation as Gwin says, "The Melder—she really is gone?"

Balvinder offers a sombre nod and Thorne just cuts a glare at me, as though I'm the one responsible.

"It's no surprise," Harlie says. "She was tired, in body and heart. We needn't dwell on it."

"Oh goodness no!" agrees Gwin. "Onward she goes—to the next life!"

I catch Thorne laying a hand on Balvinder's shoulder, which is probably the only sign of sincere affection I've seen him attempt.

Then I notice Harlie following the line of my gaze. "Balvinder was her favourite," she tells me.

"Of course he was!" Gwin throws her hands in the air. "He's my favourite too. Let us be honest with ourselves, shall we? Ah, yes! Harlie, the most honest of us all—who is *your* favourite?"

"It wouldn't be you Gwin, I must say," Harlie replies, her sharp chin lifting a tad. "The constant state of ignorant bliss is rather exhausting. However Thorne speaks mainly of himself, and one can only feign interest for so long. So yes, I quite enjoy the company of Balvinder. And if I were required to pick one from amongst the lot of you, it would be him."

There's a moment of silence around the table as Thorne glowers at Harlie, Gwin nods triumphantly and Balvinder just smiles. "Our last Melder was particularly special," he says, setting his eyes on me. "And so are you."

Everyone looks my way, each gaze intense and curious. Just as my cheeks start to burn, Zac—bless his heart—breaks through the silence.

"It seems to me that we should tread carefully," he says. "If the Essence of Evil really has escaped, and for whatever reason has set her sights on Abbey, we need to protect her."

Thorne grunts. "You don't know the half of it, boy."

Without warning Gwin springs to her feet and Zac and I fall into the space she leaves. "Lunch!" she bellows. "I hope you like rabbit."

While she dashes downstairs in a flurry of pink, Balvinder and Harlie start up a debate on the slaughtering of animals for meat.

"You will eat them," Harlie says. "But you refuse to kill them yourself?"

"*Exactly*," exclaims Thorne, slapping the table. "Is that not the most absurd contradiction you have ever heard?"

Harlie gives a rapid shrug. "Not the *most* absurd."

"There are certain acts my Essence disallows me to do, and killing is amongst them," Balvinder explains. "But once there is no life left, I can eat the meat to sustain my human form."

Thorne snorts. "So we do the dirty work and you reap the rewards? How noble of you."

At this point, my nostrils curl with the smoky scent of something burning. Gwin returns with a large platter in one hand and several serving plates in the other. She sets it all on the table with the main, charred-rabbit dish in the centre.

"You burnt it," observes Harlie, inclining forward to inspect the meal closely.

Gwin lets out a hoot of laughter. "Must have overestimated cooking time! Ah well, it will taste the same."

"No, charcoal is rather distinct in flavour." Harlie straightens up and adjusts the neck of her shirt, concealing her pale collarbones. I notice Thorne watching the movement, his brows furrowing a little. His eyes do a rapid loop of Harlie's frame before he looks away, reverting back to his usual air of scorn.

Gwin cuts a piece of the meat for each of us, while I study each of the Essences in sequence and contemplate the extreme variances in their behaviour.

Gwin—unshakably joyous. Harlie—bearer of truth, no matter how uncomfortable. Thorne—an eternal pain in the arse. And then there's Balvinder, calm and kind and articulate.

It's like peering into an enclosure at a zoo where animals of different species have been thrown together and forced to mix. Fascinating, and a little unsettling. I want to be standing a safe distance from the fence, but somehow I'm right up the front with nowhere else to go.

The sound of the front door triggers a squeal from Gwin that makes me yelp and Zac jump. We exchange a startled look as she tosses the knife she was holding—sending it clattering across the table—and dashes down the stairs.

Thorne slams his palm over the knife's handle as casually as if it were a stray spoon. The blade would've struck him had he missed it, although he doesn't seem overly perturbed.

"Peirce!" Gwin cries from somewhere below us. "You came! I had Kayna on the mind. Thought you might be her!" I hear shuffling feet and an uncomfortable groan, like the noise of an unwilling participant in a too-tight hug.

"Kayna?" A flat, male voice. "Isn't she—"

"She might have escaped." Gwin sighs. "Apparently there are apparitions in the forest again."

"Oh, fantastic," the man replies. There's a brief pause—a sniff. "What did you burn this time?"

"Now why would you presume it was me?" Gwin retorts.

"I could smell the smoke from my oasis."

"Oh Peirce, don't be such a bore. You always give me that look. The human face is relatively malleable, you know. We must continue your smiling lessons. Like this—see? There is a new Melder to impress."

Thorne shakes his head as the stairs creak, and soon enough Gwin stamps onto the top level, dragging along a frumpy-looking man dressed in a crinkled, black cloak.

He bares his teeth. I think it's intended as a smile, but I can see the corners of his mouth twitching, like the weight of bringing it to fruition is almost too much.

Greasy, black hair flops across the man's face and obscures his eyes, hanging lankly beyond his shoulders. Gwin seems to register this as I do. She stands on her tiptoes and sweeps the hair back to expose a pair of dark, beady eyes.

"Abbey and Zacharias," she says. "I'd like you to meet Peirce, my best friend."

TWENTY-SEVEN

ZAC LOOKS TO ME FOR GUIDANCE, TRAINING his eyes roughly to where mine indicate Peirce is standing. Another Essence, then. But how many *are* there?

"Shake her hand," Gwin whispers into Peirce's ear, though I'm sure the whole table heard it.

After a beat of hesitation, he extends a limp hand. I stand and take it firmly, even though his fingers are cold and feel a lot like a fish on a line, wriggling to free itself.

"I'm Abbey," I say. "Shader."

"Shader," he repeats, dark eyes searching me. "How morbid."

I hesitate before taking my seat, wondering whether his observation was a reference to my name or our meeting. Peirce rounds the table and stops behind Harlie, laying his hands on the back of her chair and fixing his gaze on Zac. "Who is this? And how can he hear us?"

"It's *Zacharias*, Peirce," Gwin says with a sigh. "Balvinder's Zacharias."

"Oh. The orphan?" Peirce frowns. "But why?"

"We are taking Abbey to Amnoralas," Balvinder says, digging a fork into his meal. "She was summoned to Emba, where Zac became involved. He already knows of our existence—has known for ten years. We can trust him."

Thorne scoffs. "That's the thing," he says. "You always *think* you can rely on the humans until they prove their deceit. Don't forget that they aren't entirely comprised of Harlie's Essence. They possess Kayna's too."

Zac lays his hands on the table, stealing the attention of every pair of eyes. "Do you really think I'd be foolish enough to share any of this? Nobody would believe it anyway."

"If you led them here, they might," Thorne replies, terse.

"And why would I do that? What would I achieve?"

"Notoriety," Peirce comments. His eyes narrow into slits. "The recognition associated with discovering the truth of all things. An escape from the solitude of secrets."

"If I wanted to spread the truth, I would have by now," Zac says, his voice edged with frustration. "I owe Balvinder a debt I can never repay him in full. But the very least I can do is keep my word, and my mouth shut."

He raises his knife and fork and begins sawing through the rabbit Gwin has served him. In the silence hanging around the table, the crunch of burnt meat is unmistakable. Zac spears a piece with his fork and pops it in his mouth without hesitation, while Gwin watches on with glee. I can almost hear the charcoal crumbling between his teeth, but he smiles and tells her it's perfect while I smile and think to myself that he's perfect.

"What's everyone waiting for?" Gwin cries. She flings her hands into the air like we're horses in stalls at the races, raring to go. "Eat up!"

Thorne shoves his plate across the table and folds his arms. I'm doing my best to gnaw on a particularly rubbery morsel—when Harlie grabs her meat with both hands and hurls it over the roof's edge. The action stuns me enough that I start to choke, but Gwin is oblivious. She hustles Peirce into one of the remaining empty chairs and returns to sit between Zac and me, looking around at us all as though everything in her world has just fallen into place.

✳

The rest of the afternoon involves a babbling stream of bizarre conversation. Balvinder leaves briefly to wash up at the creek, during which time the Essences seem to heighten and aggravate each other even more than before.

Gwin takes to playfully slapping Zac's back every so often too, which always startles the heck out of him, since he never sees it coming.

It's strange to think of what Zac sees, or doesn't see. To him, the only person around this table is me. His eyes flit toward me fairly often, as if assessing the actions of the others by my own, scrutinizing me more than he would otherwise.

The interactions I catch between Gwin and Peirce intrigue me most. Or maybe they're just the loudest.

"I'm telling you Gwin, I would rather DIE right here, right now, than eat that," Peirce says, frowning down at the rabbit she insisted on serving him.

"Oh, come now." Gwin laughs. "Don't be so melodramatic." She squeezes the back of his neck.

"I'm being realistic," he says, drawing out the last word as he slides the plate away. Gwin shakes Peirce's shoulders and he quivers like a bobble-head.

"We both know realistic isn't the word," she says. "Come on! For me, yes?" She brings her face an inch from his, as if that's sure to convince him.

"No," he replies.

"Yes!"

"NO!" This goes on for another few seconds until Harlie breaks her conversation with Thorne to intercept theirs.

"*Stop*," she chides, louder than I've heard her voice all day. "Gwin—the rabbit is burnt to a crisp. Peirce does not want to eat it. Enough."

Balvinder returns then and I release a breath I wasn't aware I'd been holding. "We should continue on before it gets dark," he says, directing his words at me but receiving the full attention of everyone around the table.

"On foot?" Harlie inquires, arching a narrow brow. Balvinder nods, and I don't have time to question the interaction because Gwin is rushing toward me.

"*I* want to come." She drops to her knees and seizes my hand. "Oh please, please Abbey. Let me come." Her beseeching eyes are a warm shade of blue, tugging me into their hopeful depths. I look to Balvinder for an answer but he seems to be awaiting mine too.

"I guess—"

I nearly jump out of my skin as Gwin lets out a yelp of delight and pulls me into a tight hug.

"Thank you, thank you! What a fun idea Balvinder—a hike through the forest! We really don't do it enough."

"For specific reasons, Gwin," Peirce mutters dully. "The forest is a dark, sinister place."

"Then you will fit in very well indeed," she says, her voice tightening as though suppressing laughter. Then she wheels to me again. "I presume you were headed for Amnoralas. I'm sure Balvinder has told you already—that the Overseer descends there for the Melder's first introduction." She claps her hands together. "I can take you!"

"No," Thorne says sharply. I turn to him in surprise, and our eyes meet across the table, fleetingly. "*I* was taking her."

"No, *I* was taking her," Zac supplies in faux defiance. I give him a look, which he returns with his crooked smile.

"If Abbey wishes it, you are all welcome to join us," Balvinder says. "We should be on guard, as Zacharias said earlier." His glance goes to Zac. "We cannot be harmed, but he—"

"He will die before you reach Amnoralas," Peirce finishes, although I'm pretty sure that wasn't where Balvinder was taking the sentence.

Gwin gasps with a horror I feel rising in myself too. "Peirce! You are simply incredible."

"I am merely stating a fact," he says. "We survive because unfortunately, we must. Zacharias is not protected by the same magic, and if Kayna is loose, don't you think she might take some pleasure in tormenting him? Particularly if she knows how it will affect Balvinder."

Zac looks around, as if in search of some follow-up shred of comfort.

"Zacharias is smart," offers Balvinder. "And we will be wary."

Silence expands between us, with Gwin shaking her head at Peirce. She smiles wryly. "Forever determined to drag the rest of us into your black hole. Oh my dear—thank the heavens that I exist too."

✳

"Shall I bring my needles and wool?" Gwin calls from a room beyond the corridor. "I have this divine violet shade somewhere around—"

"No," Peirce and Thorne return in unison.

We are waiting in a cluster by the open door of Gwin's cottage. Balvinder, Thorne, Harlie, Peirce, Zac and me. She insisted on packing things for the journey, even though—according to Peirce—she has no real need of anything.

The Essences don't require much, I've noticed. Food, sleep and comfort seem low priorities.

Gwin appears in the lounge room hoisting a large bag over her shoulder. Knitted flowers of yellow and white are stitched to its front. She jumps on the spot. "I'm ready! Have you decided, Peirce dear?"

Under his greasy web of hair, I see his eyes flit lazily toward her. "Must I?"

"Oh yes." Gwin trots forward and wiggles his limp arm into an unyielding lock. "You must."

"I will come too," Harlie says. Her eyes slide from Thorne's face to mine. "I would like to acquaint myself with Abbey before the first Breathing."

"Abbey is leaving Ethra," Thorne says. "Supposedly." The words jar against the lot of us, myself included. It's not a surprise—home has been my end goal all along. But somehow it feels uncomfortable to voice aloud here and now, since the six pairs of eyes that have fallen over me seem shaken by the fact.

I pull myself a little straighter as if to assert my conviction. "Yes, I'm leaving." That stirring feeling picks up in my chest. "I can't stay here. It's just not—I have to get home as soon as possible."

"We are still a month away from the next Breathing," Balvinder says calmly. "If it is Abbey's choice to leave, she must. You all know very well that the Overseer foresees all things. Perhaps there is another reason she was brought here, and another Melder will be sent for when she goes. One that will stay."

Harlie doesn't look all that convinced. "It has never happened this way before." She turns sharply toward Balvinder. "You are right, that the time of Melders past has varied. But every one of them has served at least one Breathing. Why would the Overseer summon a girl from Earth only to send her straight back?"

"Oh, how I have missed your sound logic," Thorne muses, the trace of a smirk at the corner of his mouth. Harlie smiles back, but only briefly, because her gaze returns to me in a blink.

"The Melder is not a role to dismiss," she says, her tone hard and matter-of-fact. "It is the highest honour bestowed by our Overseer. You have become an immovable bridge between two essential layers of the universe."

My skin prickles as I struggle to muster the right words. I feel suddenly weak and jittery with the intense scope of Harlie's attention wholly on me. "I—I have—well my Mum, she's still ..."

"The Overseer can choose," Zac interjects, swooping in to save me. "But Abbey can choose too, can't she?"

The Essences fall silent at that. With Mum in mind, I start wondering how she would advise me in this situation. Assuming the theory is true, and I'm here for a reason, would she tell me to let it all go? Hurry home? We've had countless conversations in the lead up to this school year about my future and the direction I might take at the end of it.

What if my direction has been set out before me now, but I'm about to walk away? The erodosphere and the Essences and the role of the Melder—I've barely scratched the surface of it all. Only a week ago I was considering a career path as a clown. Becoming a *bridge between two essential layers of the universe*, as Harlie puts it, would be quite the step up.

It seems so impossible, but when I stop to acknowledge my curiosity, I feel it skyrocketing higher and higher with every word they say and every strange corner of this place I lay eyes on.

"We will pass my oasis before reaching Amnoralas," Balvinder says. He looks to me—his eyes mottled and gleaming blue like the shallows of an ocean in the afternoon light. "Abbey, would you care to visit my home before returning to yours?"

Gwin starts shrieking her excitement and Thorne mutters something about his own oasis being worth the detour—but I hold Balvinder's gaze and let the other voices ripple away.

"Yes," I tell him. "I'd love to."

TWENTY-EIGHT

THE TREES DON'T SEEM SO GREY WITH GWIN
waltzing between them, filling the forest with her chatter and
rowdy sing-alongs. I notice Peirce clasping his hands over his
ears more than once, and Thorne nudging Harlie to roll his
eyes. Balvinder is the only one who pays Gwin much attention, entertaining her wild stories and melodies with laughter
and enthusiasm.

Zac and I hang at the back of the raucous, seven-person,
travel party. We seem to have gravitated there—a safe distance
away. But my attempts at conversation fizzle quickly, and it
doesn't take me long to sense his rising agitation. The way he
looks back over his shoulder. His dagger, out of its sheath. The
downturned corner of his mouth. He's wearing his dark shirt
again, without the hooded vest. The toggles at the collar hang
loosely enough that I catch quick glimpses of that shining tat-
too every so often.

"... so Tyler drives me to school most days, because Mum
works morning shifts," I'm saying, when Zac turns again. "You
have to be eighteen to get your license, and he has his already,
but I ..." Realising I'm not receiving much of his attention, I

stop. Then I reach out to touch his arm. Zac whips around to me, blinking back to focus. "Hey," I say, softly. "Are you okay?"

"Yes, yes of course." He offers a smile—and although I don't know him inside and out, I do know him well enough to see the artifice of it. The expression slips into a perplexed frown. "What is a car?" he inquires. I laugh, only to receive another blank look.

"Uh …" I try to wipe my astonishment away. "What is a car?"

Zac nods his head.

"Four wheels," I say, working hard to steer my voice away from condescension. "And an engine. It's … a mode of transport."

Zac nods absently, before looking around again. I'm not sure my words even got through.

"Okay, what's wrong?" I grab his arm, this time bringing us both to a sudden halt. "You've been distracted ever since we left Gwin's."

Zac glances at me, his brows twitching upward. I release my grip on him.

"Kayna isn't the only beast to watch for around these parts," he whispers. "I'm concerned about … others, too."

"Kayna," I repeat, the word sparking on my tongue like fire. I guess I should be just as worried, if the Essence of Evil really is running rampant and in pursuit of me specifically. I can't quite wrap my head around the thought, though. That night on the plateau, the black smoke luring me away from the others—it still feels surreal. Even the apparition charging toward me seems like a dream clouded by a series of others that are equally improbable.

But it all happened, I tell myself, forcing reality down with a hard swallow. Kayna is trying to find me, for whatever reason, and she doesn't seem to want the other Essences getting in the way. Since I met her in Emba, she hasn't revealed herself in full. She called for me through the apparition, and led me away from the others while they slept. So ... I'm safer with them than I am on my own. So long as we stay close.

A groan up ahead catches my attention. Gwin has trapped Peirce in a surprisingly effective headlock. "Sing with me!" she cries.

He twists and ducks out from her grip. "No chance."

Gwin prances away, unperturbed, the pink train of her dress trailing behind her in the dirt. "Will you sing with me, Thorne?"

"Not today," he says, and then mutters to Harlie, "This is why I avoid the forest."

She casts him a thin smile. "You prefer to revel in your arrogance?"

"Precisely."

Deep in my mind, something tweaks. A piece falling into place. I find myself moving away from Zac and striding toward Thorne. "*Arrogance*." The word is out before I can think twice.

The entire group of Essences slow and turn to me.

"Your Essence," I say, clearing my throat. I'm not sure where the certainty comes from, but it barrels through me now, demanding escape. "Your Essence is Arrogance."

Thorne looks a little stumped. But he recovers quickly, arching a lazy brow. "I prefer Pride," he says. "It is a common misconception that we Essences are confined to one descriptor. One measly, human word. We encompass much more than that, little Melder."

My mind is whirling too madly to be affected by his snarky tone. So there *is* a reason why the most I often see of Thorne is the underside of his nose.

Zac strolls along beside me, still holding his dagger, but he appears to be more focused now on the conversation. And he looks just as baffled as I feel, aligning his gaze with mine toward the Essences.

Thorne's kiss in the forest—he expected it to be reciprocated because he couldn't expect anything else. As the Essence of *Pride*, or Arrogance, rejection is beyond comprehension. He wouldn't have the capability to expect it, or the dignity to go down without a fight. It also explains why he couldn't bring himself to offer a proper apology.

Thorne's eyes turn to slits on me as we continue to saunter onward, as if he can sense my analysis.

"Thorne is a Minor Essence," Harlie says plainly. "As am I. He is neither Good nor Evil. Pride is rather a motivation. It possesses many facets, and many consequences."

"Minor is a gross understatement," Thorne snaps, clearly still caught on the word. "Our terminology is flawed. It always has been."

"No human word will ever describe us adequately," Harlie says. She lays a hand on Thorne's shoulder—more emphatic than sympathetic. "Our Essences are vast but our tongues are limited."

"What are the rest of you, then?" Zac inquires, his gaze darting around brightly. "If we know Honesty and Pride, can it hurt to know—"

"*You* should know *nothing*, Nellerwood boy," Thorne cuts in.

"He's right," Peirce contributes, arm-in-arm with a giddy looking Gwin. "Our identities are hidden for a reason. If Abbey stays, she will find out in due course. Until then we should all keep our mouths shut about it."

Thorne nods his assent, whilst looking a little surprised to have agreed with Peirce.

My eyes meet Balvinder's. He offers a smile that seems to be just for me. *You will figure it out*, it seems to say.

✳

"The Breathing House is close," Harlie says. At Peirce's relentless insistence, we have made a rest stop and are now sitting in a wonky circle splitting a loaf of bread—courtesy of Gwin. To my surprise, it's quite good. Dense and filled with a variety of grains. Apparently she can fluke a success every now and then.

"Breathing House?" I repeat, through a mouthful. "Shouldn't you be able to breathe in every house?" It isn't a very funny joke, but Gwin has mercy on me and giggles anyway.

"Not the ordinary sort of breathing," she says. "We congregate there every second full moon with the Melder— *you*—who proceeds to balance us according to their spirit. It's quite the spectacle for human eyes."

I stare into the trees, more mystified than before, and wonder over the process and the house and what it might all look like. A sudden urge pushes me to my feet.

"Can I see it?" If there is more visual evidence to what I've been told already, I need to witness it for myself. Now.

Oddly enough, it's Thorne who answers. "Yes," he says, rising too. "I will take you."

I cast a sidelong look at Zac, just long enough to catch Balvinder resting a hand on his shoulder. He whispers, "It isn't far."

Worry is written all over Zac's face, though I'm not sure where it stems from—me being alone with Thorne, or the possibility of my encountering Kayna or something equally unpleasant without Zac there to protect me.

As I follow Thorne away from the group, the proverbial saying *Pride comes before a fall* springs to mind. I feel in my gut that I'm inching closer to the edge of a drop. I just hope it's a soft landing.

TWENTY-NINE

THE FURTHER WE GET FROM THE ESSENCES,
and Zac, the more my nerves begin to buzz. I keep a few feet
behind Thorne in case I need to make a run for it—in case he
tries anything, or leads me into a trap. He obviously notices
my caution, because he turns an eye on me and says, "What
are you doing?" A vague edge of amusement laces the inquiry.
"Is there some reason you are trailing after me like Peirce on a
down day?"

"No," I say quickly. But then I think of Harlie, and how
she seems to relate to Thorne. From what I've seen, I might
even consider them friends. Maybe he respects Honesty.
Maybe it's a language he can understand or respect. And so I
decide to harness it. "It's just, I don't know whether I can trust
you," I admit. Or rather—I don't know whether I can trust the
very embodiment of Arrogance. Pride. Whatever he is exactly.

"Oh." Thorne turns away, hiding his expression—but I
still catch the troubled frown. He says nothing else as we walk.
I start to wonder if I've offended him somehow. But then it
couldn't come as much of a surprise, could it? He advanced on

me without any indication of my wanting him back. He tried twice. Two times too many. What does he expect?

"I cannot apologise," he says. The words are stiff, unflinching, like his teeth are gritted against them. "I will not, because I cannot."

I stare at the back of his head, trying to dissect the comment. "Apologise for ..." Thorne makes no move to aid my guess, so I press on. "For that night—"

"Yes," he snaps. "For that night."

His declaration, wherever it comes from, makes me curious enough to neglect my caution and bridge the distance between us. I fall into step beside him. "Was that meant to be an apology? Telling me you can't apologise?"

Thorne keeps his gaze set ahead. "In a sense."

"Huh." A pretty shitty attempt, if you ask me.

"There are certain contradictions," he goes on. "As Essences, we are guided by a single motivation. It pulls us in certain directions, making our actions ... complex."

Pride doesn't apologise, I realise. For a moment I slip into his frame of mind to try to understand it. My rejection confused him, because Pride is smothered in self-importance. But my claiming not to trust him because of it might have struck another nerve. Pride can manifest in a whole lot of ways. It will forever justify itself, but if Thorne now realises how his own actions might have impacted *my* Pride, he might feel some sense of regret about that. Maybe that's what he meant by contradictions.

There is no time to further the discussion though, because ahead of us the trees have cleared to expose what I presume is the Breathing House—a towering, circular structure rising up to a bottleneck roof. The walls are built from thin shards of layered stone like that of the trees, blending seamlessly into the forest. Two smooth columns polished to a gloss mark the front of a shallow portico.

We approach it, some instinct slowing us both.

"In the beginning, the very first Melder built this House with the help of the Essences," Thorne explains. His voice has shifted into a shade of reverence. "Well, those willing to help."

"I'm assuming you weren't one of them."

He turns his furrowed brow on me. "I was the one who led the undertaking," he says, and then with a little more venom, "I could hardly leave it in the hands of that unequipped pack of imbeciles."

"How long ago was that?" I ask, tentatively. "When did the first Melder arrive here?"

"Longer ago than you would care to know." Thorne grins, an aged sort of mischief dancing in his dark eyes. "I will say this much—we are older than we look, sweetheart."

I've realised that the Essences are many things ordinary people aren't, but I'm still stunned to hear that *immortal* might be one of them. It would explain how Balvinder could act as a sort of father figure to Zac, despite looking barely a few years older than him.

Thorne brushes past me, his crossbow knocking against his shoulder as he sweeps up onto the portico. He reaches out and twists the doorknob. It doesn't budge.

Grunting in frustration, he kicks the door once with his boot before standing aside to brush his hair back.

I hesitate at the portico's edge. "What's wrong?"

"Essences aren't permitted to let themselves in, by any means." He looks as though he's trying hard to keep annoyance out of his tone, channelling nonchalance instead. "I wondered if it would be different now, considering our current Melder has no desire to *be* our current Melder."

I study his face, which twitches and tightens as I hold my silence.

"Evidently not," he growls.

I take a breath and step up into the portico. An unfamiliar thrill runs through me as I touch the doorknob—and a lock clicks out of place, allowing me to push it open.

✳

I'm first struck by the plainness of the room. It's bare, the walls encasing us in a smooth, rounded, sheet of polished stone. But then I see it. A blur of shifting clouds. Wisps of blue, brown, yellow, red, green, pink, orange, purple and black—mingling and crossing and twirling together and then apart.

Immediately I'm taken back to the office of the career counsellor. That streak of glittering blue in the sky. I could almost explain it away then as a trick of the eye. But here and now, there's no doubt about it. The colours are real. Like a vast mixing pot of visible, intertwining gases.

I cut a hand through a wisp of purple and watch it split in two, then merge together again and glide past me through the open door. As my eyes trail its path, something bright catches in my periphery.

I jerk back.

A brilliant green vapour radiates from a suspended source of translucent light in the centre of the room. It glides toward me like a shapeless ghost. Heart racing, I retreat until my back collides with the opposite wall. Thorne has disappeared altogether.

"Hello?" The word catches in my throat and comes out in a croak. "Thorne?"

"Little Melder?" The voice emanates directly from the vapour—a distant echo, but a familiar one. Somehow I'm left more disturbed than I would have been without a response.

"You're, you're—"

"I'm—I'm—an Essence, yes." His tone drips with distinctive scorn, but there's no trace of the irritated expression that usually accompanies it. I rake my eyes through the green haze, unable to believe it.

"Really, you mustn't act so shocked," Thorne chides. "If I were to tell you that you were a girl, or that you have blue eyes, or that you barely close your mouth when you chew, would you be so surprised?"

I frown at the smoke. "Maybe about that last one."

"Well, I urge you to think twice before cowering from my true form. Unless you wish that I cower from yours."

I shake my head to dispel a retort about his *true form* being just a tad more confronting than mine, and order myself to relax. Edging closer, I lean into my curiosity, which soon overrides any remaining traces of fear.

I reach toward the green vapour. It threads around my fingers and circles my wrist, then slinks up to my face. It takes me a few seconds to realise where it went. I step back and huff out a sharp exhale. A wave of green streams out with the breath.

"Your spirit desires me." Thorne's echo seeps from the extended threads of smoke, half inside my own head. "Unless you wish to deprive yourself of my Essence, we are forever bound."

I stare at the green ghost, mortified. "Forever?"

A deep chuckle rumbles from Thorne's Essence. "You are Proud, little Melder, more than you know."

A trail of black snakes right by my eyes. I shoo it away, my attention drawing again to the coloured fog enveloping us. "What is this, anyway?"

"An opening in the erodosphere," answers Thorne, "designed by the Overseer for the Breathings. Here you would meet with us, breathe us into your spirit and breathe us out into the will of humanity."

"Easy enough," I say breathily, staring around at the Essences. "How would I do all that, exactly?"

Another chuckle. "It's rather simple—your spirit fulfills the task. Trust it." A strand of green smoke rises upward like a finger and I follow its trail to the narrow ceiling, which I now see opens to the sky. "The House is only a starting point," Thorne says. "You are taken far from here when you breathe, to a place your spirit can perform its duty as the erodosphere requires."

I stare up at the opening above, trying and failing to shape Thorne's ambiguous explanations into logic. The colours distract my musings, getting in the way of each thought process before it can define itself. A murky rainbow of confusion and spectral beauty.

Dizziness seizes me suddenly. I stagger back to the wall, reaching a hand back to steady myself—just as a stream of blue arcs toward me. I gasp. It spirals between my lips as if seizing an opportunity. The vertigo clears and my muscles heat through to my bones.

A gentle whisper works its way through me, the speech rapid but indistinguishable. Still, I somehow sense the tone of it. A cadence I instantly recognise.

"*Balvinder*," I whisper.

The blue smoke pulsates with the beat of my breaths—rushing forward with the inhale; slipping out with the exhale.

I think of his eyes, bluer than I've ever seen. Translucent kindness, patience and wisdom—the surface of an unending calm. Awe flows over me like a cascade of cool water. "He's Good. Balvinder is ... Goodness. The Essence of it."

"About time," Thorne's voice comes rather sharply against the elation I feel rippling through me.

And Kayna. The Essence of Evil. Balvinder's opposing force. The two Major Essences. It makes so much sense, I don't know how I didn't put it together before. I guess the full picture was a mystery to me, and Balvinder's identity was a solitary piece of the puzzle I had no idea where to place until now.

"You might hear the others refer to him as a *Major* Essence," Thorne says, as if reading my train of thought. "Though he is no more complex than I am." I can't see his face, but I know exactly how it must be contorting now.

"I am a single motivation and yet Balvinder is a collection of traits," he goes on, the words hurried and urgent. "The difference being that he is confined by morality. I exist between Good and Evil—for I am a motivation without limitations. Balvinder and Kayna are dictated by a fixed compass. The term *Minor* means nothing. Balvinder might have more power at his disposal, but the rest of us have the ability to choose our own definition of right and wrong."

His words sound practised, and I find myself wondering whether he has ever repeated them to himself in the mirror.

I think I already knew it—that Balvinder was the Essence of Good. Knew it but hadn't acknowledged it. One look into his eyes is a dive into the deepest, most profound sort of comfort. I trusted him right from the start. Before I knew him, I *knew* him. Because he is everything Good—everything tranquil, benevolent and strong—framed in a single body.

The angelic, silver hair was a dead giveaway.

And there were other signs too; his tolerance of the Minor Essences, his inability to hunt or end a life, however small, the river water calming in his wake, the flames conjured at his command. It's so obvious now.

"Tell me the others," I say, searching the green vapour for more answers. "What is Gwin?"

"We call her Optimism," Thorne drawls through the green smoke. "Though she encompasses all shades of it—Hope, Faith, Buoyancy ..."

I grin, thinking back on all her inappropriately timed quips, never diminished by an unenthusiastic audience or a dire situation.

"Peirce is Pessimism," he says, before I can wager the guess. "Caution, he sometimes prefers. Our perpetual wet blanket."

A hysterical laugh bursts out of me. "That makes sense."

What I don't tell him is that a lot of it is starting to make sense. More than I'd care to admit.

THIRTY

I'VE ALWAYS THOUGHT THAT IF YOU'RE surrounded by a collection of sincerely Good people in life, on a semi-regular basis, you got lucky. There's no saying who they'll be either. Sometimes you don't even find that reliably *Good* person in your own father. It can be a teacher, a family friend, even the woman down at the bakery who asks how your day is going each week as if she truly cares.

For me—it's Mum and Tyler. They have hearts that reach all the way around me without leaving gaps.

There's something different, though, about strolling behind the Essence of Good itself in a forest I can now say with ninety-nine per cent confidence does not exist in the world I know. Something both frightening and thrilling.

The phrase *not a bad bone in his body* is too literal a thing when it comes to Balvinder. The kind arch of his brows is more noticeable to me now, like that alone was an indicator of the Essence I should have guessed sooner.

The others have taken on a new light too. Gwin—Optimism in its purest form. Peirce—Pessimism, or Caution, to put it kindly. Everything they say has become ten times more entertaining with the revelations in mind.

The first thing I wanted to do when we returned from the Breathing House was rush toward Zac and tell him everything I learnt. But something stopped me. Not just the fact that Thorne would probably imbed one of his arrows in my back—but that it didn't feel like the time to share it all.

As we prepared to set off, Zac asked about the House, but I didn't offer much. "I've only seen it from the outside," he told me in a hush, as though he knew one of the Essences would be bound to make a fuss if they knew. "Balvinder took me there once."

"Well I don't exactly know how to describe it," I said slowly, chewing on my lip as I recalled the room. "Thorne called it an *opening into the erodosphere*. There were all sorts of colours, or Essences. And Thorne himself changed—he was different there. A vapour, more than a person."

Zac's eyes were wide on me as I spoke, entirely absorbed by every word. The details were important to him, I could tell. Half his life he has believed all this, even without the visual evidence I've experienced. Maybe only having Balvinder's disembodied voice to go by grounded his belief in the unseen. Set him up to believe the rest.

Still, I can see the yearning to know more lighting his eyes. He must be exercising an unbelievable degree of self-control, if I'm the first person aside from Balvinder that he has ever been able to question.

As we continue on our way to Balvinder's oasis, Zac walks with Balvinder while I bring up the rear between Gwin and Peirce. Thorne and Harlie are involved in a heated discussion in front about the Essences' concealment, with the occasional input from Peirce who mostly agrees with Thorne.

He blows an exasperated sigh beside me. "We virtually *live* for their sakes, Harlie, and yet they don't even know we exist—aside from fanciful tales and folklore that failed to pinpoint the real truth. How is it fair?"

"It is necessary," she retorts simply, tossing her sandy hair. The line of the cut is so clean and straight that it almost looks unnatural. A bit like Harlie herself. Unashamedly blunt.

"And don't get me started on Earth," Peirce drones on, as if she didn't speak. "We may as well not be there at all—the humans wouldn't know the difference."

"Yes, they would," Harlie says. "They have never met us explicitly, but that does not mean they don't know us."

Thorne snorts. "I'm with Peirce on this," he says. "A little appreciation wouldn't go astray."

"We are not here to receive appreciation." Harlie's tone tightens. "Your Essences blind you."

Peirce looks utterly miserable, and for a moment I find myself pitying him. Wearing the label of Pessimism for eternity feels to me like pulling the short straw.

"I have been thinking, Abbey," Gwin begins, shifting my attention as she grasps my arm, "that you would be a brilliant Melder." She gazes up at me. "I just know it." Of course. She could know nothing else as Optimism embodied. She would probably say I could be a brilliant dancer too, or a brilliant architect. In fact Gwin would make a pretty-damn-good, career counsellor.

Looking down at her bright, eager eyes, I feel a numbing truth pass through them and into me. For a moment I wonder whether one of those invisible strands of colour has worked its way to my core and allowed me to share her hopefulness. The thought is totally insane, and what's even crazier is that now I can almost believe it.

Instinct has me reaching around to my pack, rifling for my old singlet. I find the brooch pinned to it and pull it out, fastening it instead to the jacket I'm wearing.

Gwin gasps, and for a second I think it's because of the brooch—but then she clutches at her braid. "I forgot to make you that flower crown! Oh dear. The buds—I left them at my oasis."

"That's okay, I don't need—"

"I promise to crown you before you leave." Gwin beams, and I realise that to resist, I'd be fighting a losing battle. So I just nod.

"I'm sure Abbey is dying to decorate herself in your flower crowns," Peirce says, glancing at me. It seems only I have heard him. Our eyes meet and I smirk at him. Then, to my amazement, I detect the faintest twitch at the corner of his mouth. I'll take it.

"Why must we live in such a dreary place?" he then whines. "Grey, grey, grey—so much grey."

"Grey! Grey! Grey!" Gwin repeats back, though in a far brighter voice. "See? It's all in how you say it Peirce, as much as how you see it."

"Though it's still the same word."

"Quite the contrary," retorts Gwin. "Change the inflection and you might as well change the meaning!"

"You are utterly absurd," he drones.

Gwin sighs and leans in close to my ear. "He's such a defeatist." Before I can so much as smile she raises a thoughtful finger. "And that's what I like about him. The challenge. I soak more out of life with Peirce by my side."

Weaving through the forest, I notice how our footsteps blend, forming an indistinct rhythm. Gwin dashes to the front of the pack and I hear her telling Balvinder that she plans to knit all the Essences a hat in the colour of their breath in the erodosphere.

At the sound of his laughter, something stirs deep in my bones—a feeling of connection I've never experienced, like I've been chosen as a centre piece and someone is forming a chain either side of me, linking to facets of myself that I've never known.

In some inexplicable way, I feel that I somehow connect this bizarre group of Essences just by being here. *That in their purpose, I find mine.* The thought seems to come out of nowhere and I shrug it away before it can settle.

*

"Interesting lot," Zac says as we leave the Essences behind. We're heading out in search of game. Well, he's searching and I'm here to observe.

I found myself jumping too eagerly at the chance to spend a little time alone with him. My sanity requires it though, I told myself. The Essences are an entertaining bunch, but the effort of analyzing their interactions seems to have zapped the energy—and sanity—right out of me.

Zac tosses his dagger in the air and catches it by the handle as we delve into a sparse area of the forest.

"They're full on," I say. "But I sort of love it."

He casts me a side-eye. "You seem different. Less ... cynical."

I'm about to argue—when I realise he has a point. I do feel less cynical. And although a huge amount of clarification is still required, there's a strange release in opening myself up to it.

"There comes a point," I tell him, "when you can't keep questioning what's right in front of you."

Zac comes to a halt. "It took you much less time than it did me," he says, and then he turns sharply on his heel. I follow the line of his gaze and spot it too—a small rabbit, oblivious to impending doom.

I press up onto my tiptoes to whisper in his ear. "Would it be wrong of me to yell a warning? Tell the little guy to make a run for it?"

"Yes," Zac whispers back. He hesitates then, cutting a crooked smile at me. His cheek is so close to mine I can feel the heat of it. I quickly lower my heels back to the dirt, re-establishing our distance.

But then Zac turns, his dagger extended out to me. I frown at him in question—then understand his intention and shake my head.

"No, no. I can't. It's a little bunny!" I hiss. "I'm not a killer. I've never been a killer."

"You killed a wolf fifty times the size of that rabbit."

"But it was *ugly*," I emphasise, realising then that my psychopathic theory of killing only the ugly animals is becoming increasingly apparent. I clamp a hand over my mouth as Zac's eyebrows arch high. We stare at each other for a short moment before breaking into laughter. The sound of it scares the rabbit away.

"Run!" I call after it. "Go! Start a family and build a home and live a long and happy life!"

"You are so odd," Zac says, still laughing.

"I know." I grin up at him defiantly. "The truth though—I have terrible aim." Throughout primary school, I was the kid who could never land one beanbag in the bucket, and during high school I was the girl who threw the netball so far from the ring that the time board had to be paused while it was retrieved.

Zac rolls his eyes and takes my hand, pressing the hilt of his dagger into it. "Aim for that tree," he says, gesturing ahead to a trunk much too narrow for my liking. I groan, but stop abruptly as he positions my forefinger along the spine of the blade and draws my arm in the arc of required motion. The breath from his nose tickles my ear and I will myself to remain composed, even though my entire body is suddenly alert.

I wonder what Tyler would say if he knew about Zac ...

Wait for him to make the first move, he'd advise. *Guys enjoy the chase. Trust me, Abbey. I would know.*

I'm all about playing hard to get. Except that most of the time, I tend to play a little too hard to get and then never get gotten.

I want Zac's hands to stay on me. I want him to hold me, like he did under the golden rain. But he steps away, and I'm left staring ahead at that stupid tree.

With a sharp breath and a brief moment of mental preparation for the incoming humiliation, I let the dagger fly. It strikes dirt—not the tree. Not any tree. In a forest full of trees.

"Right." I set my hands on my hips. "Exactly where I wanted it."

Zac's smile widens. "You're a natural."

"You try," I shoot back. "And don't look so sure of yourself. It's very unappealing."

Zac's unbridled laughter fills the forest, reaching levels of silliness I've never heard from him before. It makes me smile enough that my cheeks hurt. Of course, he sinks the dagger into the very tree he set out for me.

I've already started to walk away.

"It's just practice!" he yells after me. I try not to look startled as his arm comes around my shoulders and he squeezes me close. "You're the Melder—you already have control of all humanity. If you had control of your aim too, that would just be unfair."

I shove him away, but my heart is still thrumming like a mad thing from his touch.

THIRTY-ONE

ONLY ONCE WE RETURN TO THE ESSENCES DO we register that we haven't brought back what we set out for. After that rabbit escaped, Zac and I became caught up in high-spirited chatter and apparently lost all sense of purpose. Or maybe my spiel about killing cute bunnies had an affect on him.

"We couldn't find much," he tells the Essences. Balvinder has already pulled out bags of food from Preo, setting them beside Gwin's bread rolls.

None of the Essences seem too bothered by the lack of meat, apart from Thorne, who gives a disdainful sneer. But it's Harlie's expression that concerns me most. A wary smile my way, like she knows something I'm supposed to know too.

I return the look with an inquiring frown.

"I told them why you left," she explains, stretching out on a knitted blanket Gwin obviously brought along, since it's a garish, pink shade dotted with white flowers. "I said you both wanted time away from us, and that the hunting was a reasonable pretext. Thorne didn't believe it, but returning with no kill to show for certainly proves my theory."

I stare at her, aghast. "That's not—"

"Be honest, Abbey," she cuts in. "If you require a private space, do let us know."

"If I—I—what?"

Gwin giggles. She's sitting beside Peirce—who is lying facedown in the dirt—and playing idly with his hair.

I don't want to look at Zac, for fear of perpetuating the air of awkwardness Harlie has helpfully contributed, but at a brief glance I can see that he's trying to keep a straight face. He approaches the food laid out on their paper bags.

Just as Zac is about to walk right into Balvinder, Balvinder extends a careful hand to his knee. It's an instinctive gesture. Habitual. And so is the way Zac responds—by retreating a foot and sinking to the ground right beside his friend. They've operated this way for ten years, with Zac blind to Balvinder's physical position. It's no surprise that it would appear almost natural now. But still, it's an abrupt reminder that Balvinder isn't ordinary, like us. None of the Essences are.

"It's a phenomenon I often contemplate, with these humans," Harlie comments. She sighs and sits upright, her long legs crossing over one another. "That their spirits don't take nearly enough of me."

Gwin drags Peirce's hair through her fingers, eyeing it inquisitively. "I feel the same thing Harlie," she says. "I have so much to offer, and yet so many choose Peirce's Essence over mine."

Peirce laughs. It's the first sound I've heard from him that isn't sullen—and yet it's also completely devoid of humour, closer to a cough or a bark. "If everyone lived like you," he says, "the worlds would explode."

"Here's the thing," Harlie says, now turning to Balvinder as though his opinion matters most of all. "Honesty equates to resolutions. Without it, both Earth and Ethra would erupt into chaos. Wouldn't you agree?"

Balvinder inclines his head thoughtfully. "Yes," he says. "Though there are times when Honesty may not equate to a peaceful resolution. In these circumstances a spirit might resist your Essence."

"I suppose," murmurs Harlie, although she seems unconvinced.

"Honesty can destroy, so much as it can heal," Thorne says. There's an underlying venom to the statement. Harlie seems to notice it too, looking sharply toward him.

I run my eyes over the faces in front of me, unable to stifle the fascination these sorts of conversations evoke.

The Essences speak as though they're performing an amateur-theatre production—one of those plays where the stage dressing consists of five seats and one spotlight, and the characters alternate dramatic monologues.

Tyler and I often check up on what's playing at lesser-known theatres around the city. Occasionally we stumble across something we both want to see, and rarely is it any good. But we thoroughly enjoy those nights anyway.

The banter of the Essences would make a brilliant, screenplay concept. Maybe I can write it up once I'm home. Have Tyler star as one of them. We did meet in drama class, after all. I smile to myself as I contemplate who I would cast him as ...

Pride? Tyler does possess shades of Thorne, in that they're both immensely confident in their own abilities. But he balances it out with a bit of Gwin's Optimism and a hell of a lot of Balvinder's Goodness.

He has a good portion of Harlie in him too, always telling me the truth even when it's hard to hear. My throat starts to burn, so I tear myself away from the thought of him—back to the Essences.

Thorne is now advising Peirce on how to redeem the unfortunate situation that is his hair, leaning across Gwin with an arrow outstretched. He is using the feathered shaft to flick Peirce's hair from his face. Something about the beady eyes that are now exposed and Thorne's unwillingness to touch Peirce himself triggers a snort of laughter from me.

Thorne glances up in surprise, before his eyes narrow. "What's so amusing?"

I shake my head at him. Where to start ...

＊

I wake to a screech. The noise was loud, but caught between dreaming and waking. I wouldn't be sure which realm it came from, if the Essences weren't sitting upright on their blankets and Zac wasn't standing with his face toward the sky.

"What was that?" I hiss, scrambling to my feet beside him.

"Bats," Harlie whispers. Another screech sounds from above, this time louder, closer.

I drag the sleeves of my jacket over my palms, squeezing them tight. "Bats?" I've always considered them to be revolting animals. I never watched past the first ten minutes of Batman. How can you trust anything that sleeps upside down? There's something super-shifty about that.

"Kayna's bats," Thorne amends, which does nothing to comfort me. Neither does the fact that his crossbow is now loaded. He holds it in a crouch.

I swallow hard as the screeches rise, deafening. Still groggy from sleep, I rub at my eyes before training them to the night sky. Sure enough—thick shadows flicker through gaps in the canopy, silhouetted by the light of the moon. The sheer volume of the cries rattles my brain.

"If we ignore them they will leave us alone," Gwin says, lying back down and tugging a yellow, moth-eaten blanket up to her round cheeks.

"I thought the same about you, once," Peirce murmurs, "but I was sorely wrong."

I pull my boots on as the other Essences—all but Gwin—stand too. I've barely tied the last of the laces when there's a violent *crack*.

Something hard strikes the back of my neck and I duck, protecting my head as rock hurtles into my back.

The canopy has crumbled. Above us the sky is now fully exposed, and large bodies perch at the jagged edges of the broken branches. Zac seizes my arm just as a dark shadow thuds to the forest floor. Peirce's shriek is almost as shrill as the bats'.

We all part quickly—even Gwin rolls away from the creature, tangled in her blanket. But she's laughing. "I suppose I was wrong too!" she caws. Nobody else seems quite so amused, because another shadow follows the first. And then another.

We extend our circle as the bats drop, thudding so heavily to the ground that I feel the force of each landing under my feet. I shrug out of Zac's grip and jerk my dagger from its scabbard. He shoulders in front of me anyway, his own blade extended.

There's a flurry of movement as the bats rise, revealing the full extent of their breadth and height. With their leathery wings spread wide—I realise how immense they are, and how small my dagger is in comparison.

The membranes of their wings are vast and thick and their eyes glint like black orbs in the moonlight. The bat nearest me suddenly shrieks. I see the shaft of an arrow protruding from its side as it writhes. I cut a look across at Thorne, who has already reloaded his crossbow. "Stand back!" he yells. "I can handle them."

"He can handle them!" Gwin repeats, just in case we missed it. She's busily rolling up her blanket as though we're simply packing up camp. To me and probably everybody else, it's clear that however great Thorne is with a crossbow, there are too many bats for him to *handle* on his own.

The other bats slump to all fours. They dig their talons into the earth and claw toward us with such unexpected speed that I find myself stumbling backwards.

Zac's dagger flashes in the dim light as the nearest creature lunges forward. I lose sight of him behind its wing for a split-second—before his blade pierces through the membrane. The bat screeches horribly and crumples to the ground. Zac springs out from its hold.

Thorne fires arrows so fast I barely see him reload. Another bat falls with an arrow in its chest, but another swarm descends—half a dozen bats tumbling from the hole in the canopy. One of them lurches straight for me. My heart thumps and I thrust my dagger out.

But in a blink Zac is there. He leaps up, driving his blade through its fuzzy head. Behind him, I see Harlie latched onto the back of one of the creatures as it rears. Peirce and Gwin stand back with entirely opposing expressions of dread and elation, and Balvinder is watching the scene with his eyes closed and hands outstretched.

Realising the direness of the situation, I unfreeze. Zac dives on a bat and is spun beneath it. I rush toward them—just as the creature shrieks and jerks away, its head lolling backward from a slash in its throat. Zac staggers out, his blade dripping. Something about his expression—an unnerving cross between serene and wild—stumps me for a moment.

Thorne's yell brings me back. I spin to see him lifted from the ground, his crossbow swinging in a flailing hand. Zac springs for the bat but misses—and is grabbed from behind by another.

I scream and run out at him. But as I leap forward, the bat propels itself upward. I roll and scramble to my feet to watch Zac lifted above the canopy after Thorne. His boots kick out at the branches, sending more stone crumbling. And then he vanishes.

I'm about to scream when my feet lose contact with the ground and all air whooshes out of my lungs. The collar of my jacket pulls tight around my throat, caught from behind in the bat's claws.

I'm suspended. Lifted higher. Past the heads of the bats and beyond the tops of the trees. The Essences disappear from sight as the creatures swarm, and I'm swept into the night.

THIRTY-TWO

IT'S TRUE THAT A WEEK AGO I WASN'T SURE where life would lead me, but soaring above a Petrified Forest in the claws of a bat with the wind tearing at my face wouldn't have rated highly in my guesses.

My instinct is to twist and pull or slash at the bat with my dagger. But I quickly remind myself that if it lets go, I'll plummet to my death. So I stop resisting and tuck my arms in tightly.

The Petrified Forest is like the fibrous exterior of a brain, a grey membrane of winding branches lying far below my dangling feet. Ahead of me, two bats fly with their claws hooked in the back of two others—Thorne and Zac.

My stomach lurches as I watch the front figure slip. I cry out in panic as he drops like a stone, smacking against the canopy with a yell before falling right through it. From up here, all I see is a black pit left behind.

It was Thorne, I realise, recognizing Zac's gangly limbs still suspended. Thorne might be ageless, but can he survive a fall like that? Both legs will be broken, at the very least.

A vice-like grip suddenly grasps my ankle and I scream. I'm jerked downward. The bat holding me shrieks as something thick and serpentine spirals up and around my leg.

Only when I look up at Zac do I realise what it is. Because a single branch has extended up from the canopy to take his leg like mine, both trees somehow come alive.

A tug of war ensues—the bats against the forest.

I hear a pop as one of the bat's claws loses its hold in my jacket. I'm spun, hanging only by the other claw. I'm a feather whirling in the wind, which quickly turns into a gale, ripping into a downward current as if to aid the branch. And then I fall.

My stomach leaps into my chest. I'm twisted around and around, catching fleeting glimpses of the bat above me screeching and madly batting its wings. My body is coiled whole in the branch that pulled me free, and it seems to slow, the world rotating in a gentle turn as I'm guided down. So far down.

I shut my eyes and pray like I never have before. Just one word, over and over.

Help.

Help.

Help.

And then I'm unravelled onto solid ground. I dig my fingers into the dirt and look around. Everything tilts, dizziness from the revolving descent setting nausea roiling in my gut.

I give myself a moment. Drop to my side. Take a few heavy breaths until the sick feeling subsides. Then I rise gingerly to my feet and study the forest around me.

Movement catches my eye—and I see the branch that saved me shrinking away. Only now, without the immediate panic of being up in the sky, I can see the texture of it. Bark—glowing from the inside like the trees of the Moonlit Woods.

As it returns to a nearby bough, shifting into place amongst the lattice of branches above, it fades again to stone. Totally still.

I hear a distant screech. Then silence.

THIRTY-THREE

MY MIND GOES IMMEDIATELY TO ZAC. I SAW the trees reaching for him, grasping his leg in the sky—but nothing more. I don't know if he landed like I did. If he was freed from the bat at all.

And if he was, where did he fall? He could be nearby. Should I look for Zac or the Essences?

"Hello?" I call out. "Zac?" And I wait a beat, before yelling again. "Thorne?"

No response.

I shake out my hands to dismiss the nerves prickling in my fingertips. So, here I am, alone in a Petrified Forest. Not to mention a world away from home. But if I panic, I'll never find the others.

I will try to retrace the flight path of the bat. If I scream loudly enough, someone is bound to hear me. We heard the bats, after all, long before they crashed through the canopy.

It will be okay.

I'm okay.

"*Shader.*"

My heart just about explodes at the sound. I wheel around, gripping my chest with one hand and my dagger with the other. Shadows gape between the trees, dense and impenetrable. I can't see a thing.

Dark, melodious laughter resounds between the trees. A chill touches my core, turning my whole body cold. The sound seems to dart one way and then the other with no visible source, until—

A soft thud makes me whirl. I see a figure hunched only a few feet away. It draws up to standing, seemingly darker than the shadows around it.

I stay rooted, watching as a hood falls back to reveal a face I know. Her face. Inky hair framing bone-white features. Black eyes gleaming like oil over a polluted sea. Just like the bats. And the apparition. I don't know her well, but I know her enough. And every bone in my body screams at me to run.

The whisper is low and cold when it comes again. "Abbey Shader." That same prickling sensation sets my nerves jumping and my hairs on end.

My tongue has gone into lockdown, like my feet. I do my best to square my shoulders. She's just the Essence of pure Evil. What's the worst that can happen?

"Well this is a surprise," I say, commanding my voice to remain level. "What are you doing out here?" I can feel myself trembling wildly all over, betraying my—*speak to her like you would an old friend you stumbled across in the supermarket and you might not die*—strategy.

There is no doubt in my mind now that she has been following us the entire way. Through the mountains, across the plateau, into the woods and the forest. The epiphany makes me shiver.

Kayna steps forward, her cloak hissing across the dirt. She looks more menacing than she did the first time I saw her. Perhaps it's the context of a shadowy forest, or the fact that I now know exactly *what* she is.

I try not to flinch at her next step. We're separated only by a few feet, but if I bolt, I doubt I'll get very far.

"It has been quite the task to free you from your ... companions," she says. Her eyes shift left, and a hopeful part of me wonders if it's any indication of where my *companions* might be right now.

"I don't need to be freed from them," I tell her. "They're taking me home."

"I was taking you home."

"Yes, well ..." A lot happened after she promised that. I found Balvinder, freed him, met Zac, hiked for a week straight, and have really started to believe that I'm here for a reason—so surely my forgetting about Kayna is relatively justified. I don't dare say all that, though. Instead I cut it at the first milestone, which alludes to the rest. "I found Balvinder."

Kayna's mouth curls, before she whispers, "He lies to you."

"What do you mean?"

"They all do. They wish for you to stay." Her grin spreads wide, exposing those disconcertingly large teeth. "But their priorities are not yours. I can take you home this very moment."

A new sense of unease stirs in my chest. It isn't fear—it's doubt. The question of whether I'm ready to go. Whether I need to see the others before I do. Whether I should trust Kayna at all.

I try to swallow but my throat is dry. "I know who you are," I say, the words scratchy.

Kayna's amusement fades, her expression hardening. "It doesn't matter who I am, or who I am not," she says. "You were summoned for a purpose you do not wish to fulfill, and so you must go."

I think back to the woods. Two words draw into sharp focus. "*Follow us*," I mutter, shuddering as I recall the horrible voice. "Did you set that apparition on me?"

Kayna hesitates before answering. "Yes."

"Huh." I feel a seed of defiance growing inside me. "Well, if you really wanted me to *follow* it, you probably should have sent something with less teeth and maybe—maybe tried for a gentler approach."

"The apparitions are loyal allies," Kayna says tightly. "The one I sent for you was simply doing my bidding." Her face darkens a shade. "And Zacharias Nellerwood killed it."

"Well, I'm sorry about that, but I'm pretty sure it was about to kill me."

"It would not—"

"Take me back," I interrupt, steeling myself. "Not home. Back to the others. I don't need your help anymore."

Silence draws out between us as shadows gather in her face like live entities, welling in the pits of her eyes. "It isn't in my nature to accommodate," she whispers, deadly quiet. "Though you do intrigue me, Abbey Shader. No Melder has refused a summoning from the Overseer." She angles her head. "I admire your defiance."

She brings her hands to the hood of her cloak, lifting it over her head again. Her fingers are thin and bony. "But if you dare defy me again—" Kayna moves so fast I have no time to react. Sudden pain erupts through me. I gasp for air that doesn't come. A hiss creeps into my ear from behind. "Remember this," she says.

My vision turns hazy, but I see her step in front of me, smiling wolfishly.

"Little Melder!" The call jolts me to attention, and I realise my hands are empty. My dagger—she took it. She stabbed me.

I'm going to die.

Agony roars across my stomach and the full weight of the realisation brings me to my knees—just as another figure strides into my rapidly blurring vision.

"Abbey?" It's Thorne. His voice is far away, even though I soon feel his hands on my shoulders.

I open my mouth to warn him. To tell him Kayna is here. But nothing comes. I can't see her anymore. The dimness of the forest is dimming further.

An instinctive breath sets my body on fire. I want to scream but I can't muster a groan. Not even as I hear Thorne huff in annoyance and then the slick exit of the dagger. I fall forward, and black out.

THIRTY-FOUR

WHEN I COME-TO, I'M FACED WITH A SHIFTING wall of dirt. My eyes drag down to thick-soled boots, and I realise I'm being carried.

"Thorne," I croak, the memories crawling back. Kayna. The pain ...

The pain? I don't feel it anymore. She stabbed me through the back. She used my own dagger against me. But now ...

I try to move my fingers, without luck. An odd sort of numbness keeps my muscles still and unresponsive. Am I paralyzed?

"Save your voice," Thorne says. "The others aren't far, and they will want to hear the story too."

"You," I go on, dismissing the order. "I saw you fall." My breath catches as he adjusts me roughly over his shoulder and the edge of his crossbow knocks my jaw. "How are you ..."

"Still walking?" I hear a smile in his voice. "For the same reason *you* are still alive. Essences cannot be killed, and the Melder cannot be killed by an Essence. I told you this only two days ago."

"I forgot," I admit, expelling a shaky breath. "I've had a lot to process. You can put me down now."

"You are too weak."

"I'm fine."

"It hasn't been long enough for the healing—"

"Just put me down!"

Although I asked for it, I'm still surprised when Thorne obeys. He easily lifts me off his shoulder and sets me onto the ground.

My knees give way and I drop like lead.

I lie on the forest floor for a moment, my cheek pressed to the dirt and my eyes shifting to meet Thorne's. He crosses his arms, regarding me with a thin smile.

"This was my intention," I mumble.

"Oh, little Melder." He shakes his head. "As tempting as it is to leave you here, I do believe Balvinder wouldn't thank me for it." I'm scooped into his arms before he marches on.

The shadows between the trees have paled from the light of the morning, but it still feels ominous. Or maybe it's just my discomfort about being held, this vulnerable, so close to Thorne. I crane my neck away from his brawny chest with a grimace.

"Calm yourself," he says, his voice a little softer. "I should be the least of your concerns."

✳

I hear the bats before I see them. "They're still here!" I warn Thorne, but he only chuckles.

"In a manner."

I'm about to question the ambiguous response when a flurry of activity catches my eye. Writhing bodies and flapping wings break into view. My heart pounds hard until we get closer, and I see that they're trapped. The branches of the trees have bent into a cocoon, like bars in a suspended prison.

Below it—Gwin, Peirce and Harlie watch on. But it's Balvinder who draws my attention. He stands the closest. His hand is outstretched and his fingers drawn in, emulating the shape of the trees. Unless ... they are emulating *him*.

I have time enough to connect only two dots—that it must have been Balvinder who launched that branch into the sky to save me—before I realise that Zac is missing.

"You can put me down," I tell Thorne. He obliges, whilst muttering something about my ungratefulness, and I find that I'm steady this time. All that's left of Kayna's attack is a muted sort of numbness in my belly, a shadow of the real wound or a physical memory rapidly fading.

I rush over to Balvinder. Gwin shrieks excitedly at the sight of me but I don't stop for her. "Where's Zac?" I yell above the cries of the bats. Balvinder turns to me, still holding the shape of the branches with his fingers.

Relief floods his eyes. "Are you all right?"

"Zac," I say again. "He fell. I didn't see where, but—"

"Oh!" Gwin's cry spins me around. She's facing away from us, jumping up and down on the spot.

I train my eyes to the point of her attention—and see him.

He's walking toward us, looking dishevelled and a little dazed, but intact. I expel a shuddering sigh of relief I barely knew I was holding and start to cross the distance between us.

But I stop short, because I'm not quite sure what to do next. Zac, however, doesn't break his stride. He folds me in his arms and squeezes me tight. It's a brief embrace, but enough to shock me into forgetting that anyone else is here, watching on.

Thorne kindly reminds me with a scoff that surpasses the volume of the bats.

Zac and I pull apart and then he looks me up and down. "Are you hurt?"

"Uh ..." I feel the memory of that blade cutting through me, and my hands fall instinctively to my stomach. "Not anymore."

Thorne appears beside me. He extends my dagger, and I see Zac's eyes latch onto it, his brow creasing. To him, it must appear to be suspended.

Gwin bustles closer. "Why do you have Abbey's blade?" she inquires, her eyes bright. Thorne doesn't respond. He just waits, regarding me carefully. But I can only stare at the dagger. I don't want to touch it, or remember where it has been.

"I know," says Thorne. His mouth bends a little to the side. "To have your own weapon turned against you is one of the cruelest insults." He draws closer, until he blocks all the others from view. "But there is Pride in reclaiming it too," he whispers, so quietly no one else would have heard, and with that—he slips it back into the sheath at my belt.

*

"She came out of nowhere."

The Essences are gathered around me, and Zac too. Their usual chatter dialled down to zero the moment I mentioned Kayna's name.

We left the bats in Balvinder's tree prison. He claimed he would release them when we were far enough away for it to be safe. We've only walked a short distance, but the moment the shrieks of the bats had faded sufficiently and we could speak without yelling, Balvinder stopped me to ask what happened.

"I think she sent the bats for us—for me—like the apparition. She wants to take me home."

"Kayna does nothing with altruistic intention," Harlie says. "She must be planning something."

I look to Balvinder, but he only taps a finger to his chin, lips pressed together. *He lies to you*, Kayna had said. What did she mean? I open my mouth to ask—then stop myself, deciding against it. If he is lying, about any of this, maybe it's best not to reveal that I know. To this point, it's seemed as if everyone else has kept an entire deck of cards to their chests, only offering me peeks at a select few. Now I have one card, and for now I want to keep it hidden.

I wince, recalling the next part of the story. "Before Thorne found me, Kayna—she took my dagger and ..." I swallow through the dryness in my throat. "She ..."

"Kayna stabbed her," Thorne finishes for me.

Zac stiffens beside me. My eyes meet Balvinder's. The blue of the irises seem greyed, swirling like a disturbed sea in a storm.

"No matter," Gwin declares. "Kayna will never drastically harm Abbey! The Melder is immune to death by the hand of an Essence—even the most powerful of us."

"Though she isn't immune to *pain* inflicted at the hand of an Essence," offers Peirce, his face mostly concealed by his dark, greasy hair.

"Where is she now?" Zac inquires, his voice contracting around the question.

Thorne barks a laugh. "Why? Do you plan on seeking revenge? Foolish boy. Kayna is the very Essence of Evil. You are a meagre human. Just ask Peirce how that will turn out."

Everyone but Zac glances toward Peirce. After a brief pause, he provides the answer—"You will die."

"Precisely," says Thorne, looking pleased. "Your melodrama has its place, Peirce."

My attention shifts to Zac, then. "What happened to you? After you fell?"

"The trees saved me." His expression softens a touch. "They brought me down and I followed the sound of the bats to get back."

"You were saved by Balvinder," Harlie rejoinders. "Not the trees."

I look at Balvinder with my eyebrows raised. He mirrors the look and I laugh. "What can't you do?"

He smiles back. "A thing or two."

"That's twice now," Harlie remarks.

Balvinder's amusement fades, and he looks sharply toward her. "Twice?"

"Yes." She gestures to Zac. "Twice that you have saved the boy."

"Two times too many," Thorne mutters.

"I watched you when the bats attacked," Harlie goes on, this time addressing Zac directly. He cuts a look at me and I nod toward Harlie, indicating the statement was meant for him. "You are highly skilled," she says. "If you were trained earlier, perhaps your parents would not have met the end they did."

A fleeting look of shock passes over Zac's face, neutralized quickly. He says nothing, just reaches over his shoulder to draw the straps of his pack tighter.

"Harlie," Balvinder warns.

To my horror, she persists. "It is the truth, isn't it?"

"He was a child," Balvinder says.

Harlie's lime eyes trace our faces, void of any understanding aside from cold logic. "Child or not—if a similar situation arose now, things would be different."

"But it did not arise now," counters Balvinder.

Zac turns from the group and sets off into the forest, leaving Harlie looking frank, Thorne smirking, Gwin red-cheeked and Peirce shaking his head.

"Oh, Harlie," Thorne mutters. "Never a sense of the line and when not to cross it." *The same could be said about you*, I think to myself, but decide it isn't the time for a jab at Thorne.

Balvinder and I exchange a momentary glance before I go after Zac.

He's walking fast, and I have to jog to catch up. "Hey," I say, nudging his arm as I fall into step beside him.

"Balvinder's oasis is this way," he says, as if to quell any questions or sympathy.

"Okay." I keep quiet for a bit ... wondering how to breach the silence. Wondering if he wants to discuss it at all. I hold to my theory that people will share when they are ready to share, but sometimes it helps to let them know you're there, ready to hear it. "Honesty," I mutter. "And to think she was starting to become one of my favourites."

"She was?" A small smile wavers at the corner of Zac's mouth. "I've always favoured Thorne."

"Liar."

Zac turns then. His green eyes fall to my face, distant, like he's seeing through it. "She isn't wrong though."

ESSENCE

I frown, saying nothing to allow him the space to go on.

"I was a child, yes. But that doesn't make the torment any less. What I could have done, or not ..." He glances away, fixing his gaze ahead. "They took me up to the woods—my mother and father. I had crossed the river into the Petrified Forest. It was a game to me. I ran and ran, expecting them to come after me. I was laughing." Zac draws a sharp breath. "I remember that so clearly."

I think back to the river we crossed. The way Zac changed when we reached the other side. His hesitation. Was he reliving the moment then?

"Eventually I realised I was alone. They were no longer following me, and when I went back ... the beast was there and they were ... gone." Zac sighs, a sound that sounds artificial, a forced attempt to lighten the weight of the story. "I was attacked too, and was badly wounded. Left for dead. But Balvinder found me and brought me to his oasis."

I feel a pang. Of course. Their odd, indefinable relationship suddenly makes too much sense. Not only did Balvinder raise Zac—he rescued him from the fate of his parents. I can see him vividly, carrying Zac's small, broken body through the very trees we're navigating now.

Zac looks at me with a tired smile, but it doesn't reach any convincing part of his face. I try to smile back, but my eyes burn and I blink away, not wanting him to see my emotion.

"What happened after that?" I ask him.

"Well, I couldn't go back to Preo," Zac says. "Physically, I couldn't go anywhere for many months. Balvinder laid my mother and father in the woods, to be discovered by the villagers, while I stayed at his oasis. I didn't feel I could face the rest of my family." Which is why Rylah was so surprised to see him, I consider. "When I was well enough, Balvinder went with me to Emba. Between Breathings he would visit me—help me start anew. A life free of the guilt and the grief."

Something in the way he says those two words makes me doubt that he's free of either thing.

I touch his arm. "Zac, it wasn't your—"

"I don't need comfort," he says abruptly.

Against every instinct, I withdraw my hand, respecting his wish. "Harlie has no filter," is all I can think to offer.

Finally Zac looks down at me again, and for a moment I see a chasm opening behind his eyes. "Exactly," he says.

And then he clears his throat, slamming the door on his sorrow and looking away before I can step too close to the edge.

THIRTY-FIVE

WHEN THE ESSENCES CATCH UP WITH US,
Harlie isn't amongst them. Apparently we were all *too afraid of the truth*—so she decided to return to her oasis.

I can comfortably admit that yes, I'm freaking terrified of the truth, especially when it has a voice and a pair of invasive eyes. I don't think Zac is sorry to see Harlie gone either. He hasn't spoken more than two words since our conversation about his parents ended.

Now I understand what this journey means for him, since our path is the very same one he took ten years ago. Watching his parents die at the river, almost dying himself, and then having Balvinder bring him to the oasis we're headed for. Is he reliving it all? Or is the only way to walk it to ignore the past?

I'm unsettled the entire way, torn between dwelling on Zac's past and the fear of encountering Kayna again. The dagger in my belt feels heavy with the memory of her attack. Steel rupturing muscles and tendons. The gasping release as Thorne yanked it out. I can hear the sounds. Feel the shock.

So consumed by the darkness of it all, I barely see the streaks of light appearing around us. It's only as Balvinder lays a hand on my shoulder that I draw sharply to attention, realising how much the forest has transformed.

The trees are reminiscent of the Moonlit Woods, lush and glowing from their trunks out through the bark. Soon enough they open to a clear spread of grass leading up to a wide, T-shaped house. It's built from pale stone, only the roof is a lattice of intertwined branches. Along the front is a garden dotted with blue flowers below tall, glass windows.

Gwin skips ahead, dragging Peirce along with her.

"Welcome back," Balvinder says. I'm about to thank him when I realise it mustn't be intended for me. Zac nods, flicking his dagger in distracted circles.

It feels like a private moment, so I slow down to give them a little space—and collide with a hard body. "Watch it," Thorne says, grabbing my shoulders and shifting me aside. Reminded of our previous and unprecedented closeness, I decide to offer the thanks that seemed unimportant then.

"Hey," I say quietly. "Thank you for finding me after Kayna ... you know. And for bringing me back."

In my periphery I see Thorne glance my way, but keep my eyes forward.

"Don't thank me, little Melder," he says, a weary note to his voice. "Believe it or not, I know what it feels like."

I look at him then. "What do you mean?"

"A story for another time, perhaps."

I get the sense that it wouldn't be clever to press him on it, so I focus on the house again. The chill of the forest has mostly dissipated, my tension easing away as if the warmth has drawn over it like a blanket.

The door to the house is carved with intricate, leafy patterns drawing into a silver doorknob, and it's wide open since Gwin has already pranced inside with Peirce.

Balvinder leads us through to a large room lit by three incandescent columns—trees, I realise with a spark of wonder, stripped of their bark. They seem to grow right out of holes in the flagstone floor, up through a ceiling of timber slates. I presume that it's their branches that can be seen from outside, cascading over the roof.

An empty, stone fireplace is set into the left wall with padded couches, and there is a kitchen bench beyond. Gwin is disappearing down the only other corridor.

"I will be in my room!" she sings as she goes.

I peer after her. "She has a room?"

"Everyone does," Balvinder says, striding toward the fireplace.

"And he means that quite literally," Thorne drawls. "I may have fewer bedrooms at my manor, but only because I am under no misconception that I enjoy the company of enough to accommodate more than two or three."

Zac still hasn't spoken, but at least his dagger is back in its sheath. He drops his pack and approaches the couch Balvinder is about to sit in. Balvinder shifts without a word, claiming the one opposite. I wonder how long it took them to learn this dance, if they've always moved so effortlessly around each other or whether Zac has never been aware of it.

Thorne takes the remaining couch and I sit beside Zac, mulling over his story. Ten years ago he was brought to this very house. He said that it was a *beast* who killed his parents, and left him for dead. He was only ten years old ... required to deal with his own near-fatal injuries, his parents' death, feeling responsible for it ... and was *then* asked to believe in an unseen erodosphere and the presence of a disembodied voice. If I thought *my* journey here was rough, perspective has put me right back in my place.

I watch as Balvinder flourishes idly toward the fireplace and wild, blue flames spring to life behind the hearth, but with no wood to burn. Despite the fact that I've seen his abilities in evidence before, I still feel a jolt of surprise.

"You will find fresh clothes in the wardrobes," he says, glancing toward me. "Your room is the first on the left, Abbey."

"Nobody ever wants to stay at my oasis." Peirce's dreary voice sounds before he appears, trudging toward the fire and dropping to the floor. Even in the way he moves, he looks like a wet rag. "Aside from Gwin, visitors are rare."

"I can't imagine why ..." mutters Thorne.

Zac glances at me, his mouth hooking at the corner. The sight of him—visibly more relaxed and closer to the humorous boy I've come to know—sets relief flooding through me.

Gwin trots into the room and I let out a garbled choke. She is bouncing toward the fire with a crazed grin—stark naked.

Thorne heaves a sigh and Peirce recoils back into Zac's legs. Zac cuts a glance at me as if to ask what's going on. Only, I'm not sure I can explain it ...

"What were we talking about? Gwin chortles.

"*Where are your clothes?*" demands Peirce.

"Oh!" She giggles, as if just realising she isn't wearing any. "It's only skin, Peirce dear. *Some* of us are comfortable in it." She looks my way as if I might support her, and I rapidly turn, deeming it a dangerous bandwagon to jump on.

Zac looks mildly horrified, an indicator that he has probably worked out for himself what we're seeing. He leans close and whispers, "Blindness has never felt like such a blessing."

A fit of suppressed laughter escapes me, while Thorne massages his temples and Balvinder seems to fight a smile, staring into the fire as though it might capture his amusement.

It's Peirce who rises and throws his cloak over Gwin, shuffling her back down the corridor. Her giggles sound the whole way—until we hear a door slam shut.

"On that note ..." Thorne wearily smoothes his silky, black hair from his face. "Shall we eat?"

THIRTY-SIX

WE SIT IN THE LOUNGE SIPPING STEW FROM large mugs. Balvinder fetched water from the creek behind his oasis—which is apparently the same that crosses Gwin's—and boiled it with vegetables in a pot over the hearth. Gwin, thankfully, is now clothed in a white gown and squished into the couch with Balvinder. Peirce remains at our feet, and Thorne is still on a couch of his own.

The ambience of the place seems to have eased all the rigid knots from my back and mind; the blue tongues of flame licking the base of the pot, the gentle simmering sound of the stew, the gingery tang that warms my throat with each sip. I feel happy, here beside Zac. Even the Essences seem to calm my nerves in some incalculable way.

"Are you always expected to escort the Melder to this Overseer?" I ask the room at large, between mouthfuls.

Thorne's eyes flash derisively in Balvinder's direction. "In a manner," he says. "Though usually it doesn't take quite this long."

Gwin giggles. "We are having *fun*, Thorne. Have you forgotten how?" She winks over at me. "The more time we get

ESSENCE

to spend with Abbey, the better. I just wish the others could meet her too."

I drain the last of my stew before casting her a frown. "The others?"

"Every Essence is required for the Breathings," Balvinder comments, rising and striding across to the kitchen bench, where he sets down his empty bowl. "If you remained, you would meet all nine."

Nine. Good Lord. I can barely deal with this lot.

"I am surprised that Harlie hasn't yet informed Westby," Thorne muses. "They have become quite close of late."

"Is that jealousy I detect, Thorne?" Gwin inquires, a mischievous glint to her eye. "A darker shade of your Pride?"

He snorts and places down his mug before crossing his arms. "Of course not."

"Who's Westby?" I ask.

"Order," Balvinder answers, returning to collect our bowls. For a moment I stare at him, thinking that his response was a demand. *Order in the courtroom*, kind of thing. But then I realise—it was an answer. A title.

"He prefers *Efficiency*," Gwin amends, beaming across at me. "I do believe Abbey would like him very much."

"There's an Essence for ... Efficiency?"

"Is that so shocking, little Melder?" Thorne chides.

"No. Just—I wouldn't have guessed it."

Zac nudges my elbow with his. "Four of nine," he says. "We are almost halfway there." I think on that. According to

Zac, the only Essences we know are Pride, Honesty, Evil, and now Efficiency. I can add Good, Optimism and Pessimism to that list—which leaves only two. But it doesn't feel like the time to blurt that out. I'm not sure I have the right, either.

After dinner, Balvinder leads us through his house to our rooms.

"Thorne, yours is—"

"Yes," Thorne cuts in. "I have been here before." With that he stalks toward a door and slams it. I fight the urge to fling it open again and whack him over the head. Nobody would take that on the chin. Nobody except, maybe, the Essence of Good.

Gwin brushes a feather-light kiss to my cheek before twirling into her room. Peirce skulks off without a goodnight.

"How do they not drive you insane?" I whisper to Balvinder as he directs me to my room. He offers a faint smile, but only shrugs before gesturing for me to enter the nearest door. Hesitating momentarily, I glance up the hall toward Zac, who is disappearing into the last bedroom.

I want to say goodnight, but the word catches in my throat and I just end up coughing before ducking through the doorway. Super cool.

My heart leaps when I see the bed in the centre of the room. I clasp my hands together and whirl around to Balvinder. "I might cry," I tell him, only half-joking. When he looks puzzled, I clarify—"A bed! Not that sleeping in the dirt wasn't luxurious."

Balvinder's face lights up. "You are welcome to sleep in the dirt tonight, if you would prefer it. Peirce often does."

I laugh, collapsing back onto the mattress with a sigh that expels every remnant of worry left in me. Beside the bed, a lamp is set up on a small table. A still, blue flame holds behind the glass, casting ethereal light that reflects in the window behind the headboard. I sit up and peer outside, but the night has swiped any chance of a view to outside.

Balvinder goes to close the door. "Hey," I say quickly, and he pauses. "At the Breathing House ... I learnt something about you."

A glimmer of humour crosses his face but fades quickly, replaced by a curious expression. "And what was that?"

"You're the Essence of Good."

Balvinder looks contemplative. "I suppose I am," he finally says, the offhanded admission leaving me a little lost for words. "Does it surprise you?"

"Not really," I say, honestly. At least, *surprise* isn't the right word. "I don't know how I didn't see it sooner."

Balvinder sighs, and his face relaxes into a smile. "There was much for you to see."

We look at each other a while longer, the silence somehow just as easy and in-depth as if it were a stream of conversation.

"You have perfect reason to feel terribly confused," he says. "But without confusion there would be no discovery, you see."

I keep quiet, considering the sentiment, which I decide is ultimately true. Balvinder pushes the door open a touch wider.

"You mustn't fear what you don't know, Abbey. There will always be things you won't understand, things beyond your comprehension, and even mine. But the process of discovery can be exciting if you let it be."

"Sounds like you're telling me to revel in my ignorance," I say, with more cynicism than I feel.

Balvinder smiles. "No," he says. "I'm telling you that the answers you are looking for won't be found by confining foreign truths to familiar moulds. The truth is much greater than anything you could possibly conceive."

I go to make some retort but nothing comes. The Essence of Good likely has the upper hand when it comes to debating the truths of the universe, especially considering it has only been a week or so since I discovered an entire layer of it I never knew existed.

"Have a pleasant rest," Balvinder says. "Tomorrow may be your final day with us."

Dread unfurls in my chest. *Final day.*

Before I can self-analyse the feeling of dismay blooming inside me too intensely, Balvinder shuts the door and I just about jump out of my skin—because there's a mirror hanging behind it, edged in a silver frame.

First I note my hair, which is in a state of total disarray, half-unravelled from its elastic. There's a smear of dirt across my chin, and Rylah's green shirt seems to have greyed.

I strip to my underwear and kick off my boots, standing in front of the mirror to inspect every familiar edge of myself. Twisting, I rake my gaze over my lower back, where Kayna drove the dagger. The skin is smooth and untouched. Impossibly so. What Thorne said about Essences being unable to inflict serious harm on a Melder must be true.

Unfortunately, the same *can't* be said for giant frogs. The scab leftover from the attack on the lake is shrinking, but it must have been a significant gash. I'll be surprised if it doesn't leave a faint scar.

A gentle rap at the door has me launching myself back toward the bed. "Yes—one second—" I grab my pants and get one leg in before the door starts to crack open. Panicking, I yank the sheets around me.

Zac appears and then disappears just as fast. "Sorry!" His voice is muffled behind the door. "I didn't—"

"No it's—it's okay." I pull the blankets closer. I'm still wearing a bra, and it isn't like the straps are any more revealing than the white singlet I've worn up until now. "What's up?"

The door eases open and Zac steps inside, wearing light, woollen pants and a dark singlet. The cozy look is noticeably different from his usual hiking-style getup. For whatever reason, it sets my heart into a flutter.

I swallow the nervous lump in my throat and watch him take a turn of the room, hands deep in his pockets. "Do you feel it too?" he asks.

Nervous energy spirals through me. "Feel what?"

"This place." Zac stops. His gaze shifts back to mine, wonderfully green. "It takes away the ache."

I'm not sure whether he means it in a physical or an emotional sense, but I nod anyway. Because I do feel it. In my mind as much as my tired muscles. "I like it here," I tell him. "Is this the first time you've been back since ... since then?"

"Yes." Zac glances away, the lamp sculpting the column of his neck in smooth, pale light. "It's exactly as I remember it."

"That must be hard."

He shrugs. "It brings the memories closer. Sharpens the haze, I suppose. But it wasn't all bad—my time here."

I feel a pang of sympathy, but can't settle on how to channel it into words. Instead I shuffle up the bed and gesture for him to sit.

Zac hesitates a moment before crossing the room and sinking to the mattress. The blanket slips down from my shoulder. I hoist it up, suddenly highly aware of the fact that I'm wearing very little underneath.

The mirror behind the door now shows us both perched on the bed together. I watch the framed image with a vague sense of disconnect, running my eyes over the profile of a striking, dark-haired boy and the girl sitting behind him in a tangle of blankets. There's an unspoken rigidity between the two. A cord connecting them, holding them in place. Near and far at the same time. I tilt my head, half-surprised to see the girl imitate the action.

With a rapid shake of my head, I draw back to myself. "I want to thank you," I tell him. Zac's curious emerald eyes meet mine, bright and magnetizing. They steal my train of thought for another moment. "I mean—" I clear my throat. "We hardly could have made it this far without you."

He laughs softly. "I'm not sure I have done much more than aggravate the Essences."

"Maybe just Thorne," I say, grinning.

Zac runs a hand through his hair, twirling the ends in front of his eyes before sweeping it back. Then he turns to me and his mouth slips into a crooked smile. "I wish you could stay."

His words echo in my head and flip my stomach, feeling closer to a declaration than anything else he's ever said. Zac angles his head, regarding me with a gentle, pained sort of bemusement.

A burst of affection dissolves enough of my reserve for me to shift toward him, tucking my feet just under his leg. "Me too," I say.

Zac seems to hesitate—then reaches a hand to my face. He curls a tangle of hair behind my ear. His touch lingers at my jaw before his fingers brush a line to my chin.

My *final day*, Balvinder said, meaning my time with Zac is running short. This could be our last moment alone. Our *final* moment. My mind shakes its head while my body urges me forward, close enough to feel the warmth of him.

All functional thoughts seem to have retreated a step— made way for something I can't quite explain. I drop my face to his shoulder, feeling the smoothness of his skin against my cheek as his fingers drag into my hair.

We stay that way for a while, my nerves buzzing from his touch.

When I finally look up, Zac draws me in. My lips part over his. He feels warm. Safe. It's different to the kiss under the rain. No distractions. No veil around or between us. Just me and him, every touch burning like fire.

My blanket falls but I don't care because he's against me instead. I can feel the hammering of his heart and I want to bring myself as close as I can to its rhythm.

We slip together down the bed—and there's a solid *knock* as my head strikes the bedpost. Zac looks startled and I start to laugh. He snorts, and that dimple creases his cheek before he brings his mouth to my jaw. I shiver at the heat of his breath and his hands, one slipping to my waist—

—before a loud bang has us wheeling apart like spinning tops. I'm a flurry of blankets and limbs as I try to gather myself into some semblance of civility. The door has been flung wide open, and Gwin is standing in the hall, grinning ear to ear.

"Gwin!" I try to steady my breathing, even though it's probably useless to pretend Zac and I were just having a chat. "What the hell are you—"

"Ah," Gwin cuts in. "Zacharias is here. That explains the laughter!"

To my surprise, she looks genuinely oblivious to the moment she just barelled into headfirst.

Zac is doing a better job of looking nonchalant—mostly due to the fact that unlike me, he's fully clothed. "What's the matter Gwin?" he asks curtly. The thoughtful fist to his cheek and the crease between his brows are the only indicators that he might be a touch dismayed by her timing.

"I heard laughter through the wall," Gwin whispers eagerly, and a little conspiratorially. Already, Zac is sighing. "So I thought I would see if I might join in on the joke!"

I turn to lift an eyebrow Zac's way. "I'm not so sure you can join in on this one, Gwin," I say.

Zac covers his mouth with a hand, but his smile shows around it anyway.

"Where there is laughter, there is Hope." Gwin sets her feet apart in a triumphant stance. "There is Optimism!"

"Not tonight," I say. "Go get some sleep and we'll see you bright and early."

"Bright and early," Gwin repeats to herself. "I quite like that. Bright and early it is!" She spins on her heel and prances away.

"She's gone," I tell Zac, who is standing very still, well away from the bed.

The intimacy of a minute ago feels long gone, and I even find myself tugging the sheets in around me again. "You should probably get some sleep too," I say, and I don't know why, because I don't want him to go.

Part of me hopes that Zac will ignore it too. But he's not Thorne. I only have to tell him once. He watches me a moment, every contour of his face flawless in the subdued light. Then he nods and steps out of the room.

The door doesn't close the whole way. It's left ajar an inch or so, a slash of dark corridor left behind to taunt me. *He's not coming back*, it says. But I stare at it for a long while anyway.

THIRTY-SEVEN

I'M WOKEN—BRIGHT AND EARLY—BY GWIN jumping up and down on my bed.

"Up!" she cries. "It's bright and it's early!"

"Gwin," I croak. "It was just an expression ..."

"The sun has greeted us with a beaming smile." She flops down beside me with her round chin nestled snuggly in her hands. "Everyone else is awake," she adds. "Well, everyone but Peirce. Zac suggested I come in to wake you both."

"Oh did he?"

Gwin's cheeks gleam rose pink. "You're leaving today," she says. "They all seem a little down about it, but I'm just glad we met at all!"

I rise and rub at my eyes. "I'm glad too."

Apparently satisfied, Gwin dashes off, her blonde mane free of its braid and swishing behind her.

Daylight pours in from the window behind the bed. I turn and squint into it. Like Balvinder mentioned last night, there's a creek running behind the house, just at the base of a grassy hill. Trees curve toward the oasis, as if to protect it or be a part of it. Their pale leaves flicker in a gentle wind, kissed with white gold by the sun.

The grey canopy of the Petrified Forest snakes beyond them, a foreboding inevitability. But right now, right here, I feel untouchable in this pod of tranquil beauty. I feel the way I do when Balvinder lays a hand on me—like I can handle anything so long as he's around.

I move over to the armoire in the corner of the room, which I haven't inspected yet. Inside I find racks and stacks of clothing. Rifling through it all, I come away with a dark pair of pants and a loose-fitting shirt that look roughly my size.

I pull on my old clothes but take the new outfit into the front room, where Balvinder offers me a cloth for drying off and a little pot of gritty-textured cream. I take a whiff, and then another, drinking in a reviving aroma of a thousand flowers and freshly cut grass after rain.

Thorne is there too, an imperious arm laid across the fireplace, which is alive with blue flames. Zac occupies one of the couches in a crisp-white linen shirt, his dark hair freshly washed and dripping to the collar. We smile at each other just as a terrible roar sounds from the hallway.

"GET OFF OF ME!" Evidently Peirce wasn't too thrilled about Gwin's wakeup call. Thorne strides to the kitchen without acknowledging me. Even his gait oozes arrogance—chin high, chest puffed and shoulders pulled back by invisible strings—with all the superfluous regality of a king stepping from his throne.

Balvinder directs me to a door behind the kitchen that leads down to the creek. The air is tinged with a clean fragrance wafting from the flowers around every wall of the house.

I trot down the hill and only look back once I'm at the water's edge. The construction of the place is certainly impressive, with the three trees featured inside emerging like a crown over the roof. There's a sort of ancient wonder about the house that has me pondering how long it has been here.

When I'm sure nobody is watching I undress and step quickly down into the water. It's warmer here than near Gwin's house, the current gentle. I'm suddenly reminded of the way Harlie appeared above me the last time I washed up in this creek. The memory has me bolting upright. But I'm alone this time, with only the rustling trees for company.

I fetch my little pot of gardeny goodness and smear it liberally over my face, hair and body. The rippling water nudges and tugs at me and I leave feeling cleaner and clearer than I have in days.

I dry myself with the cloth Balvinder gave me before changing into fresh clothes. The pants are a better fit than the moleskin pair I was wearing before and the shirt hangs nicely. I pull my leather jacket on over it, marching back up to the house feeling like I might even look half-decent.

Everyone is seated around the fire now, even Peirce, who appears to have quite literally rolled out of bed, cocooned in sheets.

We share around a bowl of berries, which I initially think to be blueberries. Only when I bite into one, the flesh is a brilliant shade of red. They burst over my tongue and set my taste buds into a frenzy, satisfying my hunger more quickly than should be possible.

Once the bowl is empty, Thorne swings his crossbow and arrow quiver over his massive shoulders and suggests we leave. We gather our packs and reconvene at the door moments later. Balvinder holds it open for us, and I turn to him as I pass through. "I love it here," I say.

He smiles, a spark moving behind his eyes. "I am glad."

Stepping outside, I can't help but feel like I'm leaving something important behind. Slamming a book shut before reading the end. I try to shake off the uneasiness, but it stays with me all the way into that maze of trees as they turn to stone.

✳

Much to my delight, I'm lucky enough to receive a comprehensive commentary by Gwin as to our proximity to Amnoralas—resulting in fierce disagreement from Peirce, who claims we are much further away than Gwin does. I guess a semi-realistic deduction can be made somewhere between their two loud opinions, in which case Amnoralas is getting close. And the portal is too. My way home.

We stop for our last break when the sun reaches a midday point in the sky, beating against the canopy and leaving sharp shadows around yellow slashes of light on the forest floor. The effect is mesmerising, as if the shady lines are fissures in the ground exposing tracks of fiery lava underneath.

There's still some dried fruit and jerky to nibble on from our market purchases in Preo and Balvinder insists that Zac and I take most of it.

While we eat, Gwin starts up with Peirce about how he ought to smile more often, because *isn't he beautiful when he smiles*. Thorne and I exchange a look.

Balvinder stands against a tree nearby, his back to us. I go over to him and when he turns to me, his eyes glint blue and silver like translucent jewels.

"How do you feel?" he asks softly.

"Fine," I lie. Balvinder's gaze holds, and I sigh. There's something unsettling about lying into the face of Goodness. "Okay. Not totally fine."

Balvinder runs a hand over his mouth. "You are nervous to meet with the Overseer? Or to return home?"

I purse my lips, mulling it over. "Both," I say finally.

Lines form between Balvinder's brows, as though my apprehension has seeped across to him. But then they ease away, melting into calm. I feel my own frown disappearing too.

"You needn't fear the Overseer," he says. "I do believe your decision will be far clearer after speaking with Him."

His words strike a nerve and I stiffen. "My decision?"

Gwin starts to sing behind us. I look over my shoulder and see Peirce covering his ears and Zac grinning. I might smile too if I wasn't still distracted by Balvinder's comment.

"You mean, whether I leave?"

He nods, adjusting the collar of his grey tunic so his silver hair is brushing it.

I grit my teeth. "I can't stay." The words feel bitter in my mouth, maybe because I'm not sure I fully believe them, or whether I want to believe them.

Balvinder touches my shoulder and immediate warmth spreads from his hand through to every inch of me. I cut a look up at him, a little alarmed by the sensation. But he isn't looking at me—he's looking at Zac, who is strolling toward us.

He stops beside me and offers a hand. "One last walk?" The curve of his smile twists my chest into a hundred knots. I take his hand in answer, and his fingers slip through mine as we wander away from the group.

I cast a quick glance back at Balvinder. A waver of concern strokes his fine features. But it's only fleeting, soon replaced by a more contemplative expression.

I've held Zac's hand before, but back then I wasn't sure what it meant. It was under the curtain of night, and a blanket, and away from prying eyes. This feels like more of a statement. An acknowledgement that we have something to lose. I'm still not certain what it is, or what I want it to be, but I do know that I'll miss it. And I want him to know that too.

"Tell me something I don't know about you," I say, once the Essences are out of earshot. "You're quite the enigma."

"Am I?"

"Sort of."

"It would be a shame to diminish the mystery." He clicks his tongue a few times. "Well, much of my time is spent either hunting, fishing, or bartending in the village."

"Oh yeah. That bar. I noticed you there."

"I noticed you too," he says, amusement lacing his tone. "You were talking to yourself, after all."

I frown at him, before the realisation starts to dawn. I was with Balvinder—who nobody can see but me. "Oh no." I groan. I was—by all appearances—sitting alone and chattering away like a raving lunatic. "I hadn't even thought of that."

"It's all right." Zac's grin widens. "I was all-too-familiar with imaginary friends, so you piqued my curiosity."

I shove my shoulder into him.

"Now tell me something about you," he says, nudging me back.

I draw arcs in the dirt with my boots as we walk, contemplating the question and how best to answer it. Again, things feel different now. I want to tell him more about myself before I lose the chance. "Okay. A week ago, I had zero clues about what to do with my life. Mum booked me a session with this career counsellor, but it didn't help much. I still don't—" I stop abruptly, letting Zac's hand go to catch at his arm.

He looks around. "What's the matter?"

I stare ahead. The shape of her seems to have materialized from a bend of shadow. She now stands tall in our path, sweeping back her hood over sheets of black hair. Her smile follows, expansive and cold.

"Abbey?" Zac has his dagger out, but he still looks puzzled.

I open my mouth to answer him—just as Kayna speaks. "He can't see me," she says, only, her lips remain unmoving, like the shapes of the words exist in a hidden slice of reality imperceptible to everyone but her. I cut a look to Zac. He hasn't reacted at all.

Kayna's wide lips curl under those empty, black eyes. "Neither can he hear me," she adds. "I require your attention only, Abbey Shader. Tell him I am here and he will drop dead before you finish."

My spine tightens, and I force myself to look back to Zac. I offer a smile that evidently falls short of any believability whatsoever, because he only looks more disturbed.

"Abbey." Zac presses a cool hand to my cheek. "You've turned pale."

I glance again at Kayna. She is reaching into her black robe, drawing out an obsidian bow and a fine arrow, its head pronged with two sharp, bone-white fangs. I don't have to look too closely to see how easily it would spear through its target.

"Tell him you need time to yourself," Kayna says, without speaking. "Tell him to return to the others. Then we will go to the portal." She raises the bow and arrow, walking a slow circle and stopping behind Zac.

My throat closes up, and I feel my eyes go wide as Kayna pulls on the bowstring. Zac twists around, looking straight through her and then back to me, his expression unmoved. Somehow, she has made herself entirely inaudible to him.

"Now." Her voice dips into a low, unnatural rumble that sounds less human and more like shifting earth and tumbling rock. I'm reminded of the wolf in the mountains, its lips peeling back over grey gums. "Tell him *now*."

"I—" I swallow down the fright barring my voice. "Zac—I need some time to—I need to think. Alone."

He angles his head, the crease between his brows only deepening.

"I need you to go back to the others," I say firmly. Kayna continues to drag the bow back, her mouth bending with it.

Zac takes hold of my shoulder, but I shrug him off. "*Go*," I urge.

For a moment, he only looks at me. I try to hold his gaze steadily, commanding the panic to leave my eyes.

"All right." Zac begins to turn, but at the last moment—spins on his heel. The throw is a flash. I hear a sharp hiss and Zac jerks back into me. I catch sight of his dagger, buried in Kayna's neck. I see her pluck it out with only a mild grimace. And then I'm tumbling to the ground under the weight of Zac's body.

The black shaft of Kayna's arrow juts from his chest. He tries to steady himself but trips over me. We fall hard.

THIRTY-EIGHT

ZAC SLUMPS AGAINST ME. I SCRAMBLE OUT from under him and support his body to the ground. My hands hover over the arrow, shaking and helpless. A burst of blue catches in my side vision and when I look up—Balvinder is there. Kayna is gone.

A cry bursts out through my shock. Balvinder crouches low beside Zac, eyes wide and electric blue as he reaches to cup his face.

Zac's features fade out of their contortion. At Balvinder's touch, he goes limp. I'm about to scream again when Balvinder grabs hold of my arm. "I have just put him to sleep," he says. "So that he doesn't feel the pain." But the circle of crimson around the arrow is growing, turning Zac's shirt the colour of death.

The other Essences suddenly pour into view behind Balvinder. Thorne, Gwin, and Peirce. Tinkling laughter fills the forest. *Her* laughter. I feel all the blood drain from my face.

"I—I'm so sorry," I gasp into the words. My eyes remain locked over Zac's—iridescent green but totally still. "It was Kayna, she was—he attacked her and—" A choked sob escapes me.

Numb with shock, I only realise that Gwin is pulling me to standing when I look to her. She's smiling. *Smiling*. Behind her, Thorne has strung his crossbow. His attention isn't on Zac, but the forest around us.

"We heard a scream," says Gwin. "Ouchy. Is he okay?" I stare at her, wondering whether I might have misheard the question.

"Is he *okay*?" Peirce repeats, mirroring my disbelief. "Gwin, the boy is half-dead!"

I'm trembling all over now and tears track down my cheeks.

Peirce droops a feeble hand down to Zac's mouth before announcing, "He isn't breathing."

I cover my face, refusing to believe it. The Essences babble on around me but I don't hear them. Their voices are muffled and blended together in toneless discord.

Feeling a tug on my hair, I look back to Gwin. She presses her cheek against mine. "No need for tears, my dear. It will be alright."

Sudden rage sets my blood boiling over and I can't hold it back. "*Clearly* it won't be," I snap at her. "Look at him! Balvinder—what do we do?"

"There will be others," Gwin murmurs. "Others might even prefer to Zac. And just think, now you won't have so much to miss when you leave."

I keep my eyes on Balvinder's face to avoid punching Gwin in the gut. He seems to realise the effort and rises to take my hands. "Go to the portal."

"What?" I allow myself another glance at Zac's body, before cringing away. "The portal?" He wants me to leave *now?*

Balvinder squeezes my hands gently. "We can fix this." His gaze shifts to Gwin, sharp and knowing. "Take Abbey to the portal, and bring the water back." He extends his palm, a waterskin appearing there.

I take it from him, my hands wobbling all over the place. "I'm not leaving yet."

"That isn't what I mean," he says. "I need—she will—" A strange look comes over his eyes, like a film of grey cloud turning the blue hazy. "*The water,*" he says through a gasp.

My trust in Balvinder, as it has from the start, illuminates instinctively. I find myself nodding and staggering away, led by Gwin who has linked her arm through mine.

Peirce moans behind us. I look over my shoulder to see Thorne rushing forward, neglecting his bow and grabbing Balvinder as he shudders to his knees.

The convulsions are worse than I've ever seen them.

Gwin looks too. "What an odd moment to fall asleep," she mutters. And then she drags me on, trotting through the trees while I hiccup and cough beside her, Zac's lifeless body projected at the forefront of my mind.

✳

"Do—not—lose—Hope." Gwin utters each word in time with her steps, setting a quick pace through the trees. Her grip on me is surprisingly steely for someone so tiny. "Never—lose—Hope."

I find myself matching the rhythm. It calms me down a fraction, my sobs easing to quivers enough that I can catch my breath.

"Why water?" I ask, wiping at my dripping nose with the back of my hand. "And why the portal?"

Gwin beams. "They—are—one—and—the—same," she answers, still in time with our rapid strides. "You—will—see!"

Before long, I notice that the trees around us have begun to bend, as though a strong wind urged them away before they turned to stone.

A grassy clearing expands beyond them, and from its centre a huge tree unlike any I've ever seen encompasses most of the space. The tree itself seems to be the force that has pushed back everything around it. Its burly-limbed branches twist and coil, the roots rising from the dirt like colossal waves in a storm.

"Welcome to Amnoralas," announces Gwin.

The tree's size isn't the only unusual thing about it. Peering up, I see white blossoms covering the higher branches. They're alive, bursting into bloom even as I watch them and then drifting toward the ground like flecks of untouched snow. Momentarily I forget why we're here and just stare, totally mesmerized—before Gwin squeezes my arm and I'm brought back to the earth, colliding again with my panic.

"Zac," I breathe.

"Oh, that's right." Gwin giggles, and pulls me toward the base of the tree.

An unusual glow emanates from a deep patch in the roots. As we get closer I see that the tree seems to curve around the glow, the trunk shaped like a protective shield over what appears to be a *pond*.

The source of the light is the water itself, radiating gently. A single, continuous ripple disrupts the surface, but as far as I can see, nothing visible explains it.

"This is your way home," Gwin says, swiping the waterskin from my hand. She dances across one of the lower roots to the opposite edge of the pond, balancing impeccably well. I stare at the pond. My *way home*?

Bending swiftly, Gwin dips the leather vessel into the water. Raining petals tickle my cheeks while I watch on. The edge of Gwin's dress slips into the glimmering pond too, but does nothing to disrupt that continuous ripple in the centre.

"The portal is enchanted in more ways than one." She skips back across the root, twisting the lid over the waterskin and jiggling it at me. "We aren't *supposed* to use it like this, but if Balvinder says we can—" She tosses aside her thick, gleaming blonde hair. "Then we will."

THIRTY-NINE

A WILTED PART OF ME HAS SPRUNG BACK TO life. I don't know what I'm expecting, but something in Gwin's hopeful stride adds a bounce to my step too.

When we return to the others, Balvinder is conscious and kneeling beside Zac, whose shirt is now mostly crimson, a dark pool soaking the ground around him. Tightness returns to my chest at the sight, squeezing out the hope that guided me back.

Thorne stands nearby with his feet spread in a wide, protective stance. Peirce is lying on his back off to one side. He looks paler than a ghost, and for a second I wonder if he's even alive. But then he turns his head toward us, his eyes narrowed.

Gwin lopes to his side. "What's the matter with you?" She smacks his cheek a few times. Miserable clumps of hair part over his face as he raises his head to look at her.

"Everyone is *dying*," he laments. "We are all going to die—die—die."

"Water," Balvinder says.

I rush forward and snatch the waterskin from Gwin, refusing to waste another minute.

"We are the Essences, Peirce," I hear her retort. "Die, die, dying is impossible!"

"Unfortunately," he murmurs back, while I crouch over Zac and thrust the waterskin into Balvinder's outstretched hand.

"Nobody is dying," Balvinder says, giving me a nod. His eyes are still a little glazed, but nothing like before. He is much closer to their surface.

"Let me do it." Thorne knocks into me. "Move, little Melder." He reaches forward to grasp the dagger, and before I can look away—rips it from Zac's torso.

Blood sprays and I cry out, ducking my head toward my shoulder.

"It's all right, Abbey," Balvinder says.

Thorne rolls his eyes. "I expect Zacharias would rather not live the remainder of his wretched mortal life with an arrow through his gut."

I bite my lip so hard I taste blood. Or, maybe it's Zac's. The thought makes my stomach turn.

"Your ignorance never fails to astonish me," Thorne mutters, but still, I can't bring myself to look.

I hear a twist of metal. A slosh. Feel a hand on my shoulder. I look up to see Gwin, smiling. "Don't miss it," she says quietly, gesturing down toward Zac.

Tentatively, I bring my gaze back to him. They have pulled Zac's shirt up, exposing the gruesome wound in full. I cover my mouth as Balvinder lets the water stream over it.

Zac's skin glows silvery white. Reactive fizzing works at the edges of the torn flesh. I watch, clamping my teeth around my finger, while the skin begins to fuse together. Threads of muscle twist into place as if at the urging of an invisible needle and thread. Gradually, the pool of blood under his body shrinks. It takes me a moment to understand that it isn't disappearing. It's returning.

Gwin and Peirce have come to crouch by Zac's other side—Gwin beaming ear-to-ear and Peirce looking as though he's about to be sick. Together their expressions are a bizarre combination of how I feel.

Soon enough, the wound is gone, with only a pinpoint of silver light to mark its place.

We all seem to hold a collective breath.

Peirce is the first to break the silence. "It's too late, he is—"

Zac gasps into waking. I just about topple backwards and Gwin collapses into a fit of giggles. Balvinder beams, and even Thorne allows a small smile.

Zac's eyes shift from his unblemished stomach to me, wide and alarmed. He presses his fingers to the place of the wound. I wonder if it feels anything like my experience of healing after Kayna drove my dagger through me. The tingling numbness and disorientation.

"Zacharias." Balvinder's voice captures Zac's attention. They would almost appear to be looking right at each other, if I didn't know Zac was blind to him. Balvinder's face is filled with such an intense, overwhelming sort of relief—I wish more than ever that Zac could see it too.

I fall back onto my elbows, feeling my cheeks grow hot and wet. Gwin pauses her laughter for a breath, and to say—"I told you it would be all right."

✳

"On we go," Thorne says, once Zac has risen gingerly to his feet. "Our little Melder still needs to meet with the Overseer, and if we see Kayna on the way, I will take great pleasure in eviscerating her."

I crinkle my nose, even though having Kayna eviscerated would probably fit her crime.

"I have had enough of her rancorous ways," he grumbles on. "And what of you, Balvinder? Do you have nothing to offer?"

All of us but Zac look toward Balvinder. The waterskin is pressed to his lips. He tips it, gulping down the last drops.

I gasp as the waterskin falls from his hand and he gazes around at us all. A new dimension whirls within the blue of each iris. Flickers of blue light explode to the surface like supernovae, and I step back on impulse.

"That's much better," Balvinder says simply. He smiles at me. If his smile was radiant before—now it's angelic. "I owe you all a long overdue explanation. I wasn't sure if this would work. Though, evidently, the portal water heals unseen wounds too."

FORTY

BALVINDER'S FACE IS A CHAOTIC MIX OF extreme expressions. Urgency. Excitement. Pain. They merge and flash one after the other, and then balance into a sombre expression. We all wait for him to speak. Even Gwin remains silent.

"Zacharias," Balvinder says quietly. "Ever since I found you, I have done all I can to protect you." He expels a heavy breath. "But we have seen what knowing the truth can do, and how pursuing it has the power to destroy. Mostly because of the one who relishes such destruction. You know enough now for me to tell you …"

Balvinder hesitates, just for a second. "I am many parts," he says, "but every one of them works for Good."

Realisation breaks down Zac's confusion. His brow clears and a smile cracks the perfect symmetry of his face until my favourite dimple shows. "The Essence of Good? Kayna's opposing force?"

"Finally …" mutters Thorne.

Gwin gives a hoot. "Could you have guessed it?"

"I suppose I could have." Zac's grin spreads so far that it crinkles his eyes. He looks my way. "Did *you* know?"

"Sort of," I admit, which might as well be a *yes*. "Back at the Breathing House, it came up. But—I didn't think I should be the one to tell you." I feel like I'm trying to justify the secrecy, which triggers a twinge of guilt.

But then of course I couldn't be the one to reveal Balvinder's Essence. The revelation was between them, at whatever time Balvinder saw fit. Clearly, that time is now, and I'm glad I didn't spill the beans sooner.

"It's true that you have never seemed to be one thing," Zac says, his eyes falling to the dirt. "I have known you ten years, and you were an Essence, at the beginning. Perhaps then I cared to label you. But now you are just Balvinder. My teacher and friend."

Balvinder lays a hand on Zac, smiling just as brightly.

"You seem more your merry self," Thorne comments. "But now that the truth is out, so to speak—" he casts a narrow look at Zac, "—you might as well tell us the rest of it. I am not a fool, Balvinder. I know you have been hiding something."

"No longer," Balvinder says, a note of triumph to his voice. "I can tell you now that Kayna is roaming free—"

"Shocking," drawls Thorne.

"—and that I was the one to set her free."

Thorne's crossbow slumps to the ground. "You *what?*"

Even Gwin and Peirce look puzzled.

"Kayna was imprisoned, Abbey," Balvinder continues, unfazed by Thorne's horror. "It was a decision we made together, years ago—after the massacre in Emba." A blaze of something bright and powerful touches Balvinder's soft features. "She killed twenty children. Piled their bodies in the square for the villagers to discover."

"We hold a memorial every year," Zac murmurs. "The killer was never found. I had no idea it was related to the Essences."

"I recall that night," Thorne adds with no small amount of venom, his arms now folded crossly. "It was a mess. Therefore I cannot possibly fathom what possessed you to *release* her and risk the same thing happening again."

Balvinder raises a placating hand. "There were conditions to her release," he says. "Information she promised to offer if I let her go. Important information. She also claimed to have reached the conclusion that civility was preferable to imprisonment, and I believed her."

"We all intervene on occasion," Thorne interposes. "Just not the way she does. We were designed to enrich lives, not to end them. Kayna does not deserve the freedom we were granted in the beginning, you know this all too well Balvinder."

So the Essences *do* reveal themselves, *on occasion*—an obvious occasion being Balvinder saving Zac in the forest. But if Kayna is *murdering* people, even children, no wonder Thorne wants her locked up. I can understand his confusion. His frustration. If she wasn't roaming, she couldn't have stabbed me, or shot Zac. So if Balvinder is the Essence of Good, what information could possibly be worth setting her free for?

"Kayna's very nature is to revolt against the rules," Balvinder says calmly. "After the massacre in Emba, I would visit her often in that house—"

"*Visit?*" Thorne scoffs. "Intelligence clearly does not fall under your Essence."

"It makes sense," chimes Gwin. She is drawing her hair into thick sections, crossing them into a braid as if the seriousness of the conversation hasn't touched her. "Kayna might be manipulative, but she will accept a bargain if the outcome will suit her. Balvinder must have had a good reason for doing what he did. He's the *Essence* of it, after all."

"Not a bad bone in his body," Peirce says dryly.

"Well—" Balvinder swallows. "I brought the Melder with me to oversee the deal, and finally it was struck. Kayna would tell me what I needed to know, and if she also agreed to keep her distance from human life, I would release my power binding her to the house." He shakes his head. "But she gave us false information, before flipping the imprisonment spell and trapping me instead. The Melder passed on shortly after."

Balvinder's eyes glisten, and he turns them on me. "Kayna couldn't have overpowered me forever, but it would take time to summon my strength against hers. Perhaps even years. If Abbey hadn't freed me, I might still be there."

"I felt like I needed to," I tell him, which is an understatement considering how taut the cord of trust between us had been even then, instinctive and unexplainable.

"Because you are Good, Abbey," Balvinder says, a smile appearing where sorrow had turned his mouth before. "You sensed a home in me."

"All right, all right." Thorne flaps his hand, as if Balvinder's words are an unbearably bad smell. "So Kayna promised to tell you something important—but then she turned the imprisonment enchantment on you. None of that explains why she is so eager to get our new Melder to the portal. If Abbey *does* leave, the Overseer will send another to replace her. As hard as she tries, Kayna cannot rid the world of the Melder."

"I have wondered the same thing," Balvinder says. "But I could never speak of it, not until tasting the healing water. As well as binding my body, Kayna bound my tongue with her dark magic. I could not say her name or utter one word against her."

"The convulsions," I mutter, remembering the way he shook back in Emba, the mountains, and only a moment ago. He was trying to warn us. To fight against Kayna's hold on him.

Zac looks at me, the same concern etched around every feature of his face. "I have heard of dark magic, and those who live by it on distant continents. Does it all come from her?"

The blue of Balvinder's eyes seems to flare. "Yes."

"There isn't much we can do about it," Thorne growls. "Many humans are drawn to darkness, and our entire existence is to allow them the freedom of will. We can minimize Kayna's destruction, but never eradicate it completely."

"What now then?" I pipe up. "Should we try to find her?"

"We will continue on to Amnoralas," Balvinder says. "The Overseer might impart his wisdom on the matter, and you can leave Ethra through the portal, Abbey, as is your wish."

I gnaw on my lip, confusion mixed with fear bearing down on me. "Gwin and I were just at the portal," I say. "We didn't see any Overseer."

The Essences exchange looks, some of dismay, others of amusement.

"We need to be ready for Kayna," Thorne says, as if my comment doesn't warrant a response. "We can keep her at the Breathing House for now, but we may need to design a more permanent enclosure."

"You could barricade her into her own oasis," suggests Peirce.

"I couldn't," Balvinder says. "It isn't possible. Kayna's oasis is untouchable, as mine is to her."

Peirce sighs. "If only I could barricade myself into my own oasis ..."

"But then I wouldn't be able to visit you!" Gwin exclaims, clearly missing his point. She flicks her braid back behind her and claps her hands together. "We can discuss Kayna and cages and all that bellytosh later. Abbey must meet with the one who brought her here. So, shall we?"

I frown at the ground, mulling everything over. The cause of Balvinder's convulsions, the healing water working its magic on Zac and loosening Balvinder's tongue, Kayna's pursuit of me ...

It's only when the silence starts to drag beyond what's comfortable that I glance up and realise they're all waiting. Waiting for me. My verdict. Even Balvinder is quietly holding my gaze.

It's a small gesture, but seems to mark some sort of shift within the group. A subtle transfer of authority. "Sure," I say. "Let's go."

"Before Zacharias gets another arrow through him!" Gwin adds, shooting me a wink. Zac's hands go to his stomach, his eyes widening a fraction.

"Too soon," I tell Gwin, shaking my head. "Way too soon."

FORTY-ONE

PETALS CASCADE OVER US, SOUNDLESS AND dreamlike. Despite already having seen it, Amnoralas still leaves me gaping. And now, without my attention diverted to the possibility of Zac's imminent death, my eyes feel more open than before.

I note the sheer size of each bough. The leathery, wrinkled texture of the trunk as it stretches to roots like aged skin pulled taut. The thickness of the foliage, and how the immediate, stone trees around Amnoralas are coated in a snowy display of white blossoms.

Everything about the huge tree buzzes with life, from the heady, floral scent down to the lichen clinging to its bark—as if the moss itself is magnetized by the same power that draws me forward now.

Thorne prowls over the roots like a slick wildcat, pausing above the portal and peering down into it.

"How will he know I'm here?" I whisper to Balvinder. "The Overseer, I mean."

"He will know," is all he says.

"Abbey Shader has arrived!" Gwin screams, throwing her arms into the air and scaring me to death. "Your Melder is ready for you!"

I glance around, meeting Zac's startled gaze. Judging from his expression, it seems I'm not the only one on high alert.

"He won't show if you carry on like that," grumbles Peirce.

Gwin offers him a wry smile—before breaking into song. "*They move in the narrows, no voices, no shadows, breath in the place of demise ...*" Surprisingly, she seems capable of holding the tune of this little number, her voice tinkling with practiced vibrato.

"Oh, but singing will help." Peirce gives me a dubious look and I smile.

Gwin however, goes on without pause. "*Colours of old, stories they mould, and from them all shades will arise ...*"

Zac cuts in as Gwin takes a breath. "Do you normally summon him with song?"

Balvinder smiles. "It isn't essential. He will arrive when he sees fit."

I scan the area, half-expecting a tall wizard with a long, grey beard and a purple robe to appear from the trees.

"Do you hear him, Abbey?" Balvinder's question sends a jolt of fear through me.

"What do you mean?" I glance to Zac for clarification, but see only curiosity in the arch of his brows.

"Listen," Balvinder says softly.

I press my lips together and close my eyes, training my ears to pick up something. Anything. Nothing out of the ordinary reveals itself—unless the rustling of a magic mammoth tree and the humming of an Essence still counts as *extraordinary*. I think I've lost my grip on the definition of the word.

Thorne's snarky voice breaks my concentration. "Perhaps the Overseer will not meet with a Melder who refuses her task."

I open my eyes to see Gwin prancing across to me, clutching her dress in fists. "Could be! He *does* know all things." She gazes up at me, her head inclined as if *I'm* the oddity to be analysed here. "What if he is offering Abbey free passage home?"

Zac drops his pack and strides toward the portal pond. His gait has lost some of its ease, tight through the spine. He stops nearby the water and stares into it. I can't decipher the look on his face.

I remind myself that he *did* just die and come back to life, which is good reason to feel more than a little tense. But I also can't help but wonder what he's thinking right now, looking into the portal. Is he upset that I'm about to leave? Does he care enough for it to affect him?

We wait. And we wait ... long enough for Gwin to construct a bracelet for each of us from the fallen petals.

The gaps between Thorne's impatient sighs become shorter. Balvinder doesn't move. I'm now perched beside Zac on a root nearby the portal. Our legs hang, Zac's long enough for his boots to touch the ground. He kicks at the dirt, flecks of it disappearing into the luminous pond.

"You are worried," he observes, accurately, in a voice low enough that I'm the only one to hear it.

"No I'm not," I lie.

Zac's eyes slide to mine. "Well, if you were," he begins, smiling his crooked smile, "I'm certain there is no reason to be. Balvinder has told me that the Overseer is fair and just. He will always give you a choice."

"That's sort of what I'm worried about," I say, cracking like an egg. "I feel like I've barely scratched the surface of this place. Like there's a whole chunk of it I'll be missing if I go home. And what scares me most is that leaving ... it doesn't feel totally right. But then I think of Mum ..." I trail off, deciding to internalize the remainder of my doubt. What good will it do, voicing it to Zac?

He ruffles the back of his hair, a resigned twist forming at the corner of his mouth. "I don't know how it works entirely, but perhaps there is room for negotiation."

"Negotiation?"

Zac shrugs. "You could agree to remain in Ethra for a short time, or request to speak with your mother before you do."

I stare at the pond, imagining that conversation.

Hey Mum, I've been summoned to a parallel universe called Ethra to become the Melder of the erodosphere and the Essences, so I'll be gone a while, okay? See you in a few years though. Love you—bye!

"What's so funny?" Zac inquires, his own voice tipping into amusement.

I sigh. "I think I'd rather just disappear, to be honest. I'm not sure how Mum would take it all. Probably somewhat like I did."

"With great suspicion?" he goads. "And a touch of contempt?"

"Hey." I jab my elbow into him, before realising some degree of care should probably be taken around the portal. A laugh bursts out of me at the thought. "Imagine if I pushed you in."

Zac grins. "That would be ... surprising."

Letting myself meet his eyes, the emerald of them dashed with silver from the pond's reflection, I feel a familiar rush of affection seize me and glance away before he can see it.

But then I remember how little time we have left.

Without thinking on it too much, I rest my hand over his, which is pressed against the narrow stretch of root between us. His skin is hard but warm. I think of how it reflects him— the ferocity of his combative skills, the careful precision of his dagger throws, the tenderness guiding a touch I haven't felt enough.

Zac doesn't look at me but his long fingers splay, allowing mine to drop between them.

We stay that way for a while—before Balvinder starts toward us and I pull my hand away.

"Perhaps you are free to leave, as Gwin said," he muses. The sunlight streaming through the leaves above us turns his platinum hair a radiant white. "When you touch the water, Abbey, the portal will open for you," he says. "Then you need only step into it."

I slide myself down from the tree and Zac does the same. Gwin skips closer, followed by Thorne and Peirce.

We all look toward the pond, and for a moment I'm stumped by the fact that I truly believe stepping into it will take me home.

I look up to Balvinder and study every angle of his face, somehow hoping to find an answer somewhere there—an answer to the gnawing angst in my chest. I've travelled all this way to do this. Why don't I feel ready? Why does it feel like a mistake?

I crouch at the water's edge, watching that single ripple wavering across its surface. The portal glows bright as I dip my fingers into it, the light so intense I find myself squinting. Looking away.

The faces of the Essences are a comical display. Peirce is all distress, Thorne has his arms folded below an impatient frown, Gwin looks as though she might burst from anticipation, and Balvinder's expression is one of curious contemplation.

Zac isn't watching me. He's looking up at the higher branches of Amnoralas, blinking into the sun with his fingers interlaced behind his head. My heart squeezes, because I can see the forced effort he's making to appear indifferent. If I didn't feel the same desire to hide my apprehension I might not have noticed his.

For the first time in a while I remember the Melder's brooch on my jacket, and bring my hand to the stone in its centre. It's cold and smooth. Everything started with this brooch. Realistically, it makes no sense. But I think I can safely set aside my perception of the realistic.

I bite down on the questions firing in my mind—

How much more is there to learn here?

What am I missing if I leave?

What if I postponed my return?

What if I didn't go just yet?

Would the portal remain?

"Hello, friends." The poisonous voice has me jerking to my feet. The Essences have spun toward the Petrified Forest too, Balvinder stiffening all over. I follow his icy gaze to a lone figure emerging from the trees.

Her ebony hair is tied back from her face, exacerbating her harsh, broad features and those pitch black eyes.

Balvinder steps slowly to the right. It takes me a moment to realise he's shielding Zac, who is scanning the forest wildly.

"What is it?" Zac hisses.

Nobody answers. Thorne marches forward, halting in front of Balvinder in a militaristic stance with his crossbow raised. Gwin links her arm through Peirce's.

"Kayna," I murmur. Zac doesn't look back at me but his dagger is out in a split-second.

Kayna seems to glide over the dirt, wraithlike. Everything about her is chillingly tempered, all the more terrifying given what I know she's capable of.

I grit my teeth and march forward, yanking my own dagger from its sheath. A hand on my shoulder tries to pull me back—likely Zac's—but I tug out of his grip and fall behind Thorne.

"I must say, it's quite surprising to see you," he says, and I can hear a smirk in his voice as he adds, "out and about."

"You are looking lovelier than ever, Kayna," Gwin offers with a note of high-pitched whimsy. I'd almost laugh, if Kayna wasn't getting so close. She stops a few metres away from us, her black eyes slinking from one face to the next. When they reach me, her mouth breaks into a full, grey-toothed smile that has the hairs rising at the nape of my neck.

Balvinder brushes past me to meet her. "What do you want, Kayna? Why are you here?"

She drags her eyes away from me, idly, as though answering Balvinder's questions is a chore she was hoping to avoid. "You are far better company in captivity," she says.

"I might say the same about you," Balvinder bites back. It's the closest to hostile I've ever seen him, which is oddly comforting. Watching him watch her, his shoulders square and his chin set high, I feel like I'm safe behind the ranks of the winning team.

If Balvinder can retain his poise in the face of Evil itself, surely that means I can too. I try to match his fearless posture.

"You speak my name," she murmurs, "though your tongue is still unworthy of it." Her eyes flit behind me, to Zac. A twitch of mild irritation affects the corner of her mouth. "The boy stands. How immensely dull and predictable—even for you, Balvinder."

"What do you want?" Balvinder repeats. "Why were you so insistent on escorting Abbey home? You know very well that the Overseer will only send another to take her place."

Kayna's lips pinch together, like she might be hiding a smile. She goes to move around Balvinder but he's quick to block her way. They stand for a long moment, staring at each other fiercely like two opposing magnets forced into close proximity. Or like the river, calm and turbulent with nothing to separate each side. In the same way, something about it appears unnatural.

Kayna's lip curls back. "Step aside." Her voice is icy and jagged. But Balvinder doesn't bat an eyelid. A dangerous sort of energy radiates from the pair.

I find myself moving before I can think better of it. "Abbey," Zac whispers urgently behind me.

I ignore him and stop right in front of Kayna. Zac's lifeless body slams into my mind's eye, the memory writhing, bloody and terrible. Balvinder makes a noise low in his throat—a warning sound. I ignore that too.

"If this is about me," I say through gritted teeth, "then there's no need to drag anyone else into this."

Kayna's thick brows rise high. "Who ever said this is about you?"

I frown. "You said you wanted to take me home to—"

Kayna's laughter cuts me short. Her mouth is wide with the sound but she remains very still, a combination that's so disturbing it has me stumbling back a step.

The laughter ceases as abruptly as it began. Kayna tilts her head in a motion that reminds me of the apparition—a quick, bird-like crick at the neck. "You are just like the one before you," she says. "Your allegiance is selective." She leans forward until I feel her breath on my cheeks, bitterly cold. "Do you plan on killing me with that blade?"

My heart races and my fingertips prickle as I clutch onto the hilt. I can't kill her, if what the others told me is true. But she can't kill me either. Not in any *permanent* sort of way.

Still, the idea of having a knife driven through me again doesn't thrill me.

Suddenly Kayna has my wrist. Her fingers are like cold iron, digging into my skin as she pulls my knife toward her own stomach.

"Enough," Balvinder commands.

I'm yanked closer—until I feel the tip of my dagger puncture her cloak. Kayna's face is so close to mine now that our noses are almost touching. I shut my eyes and hold onto a breath to stifle the nausea as she guides the blade.

"You want to, don't you?" she whispers, just loud enough for me—and probably Balvinder—to hear. "You want to inflict the pain I inflicted on you, and the boy. Harness your hunger for revenge, little girl. Show me your strength."

The dagger is jerked closer, Kayna's bony fingers unrelenting over mine. I feel the resistance of skin. Muscle.

Bile rises in my throat. Mostly because Kayna isn't the only one forcing the dagger now. It wouldn't take much to drive it through her, the way she did to me. The way the arrow shot through Zac.

"Enough!" Balvinder bellows, louder this time.

Kayna jerks the blade away with a deranged cackle, and I stagger back with it.

"Abbey!" I whirl around to Zac. His eyes are on me, wide and frantic. It must have looked as though I was hurt.

I open my mouth to tell him I wasn't—when my neck is struck hard. I drop instantly, my blade falling to the dirt and agony blazing through my head and shoulder.

Balvinder is by my side in an instant, his face distorted behind my watery eyes. I see enough to detect his rage though.

He wheels around. I look up to see Kayna bolting past us. Even as the pain reaches unbearable heights from my movement—I turn to watch her. Thorne swiftly loads an arrow and lets it fly. But Kayna is fast, and she's making straight for Zac.

He wields his knife and his eyes move frantically over motion invisible to him. My neck throbs and I feel myself growing fainter by the second. Too faint to muster a single word of warning.

I'm vaguely aware that whatever Kayna used to knock me down is still protruding from my neck. A blade. Not mine. A shorter dagger she must have been hiding. It's hilt-deep.

The world seems to slow down. Balvinder, in a stream of silver-blue light, has taken off after Kayna. Her cloak whirls behind her like a trail of black smoke.

Peirce appears to have fainted, and Gwin is screaming gleefully beside him.

I go numb all over as Kayna approaches Zac and he slashes at the air, missing her by a few inches. My head buzzes and the forest dims.

Kayna pushes Zac with an impossible degree of force. I could swear a spiral of shadow extends from her hands, slamming him back into one of the tree's giant roots.

Balvinder stops running. He watches her as she moves to the portal's edge.

Kayna's skin is paper white and just as thin over her prominent bones. Her hair falls in a dark sheet down her back, seeming to swallow the dappled sunlight. Another one of Thorne's arrows whizzes toward her, but she catches it right before it lands, tossing it aside like it's as harmless as the petals continuing to fall over us.

And then her attention rises to Balvinder. She flashes him a roguish smile—before leaping into the portal and vanishing from sight.

FORTY-TWO

A LONG, EERIE SILENCE HOLDS. I BREAK IT with a cry as I yank Kayna's dagger from where she drove it through my neck.

Gwin is suddenly there, hauling me to my feet. I'm still weak and shocked enough that I find myself drooping over her narrow shoulders. Zac dashes across to me, limping a little from the impact of striking the tree. He slides a hand around my waist from the other side.

"I'm fine," I tell him breathlessly.

He casts me a wary look, which somehow makes me smile, despite everything.

Thorne and Balvinder are staring at the portal. "Abbey unlocked it when she touched the water," Thorne says. "*That* is what she needed. It had nothing to do with taking her back to Earth—only opening the portal."

"*She* wanted to go to Earth?" I ask, alarmed. Terror grips me as I think about Mum and Tyler, and Kayna lurking in the shadows around them.

"It doesn't work like that, little Melder," Thorne says. "Our bodies only exist in Ethra. On Earth, we are vapour.

Indiscernible. Entering the portal means giving up her physical form." He frowns, looking back to the pond. The water has turned a murky grey, the light from before entirely absent. "But why would she give that up?"

I try to take a few steps but my legs are a little shaky. Zac and Gwin walk me up to the portal, supporting each arm.

"Oh, but of course," Gwin says. I note the heaviness of her breath and try to lean more against Zac. "It makes sense! Kayna is willing to give up her physical form because she *knows* we would never let her roam free here. If she gives herself over to the erodosphere in full, she won't be restricted by anyone in the same way. Think about it—she *hated* her confinement, and for whatever reason she seemed to hate us too. This way, she doesn't have to deal with bars *or* us!"

"But our bodies," Thorne murmurs, "they're a potent culmination of our Essence. If Kayna stepped into the erodosphere, wouldn't she ..."

"Disrupt the balance?" Balvinder finishes for him. He absently runs a thumb and forefinger along his jaw. "Yes," he says. "She will dominate it."

As if in response, a rumbling groan resounds through the forest. Balvinder and Thorne pull in closer to us. Peirce is still lying facedown in the dirt.

I let my arms drop from Zac and Gwin. The pain is excruciating through my neck, but I try to ignore it, because I know it will heal. And I have a suspicion it isn't my biggest problem right now.

The groan becomes thunderous, still unidentifiable. It seems to rear up to meet us like a crashing wave, rattling every bone in my body.

And that's when I see it—the canopy shifting.

The typically static, stone branches surrounding Amnoralas are moving. They slip over one another, twisting like a thousand snakes caught in a blind rage.

An ear-splitting *crack* makes me duck on instinct—before the rain strikes. It isn't like the enchanted golden droplets from last time. It arrives in cloudy streams, almost as cold and brutal as dry ice against my skin.

Everything turns dark and lightning flashes above us, cutting through the thrashing trees. Amnoralas, which looked so lush and lively a moment ago, is now too still. Its blossoms have stopped falling. Black veins begin to creep along the roots.

I look around at the others for some sort of indication of what's going on or what to do. Gwin is just kicking the mud and waving her arms under the downpour, her head tipped back to receive the murky droplets on her tongue. Peirce has finally sat up, but judging by his expression, he's sorry that he did.

Thorne is shaking his head, his dark hair tracking wet lines down his face, and Zac's brow is furrowed in confusion while he holds his dagger limply, as if accepting there's little it might do to stop a storm.

It's Balvinder that arrests my attention. His eyes are illuminated like ghostly lamps. The silver of his hair seems to have lit up too, gleaming liquid metal.

"We're all going to die!" I hear Peirce wail, just before a huge wind gushes against us. Zac reaches out to hold me steady, and I cling to him without reservation.

Peirce's declaration rings in my ears as a cluster of dark shapes appear between the thrashing trees. They grow larger, get closer, until I can make out faces. Our faces. Half a dozen apparitions. The picture is a perfect mirror-reflection, save for the hollow, black eyes and animalistic movements. And there's another row of duplicates behind the first.

Zac steps forward, guarding me against his back. His eyes are trained to the monsters ahead. I've rarely seen his focus so acutely tuned to any target before, given that the apparitions should be invisible to him.

It's then that I realise— "You can see them?"

An answering nod.

The sky unleashes another roar. A blaze of lightning catches the macabre masks of the apparitions as they lunge for us.

＊

The apparitions disperse, seemingly drawn to whichever one of us they represent. Zac stalks forward to the four coming our way—two of him and two of me. I run after him, grabbing my dagger from where it fell earlier as I go.

I can't feel any pain where Kayna stabbed me. Whether it healed over entirely, or the ice-cold rain has numbed it, I'm not sure. All of me feels numb.

Thorne's crossbow twangs behind us, and there's a shriek as one of his apparitions falls. Balvinder catches my eye even as I run after Zac. His hands are outstretched, and silvery threads dance between them. Before I have time to process what I'm seeing, the threads shoot out to meet Zac, winding around his entire body as he ducks to avoid a gnash of teeth. Zac doesn't seem to notice, but manages to leap onto the creature's back. Swiftly he brings his blade down through its throat, still encased in Balvinder's fluid, silver shield.

I feel some sense of relief, but it's only fleeting. My apparitions have their sights on me. A shiver of energy runs the length of my spine. They're so close I can see flashes of lightning reflected in each glassy eye. I dart away from Zac, realising that it won't help either of us to stick together.

Whirling around to face my two apparitions, I hold my dagger steady, internally wishing I'd asked Zac for a few lessons in combat training before now.

I try not to let my ignorance trigger any doubt. Instead I pretend I know exactly what I'm doing and rush at the nearest version of *me*, just as it exposes those needle teeth. I thrust my dagger into its shoulder, squinting against the resulting, tear-inducing cry that ascends from its gaping mouth.

I'm struck from behind. I yank my dagger free and whirl to see the other apparition lunging for me again. I leap aside, avoiding its talons by millimetres. Then I spin around and lash out with the blade, striking the hard flesh of its back.

As the creature falls, Zac appears behind it.

No.

Not Zac. His mouth bends into a gruesome smile—another of his apparitions. Before I can scream it swipes at my dagger, knocking it from my hand.

I retreat a step and trip. The mud makes for a softer landing, but I still find myself a little winded. The creature drops to all fours and scrambles for me.

This time I do scream.

It springs forward and slams into me—limp, with Zac's dagger buried in the back of its head. I watch in horror as it shrivels right down to its decaying, foetal form over my chest.

Zac is there in a blink to kick it off and reclaim his dagger. The silvery shield Balvinder drew over him has disappeared. His shirt, soaked from the rain, is twisted and glued to every plane of his torso. I gasp as he drops over me, dagger raised. There's a hard glint in his eye that I've never seen before. A spark of madness.

"No! Zac!" I grab at his shirt. "It's me!"

He blinks through the rain, his eyes shining a dull green and his lips parted over heaving breaths.

She disrupted the balance.

Kayna's Essence isn't just dominating the forest, but Zac too. The entire erodosphere. I think back to those swirling colours in the Breathing House. The dark licks of shadow weaving amongst blue, orange, pink, red, purple ... even if Kayna is more potent now, the others still exist. Good still exists. And Zac is more than Good.

"Hey." I squeeze his sides, urging him to harness the better part of himself. "Remember Balvinder," I say. And then I repeat it, over and over, until the cold gleam vanishes from Zac's eyes and he lowers his dagger. He gets to his feet, and then pulls me up too.

His lips slam together and his nostrils flare wide. The shock is plain in his face before his attention snaps right, back toward the others.

Three apparitions skulk toward the group—two of Gwin and one of Peirce. Peirce himself is cowering over by the base of Amnoralas, but Gwin is strolling right toward the creatures. "How marvellous," she says, laughing. "My name is Gwin, though you must already know that."

"Shut it, Gwin!" barks Thorne. "Move aside!" He fires an arrow into one of her apparitions, loading another as Balvinder steps in to unleash a stream of blue light. It knocks Peirce's apparition back. Thorne's next arrow takes down the last apparition.

Zac and I go to them, and nobody speaks as glances are cast around the group. Grey, coiled corpses lie motionless, mouths gaping like fossils drawn out of the mud.

The rain has eased a little, replaced by a chill so fierce my teeth are already chattering. Thunder continues to growl and the stone trees writhe furiously as if we've sent them into a blind rage.

A loud screech rises above it all.

We look up to the stormy sky, only to see a flurry of wings and bodies silhouetted against it. Lightning cuts the shapes of the bats into ghoulish displays of chaos. There are hundreds of them. Possibly thousands. Terror seizes me, and for a moment I consider what might happen if I slipped into the portal while nobody was watching. But then, who's to say I'll be safe anywhere else? The entire world might be affected.

Instinct has me looking to Balvinder. If anyone can make this right, it's him. Something tells me that what I've seen of his powers is only the half of what he can do.

He must have moved while my attention was on the sky, because now he's standing at the portal's edge. The rain draws his silver hair into sheets that hang either side of his face.

"Balvinder," snaps Thorne. "What are you doing?"

My heart hammers against the walls of my chest as Balvinder's gaze rises. His eyes lock with mine—the calming, resigned blue of waves moving for the shore. Then they shift to Zac, and a sad smile touches the edges of his expression.

The bats reach the canopy of the forest. Their claws scrape against the shifting branches in an effort to break through. The branches seem to assist them, coiling around their bodies and spinning them onto the ground. Dozens of the bats begin to drag themselves through the mud toward us, followed by hundreds more.

Thorne puffs his chest and extends his crossbow.

"No," Balvinder says, raising a hand. All of us, including Thorne, glance at him in surprise.

Balvinder's gaze sweeps over us, tracing every face. Then he brings his hand to his chest. His eyes flutter shut. Realising too late his intention, I gasp, while he steps forward and falls beneath the surface of the water.

FORTY-THREE

THE SKY RUMBLES INTO SILENCE, TURNING A tranquil shade of amber, dashed with periwinkle blue.

Balvinder is gone.

The portal is as it was before Kayna leapt into it—light radiating from its centre where a single ripple breaks the surface.

The bats have vanished, and the Petrified Forest has stilled.

Above us, the highest branches of Amnoralas are blossoming again. A steady shower of their petals descend. The first of them are a brilliant blue, like Amnoralas is shedding tears, before they return to pristine white flakes.

"Accord," Gwin whispers. "Perfect accord."

I catch an inquiring look from Zac, and my throat grows suddenly tight as I realise—he didn't see any of it. "He's gone," I manage to say.

His brows furrow, but when he looks to the portal, an awful look of realisation replaces the confusion. "He jumped?"

I swallow hard and nod.

Perfect accord. As much as I wish I didn't, I understand it. Kayna jumped to disrupt the balance. Balvinder jumped to

HAYLEY GABRIELLE

restore it. A sacrifice on both sides, leading to the eradication of their physical forms.

Had Kayna anticipated that Balvinder would jump too? Was all this a cunning ploy to force him into giving himself up? Or did she truly believe she would dominate the erodosphere? Perhaps she couldn't understand the sacrifice Balvinder was capable of. Selflessness at its purest.

"We will never see him again," Peirce mutters.

Thorne tosses his crossbow to the ground. "Only in flesh." He rakes his hands through his hair. "He is only gone in flesh." Despite his attempt to sound frank and untroubled, I can see Thorne's shock in the way his fingers tremble before he locks them under folded arms, the muscles in his huge jaw pulled taut.

"The Overseer might bring them back," Gwin hazards, her fine eyebrows raised hopefully.

"No." Peirce slams her suggestion. "I think he knew this was to happen. Major Essences are different to us. More difficult to preserve as physical presences." He shakes his head, a mess of wet hair falling across his small, dark eyes. "Think of all the times Balvinder has had to deal with Kayna's destructive habits. Think of how she enjoyed tormenting him by tormenting others. Perhaps their reign is better off served in the metaphysical layer."

I pinch the bridge of my nose, a sudden and intense feeling of loss weighing down on me.

"Does this mean we must jump into the portal too?" inquires Gwin, her bright eyes flitting between us.

"Of course not," Thorne retorts, gruffly. "We have done nothing to warrant the abolition of our bodies. I plan on keeping mine."

"Balvinder didn't do anything to warrant it either," I say.

"No," Thorne concedes. "He made a necessary sacrifice. I am sorry to see him go, though I can't say the same about Kayna. Balvinder did what was right, and Ethra will be better for it."

"What happens with the Melder then?" Zac asks. His voice is flat and only mildly curious. A weight of sorrow hangs over it. Even his eyes have lost their spark. "Will the Breathings go on?"

"I would assume so." Thorne straightens his cloak. "We still require balancing. That much hasn't changed."

"All right, well ..." Zac glances at the portal. "What now?"

The Essences look to me. I feel a hard twang in the pit of my stomach.

"We send Abbey home and get on with things," Peirce says. "Yes?"

I avert my eyes from the four pairs on me, looking instead to the portal. I can easily step into it. I would be gone in a second. Home in a second.

But it doesn't feel so simple anymore.

I don't know exactly when it became complicated, but it did. And now I'm stumped over what to do next.

What changed? Why does the decision feel suddenly impossible?

I look toward Zac, hoping to source some sort of answer from him. But he shifts his gaze away.

It isn't just about him. It's this place. The Essences. The role of the Melder—which is supposedly designed for *me*. Or, I'm designed for *it*.

Fully understanding my world has been close to an obsession in the past. This new world—I understand so little of it. Staying feels wrong. But so does leaving.

What exactly would I be passing up?

"Abbey." Gwin's voice breaks my daze, quiet and careful. She has come to stand right in front of me, and when I look at her, she pulls me into a hug. "It will be okay," she whispers. "You will choose right."

I hang loosely in her embrace. My eyes start to burn from the pressure rising inside me, threatening to draw me apart.

And then I do. I draw apart.

I feel my consciousness cleave between my sight and my streaming thoughts. A new space opens up, and an unfamiliar presence fills it. A presence that isn't my own.

＊

Abbey Shader.

It resounds from one side of me to the other, in this foreign in-between. I don't recognise the voice, but it feels closer than my own. A whisper powerful enough to bend time and sense.

I can see myself sagging to my knees, see hands reaching for me, petals settling over mud—but it's an untouchable picture.

My thoughts are equally distant. At least, the chaotic mess of them is. Memories of home, all my doubts, confusion, and analyses—their echoes are lost in a faraway place.

I can breathe here. I'm open. And I'm not alone.

"*Yes?*" I channel the word into the empty space, out to the voice that somehow knows my name.

Welcome.

"*Who are you? Where are we?*"

You know who I am.

"*The Overseer?*"

The voice offers an answer with silence.

"*Then where am I?*" I ask. "*Am I dead?*"

You are between spirit and body.

"*Why didn't you show up before? We were looking for you.*"

My timing is not your timing.

"*Clearly. I didn't exactly ask to be brought here.*"

Didn't you?

"*No.*"

Every Melder possesses a spirit intended for this place.

"*I want to go home.*"

Do you?

"*I don't know.*"

A length of quiet draws out, murmurs babbling either side of it from the reality where the Essences and Zac fuss around me, and the endless chatter of my fears.

"Why didn't you stop Kayna? Why let Balvinder go after her?"

The Essences were granted bodies long ago, the Overseer answers. *It was a gift, not a necessity. Evil cannot function as the others do. The time had come for her to depart from the tangible, and the way she chose to go, required Good to depart too.*

I don't respond. Everything draws further away, enclosing us in the safest space I've ever existed.

Good is as present as it ever was, the Overseer says.

"Couldn't you just get rid of Kayna altogether? Why create her in the first place? If there was no Kayna, there would be no problem."

And no free spirits.

"Okay ... so how do I fit into this? Why am I here?"

Your spirit is the key to the next chapter. You are what my worlds demand.

"I don't really understand."

You will.

"And if I decide to stay—just for a while, what then? Will the door to home close?"

I don't close doors.

"So I can go back?"

Your decisions are marked in space and time beyond what you know. You will do what you will do at a time I have accounted for.

"Is that a yes?"

Yes.

I let the emptiness take me over, feeling it shudder against the walls of my eyes and my mind, which are both insisting I return to them.

"*Okay,*" I think at last. "*I'll stay. For now.*"

FORTY-FOUR

THE VOID SLAMS CLOSED. THOUGHTS AND sensations collide against the forest with such force I'm knocked backwards. The Essences stare at me curiously. Zac is closest, looking the most alarmed.

My heart pounds in my ears and fingertips, as if jolted back to life and making up for missed beats.

"Is she alive?" Peirce drawls.

"Of course she's alive, you imbecile," snipes Thorne.

"She is positively glowing," Gwin says, beaming at me.

Then I see more than faces. I see it all. The threads of colour dancing around us like liquid gems, encircling me, and Zac, propelled through his parted lips as though invisible hands are tugging them in.

Sapphire. Gold. Amethyst. Emerald.

A wisp of the brilliant blue rushes by me and triggers a dazed smile.

"The girl has lost her mind," murmurs Peirce.

"No, dear one." Gwin trots forward to crouch in front of me. "She sees us. The real us."

With my next breath, the thread of blue changes course and advances, in through my nose and mouth. It spirals around my racing pulse and calms it into a steady beat.

Gwin offers her hand. I take it to rise, watching the colours vanish as though they were just a trick of the light. But I know better now.

"It's as I thought," murmurs Gwin, her eyes crinkled in delight. "You have chosen to stay, haven't you?"

Thorne's mouth wavers in an almost-smile, and Peirce looks thoroughly confused. I glance Zac's way as I nod, watching the thrill of shock flash across his face. He recovers quickly but seems to be working hard to keep from smiling too broadly, turning it endearingly lopsided.

A burning sensation sears against my chest. I press a hand to it with a gasp. Gwin starts forward to fiddle with the buttons of my jacket. I try to shove her away, but she flaps at my hand.

"Oh, Abbey," she huffs. "Let me."

I watch cautiously as she unbuttons further, then drags my shirt down low enough to expose the source of the fiery feeling.

Any discomfort I felt about showing bare skin is cast away the moment I look down.

Imprinted on my skin—just above the sternum—is a pale mark. I recognise it immediately.

"Air," I breathe. "The alchemical symbol for air. I know it."
And I've seen it on Zac, too. The upward-pointing triangle,
bisected by a single line.

"We know it as a mark of the Truth," Zac says, his expression so bright I find it lighting up mine. "The Insignia." He
pulls at the laces of his shirt, revealing the symbol in full.

Thorne's snort breaks the wonder of the moment.
"Sickening—the mere sight of the Truth on such a commoner."

"Zacharias is hardly common, Thorne," Gwin offers, looking between Zac and me with a wide grin. "Neither of them
are."

"Can we go back to our oases now?" Peirce whines, matted hair still covering his eyes.

The question brings me back to a sharp, cold reality. I'm
staying. Home is a few steps away, and I'm turning from it. I'm
leaving it behind. Leaving Mum behind.

I grit my teeth at the thought, letting the Overseer's words
fill me.

I don't close doors.
I don't close doors.
I don't close doors.

My tension is eased somewhat as Gwin quite literally
squeezes it out of me in a suffocating embrace.

"You're going to break her," Peirce warns. But Gwin ignores him, releasing me only to pirouette across the mud and
hoot into the ochre sky, opening her arms to the hail of petals
from Amnoralas.

"Little Melder," Thorne says, "you have made the right choice." His dark eyes shine for a fleeting moment—before he throws his crossbow over his shoulder and turns to retrieve his scattered arrows. Peirce leaves us too, going after Gwin in an attempt to rein in her enthusiasm. I laugh, as he instead becomes an unwilling prop in her elaborate dance.

When I turn back to Zac I find him watching me. The corner of his mouth is hooked up into that half-smile that leaves me jittery every time it appears. My fingernails bite into my palms as I hold his emerald gaze.

"When was it?" he asks, stepping closer. "When did you decide to stay?"

"I'm not sure," I tell him. "But the door isn't closed. I'm on this side of it for now, but home isn't going anywhere. It can wait." The sentiment isn't as convincing as I'd like it to be.

Zac's lips press together, as if to hold words back. I don't want to know what they are. Dealing with my own doubts will be trouble enough. I'd rather remain oblivious to anyone else's opinion if I can help it. It was mine to make, and only mine.

My hand goes to the symbol shimmering pale against my chest. Zac follows the movement and his expression softens, that dimple I've come to adore making a brief appearance below his cheekbone.

Behind him, the three Essences are gathering. Gwin is trying to braid Peirce's hair, despite his efforts to pull away. Thorne looks like he'd rather be somewhere—anywhere—else.

There are more, I remind myself. More Essences to meet. There is so much more to learn. About Ethra. The Breathings. The Overseer.

But when I draw my chin up, up to the sky, the fear ripples away. The sun has gilded the clouds over streaks of cerulean blue. The colours are more vivid than any I've ever seen. I'm not sure what changed—the sky itself, or my own eyes.

Amnoralas seems to loom closer, its enormous roots and soaring branches taking on another dimension. Even Zac and the Essences have sharpened, as if before they were only cut-outs in a storybook but now they're living, breathing beings, real enough to extend beyond the pages I found them on.

The clean, white Amnoralas blooms twist and turn, riding on a wind that urges me to move too.

ACKNOWLEDGEMENTS

This book would not have come to be without the continuous support of a select few.

Maia, who took the time to meet my characters and offer an important seed of insight. I have no doubt that your talent will soon see you with a booming readership, and I'm ready to lead the charge.

To Sarah Pradolin, for the many hours we've spent marvelling over books without pause. You are a rarity and I value our conversations (which are never long enough) more than I can say.

My beautiful mother—your meticulous, speedy and honest edits drove the progress of this book, and your company made it a joy.

To my grandparents—your unconditional interest in my writing has nurtured a willingness to share it. Thank you for the sincerity of your questions and wisdom. And my dear grandmother, whose intelligence and grammatical wizardry has once again played a huge part in polishing this edition of *Essence*.

A big thank-you also to my dear friend Sarah Hegarty, who shared my excitement at every stage and never forgot the golden rain, even seven years on.

Mitchell, my love, and fount of never-ending encouragement—when I saw a flimsy word document you saw a published book on shelves with a film in the making.

And finally my genius father, without whom this story never would have launched itself into existence.

ABOUT THE AUTHOR

HAYLEY GABRIELLE is a Melbourne-based writer with a passion for fantasy and science fiction. She has seen works published across a range of journals and anthologies world-wide, claimed a place in the AMP Tomorrow Maker program, and won the 2018 Alan Marshall Short Story Award.

The Essence Chronicles pave the way for her longer works of fiction.

To keep up to date with Hayley's latest releases, subscribe at www.hayleygabrielle.com

or check out @hayleygabriellewriter on Instagram to follow Hayley's writing journey.